RACHEL'S GARDEN

LOUISE WORTHINGTON

BLOODHOUND BOOKS

First published in 2021 by Bloodhound Books.

www.bloodhoundbooks.com

Print ISBN 978-1-913942-24-3

To my family with love.

PROLOGUE

Your legs carry you to the familiar depths of the wood where the trees are so thick and dense the sunlight barely finds its way to the earth. You pass like a shadow beneath the trees, merging with them, moving further and further away from Maple Cottage, from your home, through long grass and the gentle enemy of holly. Your footfall is the only terrible sound over twigs and fallen branches, over patches of ivy, monkshood and death mushrooms.

When you are satisfied you have found the best place, you begin to forage amongst the chaos of trees and rotten wood, the flora and the deadly. Your wax jacket has ample pockets. Perhaps it is late morning, and you haven't eaten yet.

Birds are startled and they flee, shrieking and unsettling leaves as they burst through to an open sky that is an indistinguishable stitched line of heaven where the eye of the sun watches, as if through a needle. Sand has been dug out of the earth by badgers making setts and rabbits building a labyrinth of burrows. The sand looks red and tangy, thrown in amongst the damp brown soil, armies of nettles and mossy stones.

You screw up your eyes when you look at the leaves and berries in the soil-stained palm of your hand where the lines criss-cross like a path that some might say led you to this place. You can smell the spice of ferns, wildflowers and the unmistakable scent of a fox, which stirs memories of feathers. So many feathers. The memory draws you further into the world where woodpecker holes are the only eyes that watch you because no one knows you are making this dark pilgrimage.

Foxgloves. Slender spires of poisonous purple signal you with their deceiving elegance and the grace of their bell-shaped heads. They travel with you from the open woodland to your garden, though bumble bees would have loved stuffing themselves into the tubular bells for pollen and nectar. A bramble claws at your hand, cuts a finger.

You make a roll-call of your ingredients and turn back. It is silent, and the walk of your prayer will soon be answered. Nature is listening and answering your footfall.

The cottage door is unlocked and open, and so are all the windows. The house waits for your return, remembering.

1

DECEMBER 2018

This month is for sorting and sifting through boxes, suitcases and bags; next year will be for mending and growing. I have it all planned out in my head and coded on a calendar in the kitchen. December's picture is of snowdrops; my code for a new start with Adam is 'F' for future, when my life will start to exist in the shape it's meant to, the way I intended it to. Not the shape it got mauled into like a second-hand pillow.

When I removed the calendar from the wall of our apartment and put it in a cardboard box, together with all the other items I was moving to our new home, I looked at the hook it had hung on for a long time. Seeing it jutting out from the bare wall, I realised the big day had arrived, but all I had that was tangible was the hook and the cardboard box. Everything else was hope.

At Maple Cottage, our new home, I have faith that my dreams will come true because my parents were happily married there. It's a special place where one has to listen to the pure silence.

The cottage is situated in a dead-end. We have one neighbour – a lovely woman called Shirley. The lane has remained pockmarked with potholes for years to discourage strangers. On one side there are Peckforton Woods, and on the other there are open fields that stretch out for miles across the Cheshire plains.

At our apartment in Altrincham, the streets were rarely spared from restless people and traffic. Sounds were constantly weaving from early morning through to night: shrill hooting of cars; dustbins rumbling; sirens, and drunken cackles lit by the firefly of a cigarette. We were close to Manchester Airport, which suited my husband, Adam, because he works in China recruiting students to UK boarding schools for about seven months of the year. But to me, the sound of a plane landing was a kind of artificial thunder.

As a part-time history teacher at Nantwich County High School, I have a much shorter commute now and three weeks' holiday to settle us in before the Lent term commences in January. I inherited Maple Cottage three years ago after Dad died. We didn't move in because Adam said that we should rent out the cottage while my grief was raw. We've sold our apartment in Altrincham now. This is our new home, our forever home, I hope.

Aided by firelighters and a lot of blowing and teasing of paper and sticks, I manage to light a fire in the lounge. Peering into mesmerising flames, I think it is possible to believe in forgetfulness. It is possible to forget that the icy breath of December is blowing between the cracks in the windows. Now that my toes are warm, it is possible to forget that there is a kind of hunger in the wind outside that has sent hedgehogs into hibernation and moles into wombs made of leaves.

In other ways, though, my memory is too reliable. I cannot forget the secrets in the wood, or the way the branches on the trees wave at me with a child's hands. I cannot forget the poppy-shaped bruises.

I've dreamed of living at Maple Cottage for the last three years. Now I am finally here, it doesn't feel completely real even after sleeping for five days under its roof. I love the way the cottage is built from indigenous red sandstone, giving the exterior a warm, rustic complexion. The decorative leaded windows and the bulbous central chimney are defining features in this characterful home. The sturdy front door is well-weathered, a familiar face from an album of hundreds of happy family photographs of my parents and me. I can't wait to climb Peckforton Hill to see the cottage from above, to see wreaths of smoke billowing from its chimney once again.

I gaze into the fire. It sizzles and hisses, licks the sticks of wood and works its tongue around a log I found in the garage. Peckforton Woods was always integral to our lives, and now its wood is keeping me warm.

When I turned thirteen, Dad's roots started to grow out from under Maple Cottage and the back garden up to the woods. Like ventricles from a heart, they pumped their way up Peckforton Hill. He spent hours there most days, became taciturn and quick-tempered, while Mum walked the landing waiting anxiously for his return when the moon was his only torch. From my bedroom I'd hear her sighs; they were like waves, sometimes coming so fast that I thought we might drown. But Dad always returned, sending us to a contented sleep until the morning.

Dad died just six months after Mum's funeral. I stripped Maple Cottage and redecorated it. House Rentals told me what needed upgrading to get a decent rental income. Cataracted by grief, I rushed through the house, packing, discarding, removing. I have repeated the same actions in China and the UK, in bedsits and apartments, because no place has ever felt right.

Before the tenant moved into Maple Cottage, I painted the

kitchen-diner a wild green because green was my dad's colour: the green of time passing, of green leaves on the trees. The green tracks he made through nettles and thistles and over the mossy stiles along the Sandstone Trail in Peckforton Woods. The green of emerald ferns and knotty weeds in his chicken coop. Before I painted the walls, I remember the room as my junior-school classroom because Mum hung my childish pictures all over the place. When she removed them, they left behind greasy blobs from the Blu-Tack. I found those, and the ruler marks of my increasing height.

I painted the main bedroom lavender; that was Mum's colour and her scent. I painted my old bedroom sunshine yellow in memory of happy summer days. But the rest of the house got stripped and painted magnolia, which I now regret. I undertook a literal kind of white washing, but I didn't do a thorough job of it because my life since has not been a linear narrative free from flashbacks. And I don't even like magnolia; it is an unborn colour.

When I returned to the house, I sensed how raw I had been from my parents' deaths – but who wouldn't be? Perhaps that was why I was happy to be swept off my feet by Adam.

At eighteen, I left for university. I visited my parents as often as I could during my undergraduate years and now, a decade later, I'm back for good. I'm married and still a little giddy from the whirlwind of it. Mrs Jordan. It still feels like a new name.

I am home at last.

Except.

Since moving here almost a week ago, I've found pieces of me, pieces of Mum, Dad, and I don't know where to put them or how they fit together. I want to make friends with my past but someone – something – doesn't want that.

Skulls.

Not just one, dozens of them.

Not human ones; they are the skulls of small creatures, trophies from Dad's pest control business. He had a gun cabinet in the garage and a lockable storage space for poisons and traps. There were shelves along one wall for the skulls of pests he routinely controlled to earn a living: moles, foxes, rabbits, mice and rats. The kind of pests that can drive people demented and bring havoc to a home or a business.

Dad cleaned his guns religiously. He touched the skulls like a rosary; he seemed to find a kind of solace and serenity in the aftermath of violence. I'd watch him rake his fingers along the silent shelves to remove the dust from his shrine. In his garage and the woods, he taught me that death is a respected part of life. For some to survive and triumph, others must die. It is a law of nature.

Why did he keep the skulls? He said he saw beauty in them, while I only saw lipless grins and heard mouths whispering. But those dead creatures put food on our table; they kept a roof over our heads. If I was a customer tormented by mice, frightened by a fox, crawled over by rats, perhaps I would see the beauty in their pearly offerings.

A few days ago, I put the skulls in a bin liner and deposited them in the wheelie bin, a symbolic act to bury the dead and embrace the future. I wanted to think of my father untainted by death.

The garage looked better for it. I placed my gardening tools on the shelves – a spade, fork, trowel, a hoe and a ball of string – all the time working my way around his beloved Land Rover, which had remained there when the house was rented out. I dusted off two watering cans and a hose, but I left the spiders' webs, the dead woodlice and fragments of charred newspaper for another day. White paint had flaked off the window ledge, exposing its rotten wood. I remember Dad saying the wood needed replacing; it was a job he didn't see to before he died.

I waited for the thud as the bag of skulls hit the bottom of the wheelie bin. Then I thought of the predator in my life and the way Dad said his work was not killing, it was control. Back in the kitchen, I washed my hands and thought that was the end of the skulls. Good riddance.

It was all so simple, so decisive.

Until I found the skulls on the back lawn.

Not randomly strewn, but arranged in a way to send me a special message.

Six separate configurations.

The grass had turned white and brittle from the frost.

The eye holes stared in horror.

At seven thirty on such a bitterly cold morning, they looked perplexed to see me – but not as perplexed as I was to see them. Despite the frost, there was a threatening pulse of life around me, seeming to tear beneath the grass and under the stiff hedgerows, scratching between the dirt, sand and stones. I could feel it, as sure as I could feel myself shivering from the cold.

Eventually, after reading each shape in turn and re-reading them in their entirety, I recognised the pattern.

It spelled a word, a name: RACHEL.

Language is a powerful thing, especially when the letters are made from dead things.

~

Rachel. Foolish Rachel. I should have taken the curtains down before the tenant, Devina Duffy, moved in; I never thought someone would steal them. Steal a piece of Mum's message to me. How foolish and thoughtless I was back then. The cottage has lost something of its shape and scent, like a favourite jumper borrowed and washed by a stranger. But it will return. It has to. I want to block out the black when I can.

Once the curtains are back, I won't feel so afraid. I've left several messages for Devina and I finally got to speak to her to arrange to collect them tomorrow.

Mum was always inside, 'keeping house' like it might run away if she went outside for too long. As well as curtains, she made quilts for the beds and matching cushion covers. There was a lot of pattern. Each one gave a message of love and femininity in every room, and there was a reminder of her in case we might forget her for a split second; even if we did, her lavender scent was everywhere, wafting from the scented candles like dust particles.

I wish I could close the curtains when darkness descends and wraps itself around the cottage and find the comfort Mum once gave to me.

The black void on the other side of the glass is unsettling, more so when I hear a fox call in the night. The skulls are back in their bin liner now. It will be Christmas Eve in a week, and Adam will be home from Hong Kong to spend Christmas and New Year with me. But just now, I hear the skulls whispering to one another and me as I watch the flames fade into flickering tongues. I can still see holes for eyes, a white stare exploring my shape like curious flies as the grate fills with ash and dying embers.

I won't run. My bones, my teeth, my splintered heart – they are staying put here, at Maple Cottage. This will be my home, even if it kills me or someone else.

2

Adam often tells me how lucky I am to have a husband with a well-paid job, and that I have a habit of taking him and his money for granted. It's true; I'm not too focused on our finances.

Mum always said you live within your means.

When I first see Devina Duffy's rented house in Nantwich, I hear Adam's voice in my ear. She is a single mum with two children, living with a soundtrack of horns and music, and babies waa-waaring.

The house is a terrace on a street of mismatched houses, like a patchwork quilt with some large, some small and some decidedly tatty squares of material. Her property has a small hanging basket to one side of the front door, recently planted with winter-flowering pansies. From her windows she can see tarmac, street lighting, an abandoned pram and litter; her neighbours don't appear to place quite so much pride in their home. A young man is leaning out of a window a few doors down smoking a cigarette, making sure all the smoke goes out of the window. The dustcart is making its way down the avenue, rattling glass bottles.

Devina answers the door wearing a pair of yellow washing-up gloves. She is a trim woman with a shiny bob; she looks out of place in the cramped hall where we hold a stilted conversation before she invites me in. There is a leather jacket thrown at the bottom of the stairs and a tiny pair of shoes. I hear a lorry drive past.

She shows me into the lounge where her teenage son, Ted, is lolling on the sofa, channel-hopping. His skinny body is all arms and legs; he looks like a giant insect feeding on the faux-leather sofa. She tells me her youngest child, Tommy, is asleep in his cot. I almost mention the mobile suspended from the ceiling in my spare room, but decide not to. I assume she left it because she doesn't want it.

'Ted, this is Rachel Jordan from Maple Cottage.'

'What are you here for?' he says, moving his eyes from the screen to read my face, generously giving me the benefit of his dirty-grey gaze.

'Don't speak to Mrs Jordan like that. She's here because I invited her.' His mother raises her eyebrows at me. 'Sorry. Teenagers. He can be charming when it suits him.' She ruffles his hair fondly. I expect him to bite her hand off, but he seems to like the affection. 'He got pretty attached to our old place, that's all.'

In a sudden mood change, Ted grabs a can of Coke from the coffee table as if it's a bagful of evidence that I am here to confiscate. 'Roughin' it a bit, aren't you, comin' here?' His eyes never leave my face: they feel like horseflies that I want to bat away before they bite. 'Do you like a bit of rough?' He winks.

Devina returns to the lounge after bustling in and out. 'Take a seat. I won't be a minute. Just need to get everything together for you.' She looks flushed.

'No rush.'

The room is so sparsely furnished that I can't find anything to compliment, and Devina is too busy rushing in and out of the room to make small talk. For a while Ted and I sit in silence.

The small room feels hot so I remove my coat, fidget with a loose button. 'So, do you know Peckforton Woods well?' I ask Ted, knowing I sound like exactly like a teacher, but that's what I am and I can't think of anything better to say.

Ted's smile is dead. 'Yeah. What's it to you? You bein' all nice to me 'cause you feel guilty about turfing us out? That's it, ain't it?'

Not correcting his poor grammar eats at me, so I reply more sharply than I should. 'No, I'm here to return the curtains to Maple Cottage where–'

There is a reality programme on the television featuring unfaithful couples talking about their transgressions to a host. The live audience looks riveted. Suddenly the slanging match erupts into a fight. Ted interrupts me. 'Get in there!'

'What's your favourite subject at school?' I ask, determined not to be ignored or give up when his mother is trying her best to do the right thing.

'I hate school. It's a waste of time.' Ted doesn't bother to look at me.

I turn my face away from him and suspect he's making rude gestures behind my back. I look at the curtains at the window; Devina mentioned they are second-hand, and I can see one pair are too long. On the coffee table, there's a leaflet promoting two-for-one for teabags at the local Spar. Something unpleasant has been wrapped in its corner. Beside it is an opened packet of chewing gum and an emptied ashtray.

'You can walk into town from here – that's handy.'

'Yeah, great if you want duffing up.' I catch a whiff of cigarette smoke. 'Mum says it's just the two of you at the cottage.'

'Yes, my husband, Adam, and me.'

'You'll be rattling around in a three-bed house like that,' he says, casting another dirty gaze over my face.

I take a deep breath. 'Which bedroom did you have?'

'The yellow one.'

For all his hostility, his intimidating black jeans and hoodie, he is a child who has been forced to move house and I feel guilty about that. I know it is unsettling to be in a place that doesn't feel like home.

Ted has a coughing fit that lasts several minutes. His phone chimes with a text and he rummages in his pocket. When he looks at it, I see the screen saver is a photo of the view from the top of Peckforton Hill: I'd know it anywhere.

'It's an amazing view up there.'

'Whatever. You're giving me a bellyache. You going soon?'

I move in my seat uneasily, wondering what to say next. The room has a harshness to it.

Finally, Devina passes the bags to me containing the curtains. Ted turns his face away as if I disgust him, and his mum disgusts him too for returning them.

'Thanks for washing the curtains and... everything, Devina.' She places the framed embroidery on top of the bundle like a fairy on a Christmas tree. 'I didn't expect you to wash them.' A fresh lemon scent is under my nose. The curtains have been pressed. 'I lost my mum, you see. She made them.'

She shakes her head and the shiny hair swings like an old-fashioned shop doorbell. 'I completely understand. It was wrong of me.' For a second, I want to stay a little longer with her.

'There are a few cracks around the windows and the owls sometimes wake you up, but we loved it there. You know, I miss having a washing line!'

'It is a remote spot, especially at night, but here you've got neighbours for company.'

'Yes, I'm still getting used to the noise and light pollution.' As an explanation for her son's rudeness, Devina says, 'He adored those woods. I did too. But we'll settle here, won't we, Ted? He can walk to school now, so I don't have that to worry about. And once Tommy is a bit older, I'll be able to get a part-time job in town and things will be less tight. Perhaps get rid of the car.'

'Is your new landlord looking after you?'

'It's my ex-husband's house. Well, one of his rentals. He and his... partner... live in Ludlow.'

'Him and her in a bloody great mansion,' Ted says bitterly, louder than is necessary. 'He's just bought her a soft top, and we can't even afford a decent TV.'

Devina shrugs. 'Have you plans for Maple Cottage?'

'If Adam – that's my husband – leaves it up to me, we won't change anything, but he does like his mod cons. He was very attached to the power shower at our last place, and the built-in sound system. He'd rather have stayed at our apartment in Altrincham, but he knows how much Maple Cottage means to me.'

'It's not that sort of house at all! How's he settling in?'

'He's working in China until the twenty-third of December.' I explain that the fair he is attending to recruit pupils to UK boarding schools happens once a year.

'So, you made the move here alone?'

'Not really. Adam is friends with a chap who runs a removal business. They took care of pretty much everything except moving me.'

'How much are boarding fees? I went to a comprehensive, as Ted does.'

'Same here. Adam says it can be anywhere from £26,000 up to double that and more, and that's for one pupil per year. Some families send two or three children for their secondary education.'

'It's a different world. Adam must be quite a salesman. I feel like crying when I open the electricity bill!'

'I'll let you get on.'

'Send my love to Shirley.'

'I will and thanks again – I'll be seeing you.' I think she looks grey and underfed and I wonder if she's taking care of herself. Her telephone rings so I take it as my cue to exit and she waves me goodbye.

The initial awkwardness of the visit, the animosity emanating from Ted and the weight of the curtains in my arms push me hurriedly through Devina's front door. As I climb into my car, a young mum and a child with a runny nose stop and stare. Their dog, a collie, crossed with something like a terrier, takes a dump on the tarmac. The mother leaves it there.

I have my curtains back. I want to get home and not think about Devina, Ted, or the winter pansies beside her new front door or the steaming dump outside her house. Finding a few skulls in the garden seems incidental.

When I get back, I park my Golf on the grass verge because a van from Hollies Nursery is on the drive at Maple Cottage. On the final trip to the car to retrieve the curtains, I see that snowdrops are beginning to fight their way between blades of grass in the verge. I narrowly missed driving over them.

I lug the last heavy bag of curtains into the kitchen. When I open the back door, I hear a peregrine falcon and see a tall man wearing a green-and-white checked shirt loose over a pair of baggy jeans. I don't recognise him and immediately feel fearful, so I hover by the back door where I can retreat inside quickly.

'Can I help you?' I shout, using my hands as a megaphone.

His hair is so fair it's almost white and his smile is broad as he waves at me. I think maybe he's been here before, or he's got the wrong address. He doesn't stop looking at me, as if I'm a curious object in a shop window, but he seems friendly. With the church bells ringing in the distance, perhaps for a christening or a funeral, I am more at ease than I was at first.

'I've come to do the tree pruning,' he enunciates like I'm stupid or deaf. He's an oak of a man: broad and robust. I watch him walk towards me, taking giant loping strides over the lawn, and for a moment, his stature reminds me of Dad.

'I've just moved in. I wasn't expecting–'

He offers me a hand to shake; it's rough, calloused but warm to the touch. 'Ollie. I did the gardening while the tenant lived here. You must be the owner.' He smiles easily.

Now I remember signing up to the gardening service. House Rentals insisted on it. I relax my shoulders and smile back at him. 'Rachel. Why don't you come in? Excuse the tip, I only moved in last week.'

He follows me inside, where his eyes immediately feast on a large unpacked cardboard box in the middle of the kitchen. 'Looks like you've travelled a fair bit,' he says.

'Be my guest,' I say. He immediately bends down and pulls out the laughing buddha and a Chinese carnival mask and handles them with a wistful look on his face. His cheeks are a little flushed. A thick brown-leather bracelet slides down his wrist.

'Have you been to Red Beach in China?' he asks.

'No, but I've heard of it,' I say as I put the kettle on. 'I worked in Hong Kong for a short time. Adam, my husband, is out there for at least half the year. That's where we met.' I twiddle an earring as I watch him feast on the objects.

'What does he do?'

'He works for an agency that recruits international students to UK boarding schools. China's a big market for them. Living in fancy hotels seems to suit him. Have you travelled much?'

'I go out to Spain at least once a year to see my folks. They've retired to Malaga. The only bit of exploring I've done is in those woods behind your house. Pathetic really – I've lived in Cheshire all my life. Started at The Hollies straight from school on an apprenticeship.'

'It's harder to stay still than it is to move around,' I say. I try to work out his age and whether we might have been at school at the same time. I guess he's younger than me by a couple of years. 'I know the woods well myself.'

'You do? They're beautiful, aren't they?'

Ollie pulls out a silk fan from the box, which I'll probably put in Adam's office above his enormous desk. 'I've been saving on and off for ages, but I won't be jetting off any time soon.' He carefully puts the items back in the box and stands up. The crack of his knees is like a full stop. I pass him a mug of tea with three sugars as he requested.

'I'm thinking about changing the back garden,' I say. 'Less lawn. There's only the maple tree for colour. It feels...'

Through the kitchen window, I see the wooden frame of Dad's chicken coop has dropped to the ground in defeat. The wire has wrapped itself around the wood like a blanket. The willow tree in next door's garden still leans on the fence, as if for a neighbourly chat, patiently waiting for my return. Or Mum's. The back garden looks back at me, nonplussed, the grass leached of light and life, concussed by the cold and its own sad history.

'I did hear about–'

'My dad. Yes, that's why I want to change the look of it.'

'I met him a handful of times when he called in at the nursery for a bunch of flowers.'

'For my mum.'

'Yeah. That's his red Land Rover in the garage, isn't it? I've always wanted one like that. Lucky it's locked – it'd soon be stolen from a remote spot like this.'

I remember watching the Land Rover drive away after a brief

and perplexing farewell at Sheffield University. I was in my final year and Mum's cancer had spread. Then I disappeared for a while. I grew invisible. When I think of myself during that final year at university, I see myself shrinking inside my green parka, the one I wore the whole time in all weathers and seasons. I still have it; there's an unopened envelope in its pocket, the soil-stained fingerprints of my father on it. I haven't been brave enough to open it.

'Is there trouble out here? Thieving or–'

'No more than anywhere else. Just keep your valuables locked up and you'll be fine. Land Rovers are desirable, especially since they stopped making them. I expect you'll know local people but anything you need, give me a ring at the nursery.'

We head outside to the back garden. 'I'm not into neat little borders, anything fussy or twee.' I can't find the words to explain that Dad taught me to love nature in all its wild, cruel and beautiful forms. The moment lengthens and passes. 'A garden that reflects my parents and me. That's what I'd like,' I say finally.

I take a closer look at the water in the bird bath and see hundreds of dead ladybirds floating inside the bowl. Some have turned over and resemble abandoned boats in the ocean. The dainty black dots look accusingly at me like a thousand eyes; symbols of fertility drowned in my water feature.

'You've got the space to work with. Here's my card. Let me know anyways. I'll do the pruning now I'm here. No charge. Good to meet you, Maple Rachel.'

Maple Rachel. The phrase sticks in my head as I shower and prepare a meal, then toss and turn in bed, thinking about changing the back garden into something special. I sometimes have nightmares about Dad's decomposing body slumped in his deckchair for the birds to defecate on – because it was me who found him.

Maple Rachel.

3

Today I will organise the garage and come up with a plan for the garden. The deckchair crouches in one corner of the garage, looking strangely ordinary beside the removal boxes and bubble wrap from our move. I remember the four divots in the lawn from the chair legs, hands clawing at the earth, scraping at it to burrow deeper into the soil for worms where Dad wanted to be. I sit down in his chair and listen to the silence.

I can hear moths thrum around the naked light bulb. The window is strewn with cobwebs and dead flies which obscure the natural light to the outside living world. I remember Dad's bonfires. When the green leaves fell then turned into golden treasure, he added twigs, sticks, lit a match and watched the flames rise into the air like words only he could hear. It was another ritual of his: the branches, the sticks, the newspaper torches, the failed attempts, the blowing. On those days, he kissed me goodnight, and I breathed in his bonfire smell and slept soundly.

Dad.

The garage remembers Dad as the gentle, contented man he

was for most of his adult life. It retains a sense of the man of seasons, a big man who wore boots, carried his broad shoulders around in a carefree manner, and was afraid of nothing and no one. And yet, on his seventy-fifth birthday, he took his own life in the back garden at Maple Cottage. He poisoned himself.

There were vast swathes of moods that changed like the sea. Once, on a walk, Dad pushed me because I was dawdling. I was fifteen. His stern voice telling me to hurry and the brutal shove on my back made me gasp in fright. Later he explained that we'd left Mum alone for too long. He insisted I 'listen', 'watch' – so many imperatives, urgency like a lesson, a test I was preparing for. Why hurry? What test? Why be so stern? I was afraid to challenge him so I kept on and kept silent, wondering where my old, gentle father had gone.

His head was forever turning like a nervous twitch to check I was close by and attentive, or it would turn side to side as he surveyed the wood, looking for something. 'This way,' he would order when the fingerpost said the opposite, so we forged a new path. Though he didn't feel the earth's floor in his solid leather boots, I did through my trainers. What was he looking for? When soil and stones came loose, I used to skid or fall. Sometimes debris tumbled and somersaulted down the hill, reminding me of more danger, but he never stopped or worried.

If Dad heard voices, he never said but I heard him muttering. I wished on those walks that we'd see other walkers, but we rarely did. Once or twice we heard voices from afar, but mostly it was just us, the trees and the creatures that liked to remain hidden with us.

Sometimes, when we got home tired and hungry after a long walk, I wanted to tell Mum about what we'd seen but he'd tell me to stay away because she was particularly unwell. Then he yelled that it was his job, not mine, to nurse her now the cancer had spread to her pancreas. 'Stay out!' His fierce love and protectiveness of Mum made me yearn for his attention all the more, but he was too busy loving and caring for her.

On a walk one spring, just before it fell dark, he asked me why I was crying. When I explained my boyfriend had cheated on me and we'd split up, he patted my back and shoulder roughly. He rarely hugged or kissed me, so the gesture was kind in its own way. I took it as a cue to talk more about how I felt. He walked by the side of me rather than up ahead, so he must have slowed his pace for once. After I'd done talking, he said nature doesn't feel sorry for itself and neither should I.

By then, the oaks and sycamores were familiar to me: I wasn't scared of their iron trunks, but when the derelict outhouse stepped out of the shadows, it was a surprise to us both. The winter had dislodged and decapitated branches. We climbed over them; twigs snapped; we clambered a lot. It was a rough den, a squalid, squat building without a redeeming feature, ugly and man-made in amongst so much natural beauty.

Sometime later, I lost my virginity in that outhouse. Dad had said he could smell the pheromones of spring: he was right about that.

I'll never know if eyes were spying on us or if it was just in my imagination. I got a sense that threats aren't always visible. My first time wasn't romantic. It was a way of getting back at Dad for his sternness, for being gentler with Mum than he was with me. It seems childish now.

Beside the deckchair is a large storage box, the kind that is meant to stay intact and damp-free even if buried underground. I remove the sturdy lid to take out Dad's overalls which still have a faint whiff of bonfires, or am I imagining that?

Dad.

My shoulders relax at the sound of his name. He is starting to come to life again, to be remembered as the man he was, not the corpse in the garden, not the source of horror and shock that gripped me that day and hasn't fully let go since.

From the box, I remove Dad's pocketknife and a plastic bag from Next. I know from the brand that the bag's one of mine, but I can't remember what's inside. The contents feel slim and rustle like paper – something I wanted to keep safe and dry. I turn the bag upside down and Dad's hand-drawn maps of his walks in the woodland tumble onto the garage floor. There are four of them. Fragile, almost transparent. The paper is virtually weightless, yet I feel weighted down by these smooth pages that have been thinned by touch. They are made from trees in every way. Fine pencil lines, symbols and annotations delineate the routes in Dad's hand. I trace a pencil line with my finger as if it were a footprint, and when I sigh the paper does too.

There's almost a quarter of an acre of lawn at Maple Cottage, more than enough to create a garden of some kind that both remembers Dad and forgets his ugly death. The hand-drawn maps of the routes he loved to follow will take me to the plants he loved, and I will grow those in the garden in his memory. Then, when I look at them, I will remember his tanned and weather-beaten skin, the man I worshipped like a god in our kingdom of hens and trees.

~

I calculate I have about two hours to explore the wood and find the derelict outhouse before it grows dark. I climb over the stile, where a familiar fingerpost orientates me. The path climbs to the left for a few hundred metres, edged by silhouettes of old friends: mature oaks, pines and sycamores. I feel like I'm setting foot on an island I've visited before where the light and sound are different from the rest of the world. I want to climb to the top of Peckforton Hill, look out across the Cheshire plains with the

Welsh hills in the distance, and see the miniature smoking chimney of Maple Cottage down below.

The gradient gets steeper. Once I get to the top of Peckforton Hill, I pause to take in the view. Dad's ashes are scattered here. I see the outline of my next-door neighbour Shirley's trees in her vast garden. Ronald, who owns Witton Farm, is out on his John Deere tractor. The fields are bereft of cattle in the winter but there are dots of soft white grazing further away. I remember the pleasure I felt when we saw smoke from our chimney that sent Dad and I hurrying home to our cosy oasis. The churchyard where Mum is buried is in view. It is a landscape that doesn't need a map because its contours are the lines in the palm of my hand.

The footpath from here is so embedded in my consciousness that I could close my eyes and still find my way. The last few remaining leaves to the side of the path and above stir as I move deeper and deeper into the wood. I pick my way through fallen branches, dry and stiff as old bones; they snap underfoot. I start to regret my bold decision to return here alone, especially where the sunlight is serrated through the trees, but I have been thinking about walking through the woods and revisiting old haunts for so long. There are many paths to revisit now that I'm living on the doorstep; I need to know them again. The map in my hand gives me the courage to press on, despite my reservations.

At the sound of rustling in the trees, I turn swiftly; a grey squirrel leaps from one tree to another. A rabbit hops across the path and dives into a bed of nettles, startling me. Its bobbing white tail disappears. Soil, deep red, is scattered over fallen leaves and roots where rabbits have dug their burrows. It's a home of a kind for more than meets the eye. It's wonderful to see wildlife again after living next door to fake grass and artificial hanging baskets. I tell myself to relax and enjoy the scenery. Those skulls could have been left on the lawn as a joke by an old boyfriend.

There's a whiff of cigarette smoke. I look this way and that, expecting to see a dog walker, but only the lingering smell remains. It hangs in the air without a signature.

By the time I find the outhouse, I'm desperate for a wee. The building still has a padlocked door, and part of its copper roof is shaped like a rack of ribs. The window, my old entry point, is still broken. Dad thought the Army might have built the outhouse for training purposes, but it has long remained unused, neglected – and yet strangely pulsing. I think back to being around fifteen, lying on a picnic blanket I'd sneaked out of the airing cupboard so Stephen and I could be comfortable for our first time.

I unfasten my jeans as I step over fallen branches, holly and blue roundhead mushrooms like blue eggs. The wall feels alive with moisture. I yank down my knickers, let the pee 'ssshhhh' onto a pile of twigs and leaves, and I sigh as steam rises. Then a waft of something unpleasant catches my nose, turning me towards the window where the smell is coming from.

The skulls are in there, strewn amidst litter and the carcass of what might have been a rabbit. If the skulls are in a formation this time, I can't read it, but still they whisper and still they stare accusingly. Holes for eyes. Everywhere there are reproachful eyes, as if I should not be living at Maple Cottage.

If more eyes are watching me from a vantage point in the wood, they see me turn too quickly, catch my walking boot between branches and land awkwardly on a pile of branches. A swarm of flies hisses away angrily as my hands yank at the branches and become wrapped in spiders' webs thick as chain mail. I panic because my ankle is stuck; all around me, the pine trees morph into prison bars, the tree canopy into concrete.

'Get off!'

My body lights up with fear as my heart disintegrates in my ribs. I run towards a gap in the trees, ragging the air with clouds of breath, puffing, a miniature ghost train that startles the birds. I am desperate to get into the light. I keep running to the sound of a protest of wings and the racket of emergency bird talk. Can I hear my footsteps, or someone else's?

If I thought someone would hear, I would scream. Spit is forming at the corners of my mouth. I keep running. Branches touch one another, battling for space and light, forming a tunnel above my head.

I run until I am close to the front door of Maple Cottage. I sense the woods are still tapping me on my shoulder. Surprisingly, there aren't pine cones and acorns on the front doormat where my feet are now sweating and where I catch my breath. Dad's feet carried the wood to our door in more ways than one. Is he haunting me?

My new welcome mat is turned the wrong way around. There's a fag butt, too. I turn to look around before I adjust the mat and pick up the butt. There isn't a lingering smell of smoke.

Inside, the kitchen tap drips, drips, drips. It's so still that I hear my own breathing, fast from running. Each sound is louder than it should be and louder than the one before. It's tempting to call out, *Mum, Dad – I'm back. Help me. Someone is following me.*

4

Mum's grave is surprisingly neat and adorned with a small bouquet of carnations. I place my small posy of purple tulips and wipe away some of the moss on her stone. It isn't the winter weather that makes me shiver beneath my wax jacket.

I'm glad my hair hangs loosely over my face when a gentleman walks by with a kneeling pad in one hand. The sight of the plastic pad makes me realise I will have dirty wet knees when I stand up. Not that it matters. The small village church and graveyard are only two miles from Maple Cottage. With a bright blue sky to keep me company, it is a perfect day to visit Mum and to tell her how much I love her.

'Hello, Mum. It's Rachel.'

My eyelashes are sticky with tears.

The oak-veneer coffin was closed, so I still think of her in pastel shades. Thankfully, there was a lid on the erosion that cancer took out of her lovely self. The dignity of the service put a lid on the grief we wept into handkerchiefs. The coffin, the prayers, the hymns we sang – religion was a brocade to muffle the pain of loss. Better that than the horror of a crime scene attacking the senses.

I said my goodbye to Mum with Dad and her friends beside me. We had known all along that she wouldn't age beyond seventy, but still Dad's grief wailed, howled, bared teeth, devoured sinew. He cried so loudly, his insides ripping, snapping. It was a snarling, devouring grief. Unlike Dad's suicide, Mum's death didn't leave the taste of shock in my mouth, but she still left us feeling bereft because we had loved her.

I picture her in the rocking chair, sewing, occasionally looking up to watch a bird in the garden or Dad with the hens. When the rocking chair in the kitchen rocks itself, it soothes me. I think it misses the feel of her wool cardie, blue with a few missing buttons. Sometimes she used that as a blanket.

The lump in my throat is so misshapen I can't swallow properly.

'I miss you, Mum.'

I stroke the key to the front door to Maple Cottage that is wedged in my coat pocket now that I am the custodian of its mysteries, sadness and its joys. There's an old ticket for the tram in my pocket too, which belongs to another world.

I remember that at this time of year Mum would be busy decorating the house for Christmas – cones, holly and foliage sprayed in white-snow paint – and putting a tree in the lounge adorned in purple tinsel. The routines of Christmas Day with just the three of us didn't change in the twenty years we shared them. I recall the soundtrack of pots and pans, laughter, the Queen's speech, Christmas carols and Sinatra – because Dad loved his voice – all coalesced in the warmth and glow of an open fire.

This year it will be Adam and me beside the open fire and I will make our nest just as homely. I will clean the grate of ashes, dust and voices; I will put a match to the kindling and we will warm our toes side by side.

'I'll be back again soon.'

The walk home is pleasant. I am buoyed up with hope and joy to be home again. In five days, Adam will be back in the UK with a suitcase, a laptop and jet lag. He will return to his new home – our new home – for Christmas. I remember on a wet day in November about two years ago he drove through a thunderstorm from Altrincham to Peckforton so I could visit Mum's grave on her birthday. He was jaded from work and the traffic was awful, but he didn't complain. Not once.

Each bend in the lane is familiar and a happy geography. Winter's fingers grip my face, chill my hands. I rub my cold cheeks. Like Mum, I have green, almond-shaped eyes and thick hair. Mum's face was longer than my heart-shaped one, and her mouth was fuller than mine. Dad used to say we were both 'vertically challenged'; he stood over six foot tall, a foot taller than us.

When I found his corpse, his mouth was open as if a fisherman's hook had plucked him from the sea. I still listened for a heartbeat while knowing he was dead. For all my sadness, I felt angry that he'd left me abandoned, choosing heaven and Mum.

I hadn't seen a dead body before I saw Dad's corpse. Amongst a riot of nature, creatures were never far from him, even in death. That day I found him, I noticed the largeness of his nose and the fullness of his lips, the unruly character of his eyebrows and the deep lines on his brow. I cupped his chin because it had dropped so much. He was unshaven and unwashed, an empty vessel of the man I knew.

All the brokenness of him was on show. How many tractors, cars and walkers had passed by or looked down from the top of Peckforton Hill on his corpse? I might not have seen him first.

Perhaps I was fourth or fifth to find the legacy of a man, all his broken bits, all the broken days he'd lived alone. I couldn't bear the thought of his unhappiness while I was shagging or poring over a textbook from the library, sleeping in, doodling during lectures, thinking there was all the time in the world for my next visit.

I walk more quickly and a John Deere tractor rumbles by. The woods come closer; they seem to throb as if they have a heartbeat. I can't wait for the bluebells, for the foxgloves and spring lambs in the fields. I think I will plant lilac by the front door and lots of lavender in the back garden. I am eager for the frosts to pass.

I think Adam and I have both been patient with one another in our own ways: I waited to move here, while he waits for me to fall pregnant. In my mind, the two are inextricably bound. A new home, a new year. It will come good.

As soon as I get home, I stride the width and length of a section of the garden, twenty feet by twenty feet. At the kitchen table, in the same place where my parents and I enjoyed meals together, I make a plan for the garden then give my project a name: *Rachel's Garden of Rooms*.

The back garden is waiting for me to transform it. I'm sure of it.

From this kitchen table, I want to look out onto the garden of rooms. I don't want to feel the vacancy of the place spread about like an abandoned house after a party, tables full of debris but the people gone, the odd balloon full of air and the odd bottle of wine that hasn't been drunk in amongst crumbs and crumpled serviettes. There is only a memory of a great party; what is left behind is the aftermath and the hangover.

If I hadn't arrived, what would have become of Dad's flesh and bones, his teeth and hair? The crows hadn't pecked his eyeballs – at least they hadn't got to him. His chair stopped him from falling to the ground, a cheap garden deckchair he'd spent happy hours in, enjoying the view, drinking tea, flexing his toes after a long day in boots.

When I found him, his skin had already got thinner, translucent. A still life whose paint had run. I had wished he was sleeping under the clouds, just taking a Sunday lunchtime nap.

Green was the colour of my father; his step was as sure and silent as the sap rising. Mum's colour and perfume were lavender – her soap, her talc, the candles in the lounge, and the soft tinkling of her voice, so like a soft wind chime in the breeze. Ideas for their rooms in the garden come easily to me. And Jen, my best friend, whose room has to be a riot of colour, a jangle of sunshine yellows and tangerine. I will create a room for Adam, too, but what is his colour? I don't know.

Room one: Dad's. Evergreens. Native, semi-wild, colourful, berries, mushrooms. Food for birds, bees, butterflies and other insects.

Room two: Mum's. Lavender. Mauve wildflowers. Colour all year round.

Room three: Jen's. Lots of magentas, scarlet and yellow tulips, orange dahlias, a flutter of pink lupins. The hues of sunsets, summer holidays, cocktails.

Room four: Adam's?

Room five: A future room for our baby?

I prepared a speech for Dad's funeral, but I was too broken to stand up and speak so Roland, Dad's good friend who owns Witton Farm, did it. Adam says not to beat myself up about that. He didn't have a father to cremate. I should count myself lucky I had a dad to write about in the first place.

The locals said why poison, when Dad had a gun? I thought the same. I said my goodbye to his poisoned corpse and all the neighbours came to the funeral. Then they went home and counted their blessings that they'd not been Dad, a widower.

And perhaps not me, either, a grown-up kind of orphan where the order of deaths was all wrong.

Having lost my parents, I was afraid there would be no one to mourn my death. When I met Adam, I found someone. He was older than me and the most thoughtful man I'd ever met, not to mention handsome, so I fell into his arms. There were never any games or teasing; our flirtation was brief because the romance was always heading somewhere. We both needed someone and it felt like we fitted together. If it weren't for Adam, I would have remained nomadic, a lost soul scared of life, uncomfortable in my own skin because it felt sore and raw. Abandoned. Dad chose death over me; he chose Mum as he always had. Adam chose me and saved me.

Hasn't he?

I drive to the Hollies Nursery with my plan for the Garden of Rooms beside me on the passenger seat. I take the bends a little too quickly because I'm excited about the project and telling Ollie about the initiative I am taking. It's unlike me to be assertive, but I feel passionate about this project, about Maple Cottage and a happier future. Adam often tells me that I should be more confident and believe in myself, but today I am assertive. I might not fall pregnant easily, but I will nurture plants and flowers and embrace wildlife.

Hollies Nursery has three enormous greenhouses and a separate shop and office. The front of the nursery is mainly a car park with a display of pots, garden furniture and a few large troughs planted out with winter pansies.

I eventually find Ollie in one of the greenhouses. He is bent over with his hands deep in the soil. He carries his cupped hands to his nose before letting the crumbly loam fall through his thick fingers. It's surprisingly intimate to watch such a big man handle the soil so sensually. Sweat trickles down his nose into his mouth. He must have been digging for a long time;

sweat stains start at the top of his denim shirt and spread to under his arms.

'Ollie! Hi!'

'You caught me hard at it,' he says. He wipes the sweat from his face with his sleeve and smiles his generous smile. 'How are you?'

'Fabulous! I've had inspiration for the back garden.'

He consults the Lilliputian plan for the garden of rooms before making tentative suggestions. 'Box hedging for the walls would give it structure. Maybe Angel's Trumpet for your dad's room? It's beautiful but deadly – and *Lavandula x intermedia*, which commercial growers use for its strong scent.'

'Yes, perfect.'

His enthusiasm is infectious and I am buzzing with excitement as I follow him into the office. We identify the wildflowers in the wood with the aid of a book, and my list for Mum's room grows to include bluebells, wild thyme and germander speedwell, all purple or deep-blue hues and great for insects. My family is taking shape once more, eradicating the grey ghostly images I've been carrying around.

'I love it! I wish it were spring so we could get going.' My feet shuffle around on the dusty floor.

'I'll cost it for you and give you a quote for the labour plus the plants. Once the frosts are over, I can start preparing the soil. If you want immediate impact, we can order decent-sized plants grown in pots.' The mention of money knocks an edge off my excitement for a moment, which he senses. 'Does that sound fine?'

Adam generally likes to keep control of our finances when it's a costly purchase or project, so I might have to find a way to get the money to make this project happen. I am only a part-time teacher; Adam is the breadwinner.

I'll find a way to pay for the best. 'Instant colour would be wonderful.'

'I'll call round once the quotation is ready. Is there a good time?'

'Any,' I say. I smile all the way back to my car, skipping over the puddles, feeling lighter and happier than I have in a long time. I pull out of the car park and, in my rear-view mirror I see the pots of winter pansies and the greenhouses grow smaller and smaller.

5

Shirley's drive sweeps to the left then to the right, like a tango in slow motion. The Bird House has an elegance to it. I love that there are numerous seats in her garden, waiting for stories between people; there's a wrought-iron bench under a mature oak, a loveseat under a beech tree, and a hammock suspended between two poplars.

I've always admired and liked Shirley, ever since I perched on her window seat, swinging my legs in white knee-length socks. She taught me the names of the visitors to the multitude of bird feeders in her magnificent garden, impressing me with the way she gave each bird a memorable personality, like the bramble-picking blue tit and the diminutive wren that she called 'the singing coach'. It seemed she knew them as friends.

The borders, mainly filled with roses, fringe the patio, which is another canvas for an elegant large table and chairs. All the chairs are empty, but the garden doesn't feel like that. The exterior of the house is wrapped in ivy and wisteria, a living wall in the spring, trembling as little birds fly out to find food to feed their young. It's been a home for Shirley's family for generations and it has kept that lived-in feel, despite Shirley's single occupancy. I can't wait to see her again, and I feel grateful for her warm invitation for tea and cake and a natter.

Before I can knock, she opens the door. She is wearing red lipstick and her fiery red hair is piled on top of her head in a loose chignon. 'You've come!' Dressed in black and a splash of white, the combination with her red hair reminds me of a red admiral butterfly. She opens her arms wide. 'I've been waiting for you to come home!'

I hug her back. 'Me too.'

'Gosh, you are so like Dilly!' Her eyes look watery for a second. 'Your green eyes and the shape of your face!' She puts a hand on my shoulder. 'Come in. I'll grab another cup and saucer. Make yourself at home.' She looks down at my feet. 'Good to see you back in wellies, back where you belong.'

'Still muddy as ever! I'll leave them by the door – like I used to.'

I make myself comfortable on the Chesterfield sofa in the lounge while she makes comforting sounds in the kitchen. A Victoria sponge cake and a silver bowl of sugar lumps take centre stage on a well-used leather footstool. My eyes drink in the room's loveliness: the wrought-iron handles; a traditional bureau in dark English oak and mahogany; curtains in pretty English-country colours; the large bay window that fills the rooms with light that has a silvery quality; a window seat, and a pair of binoculars. I recall feeling a draught from that window and I see that it still doesn't close properly. A Chinese split-bamboo blind hangs at another window as if drunk, and a concertina of unopened mail is piled on the sideboard.

'Won't be a moment, darling! It's a kettle with its own deadline,' Shirley calls from the kitchen.

A bottle of HP sauce has made itself at home on the mantelpiece, dribbling a little. I feel a trickle of jealousy at the lived-in permanence of this house, this life. It's a masterpiece, although it does need a touch up or tidy up in places. Still, if it were perfect it wouldn't have such charm. A pot of tea and a delicate cup and saucer of mismatching hues balance on a coffee table beside Shirley's chair.

'I love sugar lumps,' Shirley says, as she manages to squeeze yet another mismatched cup and saucer onto the coffee table. 'I'll pour, you cut.' She passes me a knife to cut the cake and two paper napkins. 'Saves on the washing-up.' We tuck into the cake in comfortable silence. I hear Shirley chomp and slurp her tea with such contentment that I find myself asking for another slice of cake.

She tells me about philopatry, nest-faithfulness. 'The swallows never fail to return year after year, travelling thousands of miles from Africa. All creatures migrate home. Including you, my dear. You're brave and wise to come back, Rachel. Your parents would be so happy to have you at Maple Cottage. I'm getting on a bit, but I'd sooner lose a limb than move to a bungalow.'

'It's lovely to be back here just doing simple things. Like yesterday, I took flowers to Mum's grave and I walked in the woods. Little has changed. And it's so good to see you. You haven't changed a bit,' I say, smiling at her.

'I visit your mum now and then. The flowers there will be from me, I expect.'

'That's nice of you.' I lean closer. 'Is that a magpie?' I ask.

Shirley's beige bra strap is showing; her cowl-neck top has slipped to one side as if she's been on a ship on a rough sea. The image of a bird is tattooed near her clavicle. She strokes it as if she's stroking living feathers. 'Russ. I'll tell you about him another day. I want to hear about you first.'

'I know about Russ. From Mum.'

'Then you know she didn't approve because he was married.' Shirley takes a sip of her tea and slips some cake into her mouth.

'I suppose you're not a little girl anymore, so might understand about matters of the heart. Your mother thought it was scandalous for quite a long time. What she didn't understand was that he was the love of my life. And still is.'

'But the tattoo? You don't sound like you regret it...'

'You misunderstand what this bird stands for. I forgive you for being judgemental.'

'Sorry. I– Is that a dead cat on your lawn?'

'If you're referring to the predator on the lawn, I shot it. It was after the robin's nest. Full of chicks. Your dad helped me get my eye in many years ago.' She takes a long sip of tea and picks up the thread of conversation. 'I'm only sorry I couldn't attend dear Russ's funeral. Now that you ask, I'll tell you. You see, it felt unfinished, so in the end I drove into town and got a tattoo while his wife prayed and threw soil onto his coffin.'

She takes a long slurp of tea to revive herself. 'I like to think the cuckquean and I shared the pain of Russell's death. Do you think I chose the magpie as a symbol of stealing someone's husband or feeling guilty? Absolutely not. To me, death stole Russ. The magpie is my symbol of loss and grief. Quite different, you see. It's surprising how we all see things differently.'

It isn't for me to judge, but I feel sorry for Russell's wife. Twenty years is a long time to share your husband with another woman. 'Yes...'

'What do *you* think of me having a passionate affair with a married man? An affair lasting longer than many marriages. At first, your mum treated me like I had an infectious disease. It was quite funny, really, but we were good friends eventually.'

'Was it like a long holiday? All romance, not real life?'

Shirley laughs. 'In some ways, but affairs are real life with great joys and sacrifices, like any relationship. I loved Russell, so I know the heartache. Being with him wasn't a break from real life at all; it *was* my life. I just had less time with him.'

'It sounds... hard.'

'Tell me about you. You're married, I see.'

I look at the large diamond ring on my finger. 'Yes, for two years. Adam. We met soon after Dad died and got married six months later. He's thirty-five, handsome, and an incredible businessman. His mum brought him up in Carlisle between working shifts in a chip shop. He looks out for me – you know, the yin and yang thing, or whatever it's called. He's the rational, balanced half.'

'Being a grafter is all very well, but is he any fun, darling?'

I put my hand over my mouth as I laugh. 'He can be! Especially in the bath!'

'Describe your first kiss. Go on. In detail.' Shirley sticks her chin out and closes her eyes to give the impression of listening intently.

I tell her it was in the revolving door to the Four Seasons Hotel in central Hong Kong where we were both working at the time: me teaching adults English as a second language, and him at a conference and networking event. We'd had coffee and pastries and were about to leave when the rain came. He pushed the door so it revolved again, then he wrapped me in his red silk-lined overcoat and kissed me tenderly for the whole three hundred and sixty degrees.

'Pssh! That's in a film! Is he authentic?'

Shirley was always difficult to impress, so I try harder. He proposed on Valentine's Day. We were married in Venice six months later. I still have the special Jimmy Choo shoes I bought for the occasion, which I will never wear again. They hurt so much I might as well have had my feet bound. I tell her I stopped being a negative in my own darkroom; my black-and-white self-image started to change. I don't tell her the rest, the bits on the cutting-room floor.

'When I find the photo albums, I'll show you the pictures,' I say. I show her a recent photo of Adam on my phone. He's wearing one of his favourite suits plus a sapphire-blue and silver striped tie. His cufflinks are the size of gold nuggets. I like the photograph because it was taken just after a romantic dinner in an artisan restaurant in Wilmslow.

'Older man. Dark and handsome.' She scrutinises the photo closer still. 'A city boy. His clothes are very sharp, I must say.'

'It's been a whirlwind romance. Adam's keen to...'

'Start a family?'

I look at my nails, which I've started to bite recently. 'Adam has expensive taste in shoes – well, pretty much everything actually. You'll like him when you meet him.'

'When will that be, dear?'

'He's due back on the twenty-third of December.'

After telling me about the party she is planning for New Year's Eve, she glances at her watch. 'Can I treat you to an early dinner tonight? I tend to eat promptly at six o'clock so I can get an early night – I need my beauty sleep.'

'I'd like that. I'll pick you up later.' I kiss her goodbye and catch her familiar scent, Chanel No. 5; she's never worn anything else.

Maple Cottage feels very modest in comparison to The Bird House but in a cosy and comfortable way. I decide against lighting a fire as I am going out for dinner. Before I get side-tracked, I rummage in my wardrobe for something suitable to wear. Anything other than jeans feels wrong on me but Shirley always dresses well, so I opt for a shirt dress and boots.

Adam phones as I am tidying away the garments I've flung on the bed. 'Hello, gorgeous wife! How are you?'

'Oh, Adam, I'm fine! I've just been round to Shirley's. She's invited me out for dinner.'

'Good. I'm glad you've got company.'

'And she's invited us to a New Year's Eve party at her house.'

'Almost another year–'

'It'll be a lovely evening, no expense spared.'

'Shall we go to the funfair at Nantwich? I remember you used to go years ago, didn't you?'

'I wasn't scared of the big rides then.'

'I'll hold your hand. By the way, don't worry about the money side of things for your gardening project. You focus on the creative. Your gardener and I will reach an understanding, if you text me his number. You let him know what you want, and we'll sort the rest between us.'

'The gardener's called Ollie – I'll text you his number now, so I don't forget.'

'You sound happy.'

'I am! I can't wait to get started on the garden. Honestly, it's going to be amazing.'

'And it's not stirring up painful memories of your dad?' He waits for me to reply. 'Rachel?'

'It's a relief to get Mum's curtains up. I don't like looking out on blackness.'

'That woman was out of order.'

'Don't be angry. Devina's a nice woman but struggling for money – and I get the impression her teenage son isn't the easiest.'

'That's no excuse. Did you say Devina lives on Gospel Avenue in Nantwich?' I confirm she does. 'I'm proud of you for coping with the move. I can't wait to be home.'

We talk about our plans here for Christmas, which include the christening for Jen's son, Will, and long lunches out as well as evenings in beside the fire.

'I love you. See you very soon.'

The Olive Tree is tucked away down a side street. Its regular customers keep its existence a closely guarded secret. Shirley says she likes the fact they have toothpicks on the table. I notice she is carrying a huge, soft Italian bag and her hair looks like a floppy petal from a wild poppy. Her skin is powdered too heavily in places, captured in the creases in her chin, so I want to dab it away. I rarely wear make-up when Adam is away but, because we are out for dinner, I've applied green eyeliner and lip gloss, preferring a natural look to anything too obviously made-up.

'This way please, ladies.'

We follow the waiter into a small room containing four tables, all beautifully laid with fresh linen and shining glasses. Shirley is wearing what might have come out of a dressing-up box or a very expensive and fashionable boutique, I'm not sure which.

'Your usual table by the window,' the waiter says stiffly, then turns to Shirley for praise.

I admire her extraordinary gold dangly earrings, which make a brief appearance from under her hair as she moves her head to smile widely. 'Perfect.'

The tablecloth on which the waiter places the menus is flawless white, which I appreciate all the more once he lights a small candle and returns with a bowl of olives. He comes and goes like the ripples of a wave, each one better than the last. 'Your usual, Ms Cashmere.'

'Thank you, Julian. You are adorable.'

As we drink, I tell her about my ideas for the garden of rooms. I can't stop myself from enthusing about the project. It's the first time we have talked in any detail, albeit indirectly, about my parents. She urges me to enter the local Open Garden Day in June next year. Before I know it, I've agreed.

Shirley's specially made pizza arrives with a flourish. 'I adore carbohydrates!' she says.

The waiter adds parmesan cheese to my spaghetti Bolognese while we talk about cooking. Neither Adam nor I particularly enjoy it; he's hard to cook for because he is fussy about food, especially when he's training for a marathon or a tennis tournament. He insists on healthy eating, whereas I'll pretty much eat anything.

'Your dad was quite a good cook, you know,' Shirley says.

'Dad? No, he rarely set foot in the kitchen. That was Mum's domain.'

Shirley adds hastily, 'Perhaps it was when you were at university.'

'I forget I was away at university.'

'Is everything all right with your meals, ladies?' asks Julian. 'Would you like to see the dessert menu?'

'Profiteroles,' Shirley says without hesitation. 'I'm low on chocolate this week.'

I order the same.

'Did you see much of Mum after I left for uni?' I ask.

'Yes. Dilly made her peace with me, flaws and all. I don't bear a grudge. Besides, she made an excellent chocolate cake. More cream?'

I shake my head, full of grief and sensing that Shirley wants to change the subject. The one thing I want more than anything is a conversation with Mum. 'Do you know if I did something to upset her?'

Shirley reaches for my hand. 'She loved you, more than you...' A blob of cream spurts out of her profiterole and rolls down her dress. 'Bugger! Such a waste.' She pulls her dress taut then expertly collects the cream and chocolate and eats it. 'Delicious.'

'Do people still talk about Dad's death?'

'Oh, your dad was a good man. If they do, it's to remember him that way. All that nasty speculation about financial ruin soon burnt itself out. People will always talk, but you don't always have to listen. It's – what? – three years ago now. There are quite a few new people who've arrived in the village since then. Pass the sugar.'

Shirley adds a lump to her coffee. A splash catches her chin.

'Why do you think he took his life?'

She thinks for a long time as she stirs her coffee. 'Your dad was lost without your mum. He'd spent so long looking after her that he didn't know what to do with himself once she'd gone.'

'I wish I'd been a reason to–'

'Your parents didn't want to burden you with their woes. That's how much they loved you.'

'Still, I would have nursed Mum, lived with Dad. I would have–'

'Exactly, and they didn't want that.'

'No.'

'It took me years to get over Russ's death and I spent more nights alone than with him. Your dad must have felt it terribly.'

'He was under strain,' I say, recalling him in the woods barking at me, sometimes even frightening me a little with his sternness. When I was testing my wings in my teens, Mum and I had the odd fallout about nothing – chores and bedtimes mostly. Dad presided over our arguments like a bird of prey and, for the most part, I felt timid in the shadow of his wingspan and backed down because he always defended Mum with a fierce protectiveness. He doted on her; if I upset her or let her down, I feared his wrath. But he was a good father. I always knew that and, when the jesses came off, I think I had Dad to thank.

What was the worst thing I did to Mum? I was ungrateful, lazy, sometimes a liar if lying got me a few more hours with my friends or a boyfriend. I stole her perfume when mine ran out. Once or twice, I puked on my bedroom carpet. But I didn't completely flunk my exams, and I didn't get pregnant when I was at school. Dad's Land Rover got a few extra bumps when I learnt to drive, but it is the kind of vehicle that looked better for a few scars.

'I hope I've done the right thing in coming back here. Sometimes I'm ecstatic about it, like it's the natural thing to do, then the next thing I'm lying awake thinking you should never go back.'

'Give it time.'

'You're right. I'm a worrier, always have been.' I take a deep breath; it's only a few skulls, after all. There is no need to report it to the police or make a fuss about nothing. 'I'll get the bill.'

'No, it's my treat. It means a lot to have you back, Rachel.'

We hug for a long time before we part company. I feel anxious about being alone for another night, but I don't let it show. She is such a lovely woman; I couldn't wish for a better neighbour.

The landline is ringing as I unlock the front door and hastily drop my handbag in the hall. I reach the phone just in time, a little breathless and agitated that someone is ringing after 10pm. If Adam were calling me back about financing the gardening project, he'd call my mobile. The hollow eyes of a skull flash before me as I pick up the phone.

'Hello? Hello? Is anybody there?'

I think I hear someone breathing, or maybe it's the sound of my own breath. A long low exhalation of air travels down the phone. I hang up. For a while I stare at the receiver, dredging through memories of old boyfriends who I might have hurt, or enemies Mum and Dad might have had. It wouldn't be Adam playing with me, surely?

The shops and restaurants in Nantwich are closed now. The wind is growing stronger outside, rattling the metal debris of the chicken coop in the garden. Shadows cast by the interior doors are hostile as I feel myself unravel. Crouched in the corner of the sofa, I hug my bony knees and focus on my breath which comes out in torn rags, yanked from inside my chest by a cruel puppet master that I cannot see.

I tell myself there is nothing to see through the windows except thick black night pouring over the roof of the cottage, and the blank face of the garden. Soon that will change. That's one thing I can control.

6

Jen phones for a gossip on her way back home from dropping the twins at primary school. While she talks, I hear Will chattering away in his pram and a horn from a nearby car.

'Fuck me, it hurt!'

'What did?'

'Have you been listening?'

'Yes, but you cut out. It sounded like open-heart surgery.'

'Are you saying I'm a drama queen?' She laughs because she knows she is anything but self-effacing. 'I had another ear piercing, at the top part of my ear. It made me feel better. I wasn't exactly at bikini-body stage, but I had got as far as thinking about a diet and exercise plan. Will is almost old enough to stop puking down my shoulder, so I was on the verge of getting my nice clothes out of the suitcase again. No need now. I won't be going anywhere. Especially not with those little side dishes that come with pregnancy, like swollen feet, heartburn and nausea.'

'How are you coping?' I ask, sensing she needs to let off steam.

'I'm on top of absolutely nothing, not the cleaning, the washing, the ironing, the kids' homework, the shopping. Even bedtime routines have gone out of the window. There is nothing left of me. Is it possible to miss oneself? Anyway, the only good thing is our dog is getting lots of walks from Jonny, who tells me he is going around the block.'

'I didn't think he liked exercise.'

'Exactly, he doesn't. I'm obviously not great company at the moment.'

I tell her I fantasise about pushing a Sainsbury's trolley round with a baby facing me, and driving my Golf with a baby face in my wing mirror. But Jen provides a reality check on family life. 'You forget about the breast pump, the nipple cream, the mangy teddy bears, the one-eared doll and the pram and all the birthday parties to come, the shit, the toenail clippings, the sick and stink and...'

'But I still want to be a mum!'

Jen speaks her mind; she is the definition of candid. Her words don't massage, they slap and tingle the skin, leave handprints. She is a year older than me and has always had a way of weighing up people that leaves me in awe. At twenty, she said I looked expensive but low maintenance; I was her favourite silent film, I had an aura like melted butter. To me she was – and still is – a waterfall of sound and movement that doesn't ever stop.

'Devina – the tenant – left a mobile suspended from the ceiling in what was her son's nursery. It gave me the creeps, hovering above nothing.'

'What have you done with it?'

'Chucked it in the garage. I couldn't bin it.'

'Why the hell not?'

'It's a symbol.'

'Rach, love, it's someone else's mobile. Plastic, probably. Mass-produced.'

The image of it suspended from the ceiling comes to me: a bird tangling among the thermals. I recall that the mobile made a satisfying soft thud as it landed on the beige carpet when I pulled it down, an end to the lullaby hush in the empty room. The fluffy clouds and silver stars stopped spinning and splashed onto the carpet.

'How's your freckle?' Jen asks.

Jen has told me that parenthood is like a juggernaut: you can't get off, with signposts like 'first word' and 'first steps' keeping the wheels turning. She says that sometimes it feels like she's behind the wheel, driving at night with the lights off.

Still, the idea of wanting something that you can't control started to do something to me a while ago. It was gradual. I thought of it like a freckle that I hadn't noticed before but, if you looked closely, changed me a little. Jen and I talk about my freckle from time to time and it helps she understands how I feel.

'No bigger or smaller. Time keeps passing and still I'm not pregnant. Soon there'll be no excuse for me not to be, now that we live here and Adam is almost forty.'

'Have you stopped manically washing up?'

'No! I can't help it!'

Jen laughs. Part of me knows how ridiculous I am being, but the other half can't stop. Time has become a tangible thing; it is the washing-up that piles up in the sink, on the kitchen units, even onto the kitchen table. Whatever I might be doing, I have to stop and wash up, get rid of the evidence that so much time has passed. Time is stuffed into an airing cupboard, only for the content to overflow onto the landing.

I guess time and I started falling out over a year ago; until then, I'd never really cared about it one way or another. Of course, I am no competition for time. Who can take time on as an adversary and win?

'Is Adam putting pressure on you?'

'No more than usual.'

'And has he paid that money back he *borrowed* from his employer?'

'Yes, of course,' I say more confidently than I feel because the topic is off limits with Adam. 'Anyway, the good news is I've got your room for the garden all planned out.'

'Really? Awesome! Go on.'

'Orange dahlias, magenta, scarlet and yellow tulips, and a flutter of pink lupins. The colour will grab you by the scruff of the neck. It's going to be fun, garish and jangling. Like you.'

'I feel better now and I can't wait to see my room. You are lovely.'

'And you're a veteran in the pregnancy department. It's going to be fine.'

'So will you and Adam be. Love you. Bye.'

I start to unpack another unopened box in the lounge. A couple of hours later, Ollie turns up in The Hollies van with a hanging basket of winter pansies and a spade. It's a cold, bright afternoon. The breeze catches a whisper of my hair, sweeps it round my head like a bandage, then playfully undoes it.

'These are from Adam,' he says cheerily. 'He was insistent that I brought them over.' He pulls out a poinsettia and amaryllis from the back of the van.

'He phoned you, then?'

'Yes. Consider your project underway.'

I clap my hands. 'Fabulous! Oh, it's going to be–'

Then I suddenly duck at the gavel-sound of gunfire, which sends our heads turning to the woods. I imagine a pheasant with an unlucky red face thumping to earth as the shooters reload guns beside the wagging tails of their gun dogs.

'More gunfire to come with it being the season for pheasant shooting,' Ollie says matter-of-factly.

'It's hardly a sport – especially when the trees thin out.'

'The pheasants are bred for it.'

The sunlight breaks through the leaves, exposing the pheasants' hiding places. With no camouflage, there is little chance of them surviving and it saddens me.

'I know.'

Sensing my unhappiness, Ollie changes the subject. 'I'll put an order in now so the suppliers know what we want. Once the frost passes, I can make a start on preparing the soil.'

'Great. Is your boss at The Hollies happy with you doing the work?' I ask.

'To be honest, it's money in my back pocket for travelling. I want to tour Europe and spend more time with my folks in Spain. Adam suggested it. If it were through The Hollies, they'd charge him more. Cash-in-hand suits me. I can work around my day job, no worries. The job doesn't pay much, though I do get free board which helps.'

'As long as you're sure.'

'Yeah. Have you got your Christmas tree yet?'

'It's on my to-do list.'

'No need. I've one in the van you can have.'

I've arranged holly, sprayed branches with white paint. It's vaguely festive, but the tree makes a real difference. We decide the best place for it is by the bay window in the lounge, near to a plug for the fairy lights. Ollie spends nearly half an hour wedging the tree with bricks, so it doesn't lean to one side. He swears a lot, which breaks the ice between us.

'It's got decent roots. As long as you remember to water it, I can replant it in the garden next year.'

'How are you celebrating Christmas?'

'At The Poacher – food, few games of pool. Nothing out of the ordinary. Might take a stroll through the woods.'

'The garden is going to be the best present I could wish for.'

'Adam's on board with it. How long is his flight home? Eight, nine hours?' Ollie speaks as if he has an image of a plane in the clouds in his mind's eye. I sense he wishes he was on it.

'It's about twelve hours. Adam suffers badly from jet lag. Sometimes he travels first class so he can sleep, but he's economy class this time. His boss gives him an amount of money for air travel each year which he has to budget.'

'When is he due back in the UK?'

'The twenty-third. I think he lands in the small hours. Sometimes he sleeps in his car at the airport for a power nap before he drives back, or he might be here first thing. It's always a surprise.'

'Your first Christmas here.'

'Yeah, I can't wait.'

'Have you got some Christmas decorations to go on this tree?'

I laugh. 'Somewhere. There's loads in my classroom at work. The children in my form group covered almost every window with some decoration or other. I usually feel a bit sad when term starts in the new year and they're still up, cheerful but redundant. I find remnants of tinsel on my desk and caught under chair legs for months afterwards.'

'Sounds like you care about your pupils. I don't remember my teachers giving two shits.'

'Of course. Children make me smile.'

'I see you're still unpacking.' He gestures at the open cardboard box, which I haven't made much progress with because it's full of Mum's things.

'Mum died of cancer four years ago. I've kept her measuring tape, even her pincushion and thimble. She was a seamstress –

she always carried a measuring tape in her apron pocket.' I kneel and pull out a beautifully embroidered bookmark. 'She posted this to me at university. It was the first bit of post I remember wanting to receive. I was made up with it.'

'Where did you study?'

'Sheffield. Mum passed away in my final term there.'

In my bedsit in Sheffield, with its small stove and miniature fridge, I lived in a doll's house; everything I needed was there, but on a small scale. It was a scale that inflicted neatness on me, not my mother's ways. I recall doing a lot of folding to make items small: towels and clothes and the facecloth beside my sink that Mum had embroidered with a poppy. I cooked a lot of eggs because I missed Dad and his hens, and I laid the table for one. I folded myself up too, like a piece of paper in the hands of an origami specialist. I needed to shrink and reshape to fit the new world I'd found myself in.

'Sounds tough on you and your dad.'

Sensitive to my mood, Ollie heads back to work, leaving me with the past pressed up against my face. I remember Mum sent a brief note with the embroidered bookmark. She said that she and Dad wanted to meet up at an unfamiliar restaurant a short walk from the train station in Leeds. I would have gladly hopped on the train home.

The restaurant where I saw Mum for the last time was nothing special; it was meaningless because we'd never been there before. It was the kind of place that reheats meals, and offers two for one during the week, not my parents' usual choice. It was a Saturday afternoon. I remember that children ran around our table and the door to the kitchen banged constantly.

The interior was countryfied; the owners had dressed the establishment with soft sofas, wingback chairs, tartan cushions, an open fire. The red-brick alcoves created cosy drinking and eating areas that concealed the true commercial scale of the pub and restaurant. It was just a few minutes from the city centre, anything but in the country, but the fake identity could be forgiven because of its convenience, I suppose.

My parents stared at me when I walked through the door. I assumed it was because I had adopted a different look since I'd seen them last. I was wearing my green parka and sweating in my DMs as usual; I wore them like a uniform. I was a student and I embraced it.

Mum stroked my hair before hugging me lightly. I'd had it cut into a bob since my last visit home. Her hair was different too.

We sat at a table for four nestled into a corner by the open fire. Above our heads was a series of paintings of fox hunting and other country pursuits. Mum positioned herself opposite an enormous oak-framed mirror on a duck-egg blue wall, but she didn't look at it once, perhaps because her skin had an unnatural pallor. She had aged since I'd last seen her, even though it was only two months ago.

'How have you been?' The words fell as soft as petals. I wanted to cry. I'd missed her terribly, but I wanted to be brave and stoical like she and Dad were.

She was wearing her best wool jacket and skirt. Dad was clean-shaven, dressed in a checked shirt and navy jumper, which he occasionally wore to go to the local pub for a pint and a game of skittles with Ronald from Witton Farm. His best gear. I would have rather seen them in their usual scruffy clothes. I wanted ordinary, familiar, but so little was.

'Great! I'm working hard for my finals. How are you, Mum? Why are we meeting here? I can easily hop on a train home. Anytime.'

Mum's eyes were on a horizon very far away where the sky and the land merged. I wanted to wave a flag, open my arms, shout, but I did none of those things.

'Oh, we thought it would be a change. I don't want to talk about me. Your dad's taking good care of me. Don't you worry.'

'You will say, won't you, if you need my help?'

I remember the food came then. Mum had ordered soup with a roll. I can't remember what Dad had for lunch, but I picked at a plate of scampi and chips. We spoke in picture-postcard sentences. *Great! Really well!* The conversation was as bland as the meal.

When a hush settled between us, temporary as a plump cushion waiting to be reshaped by a head or a back, I wittered on about the vast number of books I'd read for the exam on the Victorian period. Aside from the library, I spent a lot of time drinking in the student union with friends. The only real worry I had was whether I pulled at the end of the night, but I didn't tell them that.

Mum touched my hand and told me how proud she and Dad were of me and how important it was to remain focused on academic work. Dad said little, but he was always taciturn and more attentive to Mum than me. I told him I'd been on a trip with the orienteering club and his half-smile said too much. His eyes didn't move; they'd been set in clay. I caught a whiff of vinegar from the next table as I took in the lines under his eyes, knots in an ancient oak's bark.

'How are the hens, Dad?' I asked, so wanting him to talk to me. 'Is Lady still the boss?'

'She is. Keeps the others in line. They're all laying.'

Mum's blue eyes twinkled. 'Even if they weren't, you wouldn't mind.'

Mum and I shared a knowing smile. A flush of joy rose through me from being part of their circle. 'Has the pheasant shooting started?'

Dad nodded glumly. He looked exhausted, frayed. I talked about my new boyfriend and the basic meals I'd been making.

Mum looked relieved, and reminisced about a birthday cake I'd made for her when I was twelve. The memory of it choked her a little. She passed a plastic bag over to me full of sachets of hot chocolate, new socks and a bobble hat for the 'bitter weather ahead'.

When we stood up to say goodbye, I took Mum in my arms and hugged her. She felt as fragile as a twig. Her cheek was damp. Something hard formed in the pit of my stomach, a warm and solid sensation like I'd had a shot of whisky that had solidified. Her head was bowed, and her eyes lowered, avoiding mine.

I wanted her to see me.

I plucked up courage. 'I miss you, Mum,' I said. 'And you, Dad. I'll visit next month when the exams are over.'

Dad felt stable and strong in my arms, but I thought there were tears in his eyes, too.

'We are so proud of you.'

Dad rarely said anything emotional to me. His ways were calloused like his hands; his words were mostly gritty. Something close to fear stirred in my mind but I batted it away as they headed to the door, to the car, without a backward glance.

Outside, I recall the air was crisp. The sky had exploded with colour, lavender-blue, burnished orange and a near-fluorescent pink. The memory of my mum walking away to the car is in colour, as clear as if it were only yesterday. I watched them drift away, so much ugly black tarmac between us, a runway lined by street lights and fake plants.

I've wondered since then how those steps felt to her. To me, she drifted away, my guardian angel in nylon tights. Dad's arm was around her waist and I thought how loving they were to one another as they walked away. She leant on him, her head tilted to one side. On his other arm he carried her handbag, like Eve's wreath.

Close to their car, they stopped. My heart skipped a beat. Were they coming back? A bubble of hope floated up inside me. I so hoped they'd return, say why not come home with them for a bit, taste some home cooking. But the gentle steps kept going, each one another bite out of my heart.

Dad opened the car door for Mum and she eased in. Her hand was against the window. Her goodbye-forever gesture. Her delicate, pallid face behind the moving glass. Was my mouth a little open? Or hers?

I was mesmerised by the image of her behind that hand, moving further and further away, smeared, blurred, her face distorted, until the hand and the car vanished.

At the time, I didn't know that was the last time I would see Mum alive. And yet, something inside me knew that the end would come soon. If only I had listened hard enough. It was our last meal together as a family. I waved long after they were out of sight. I felt like I had forever lost the smell of smoke and lavender hanging on to my skin and replaced it with the restaurant's stench of chips and vinegar.

I could have walked to the station and caught a train back home to Sheffield – or even a train to Crewe. Instead, I walked back inside The Wheatsheaf, ordered a pint of cider and sat at our table again. I remember how the wine glasses remained shiny and empty on our table.

I replayed the meal in my mind, the words we'd exchanged. I had never felt so lonely or hollowed out. I was young, selfish and fixated on how Mum had forgotten how many sugars I take in my coffee; I thought that was a sign she'd forgotten all about me.

In the ladies, I tried to gather myself by staring in the mirror above the sink to stem the tears welling up in my tight throat. The corrosiveness of a brief absence had made us strangers. After knowing each other intimately for twenty-one years, it seemed like two months apart had undone so much. It had undone stitches and seams of time; picked holes in memories. It was proof that I wasn't important to her anymore and my heart broke. Not feeling that I knew them anymore made me feel like I didn't know myself.

I bought a packet of condoms from the vending machine in the toilet. I knew I'd get drunk and sleep with my new boyfriend later that night because I needed to be next to someone.

In the mirror that had reflected my mother's new wig, her white face like a cut flower, I eventually waved myself goodbye and left for the train station.

7

Ollie's bulky shoulders make light work of the heavy wooden shelves he is putting up in the lounge. His red socks peek above his workmen's boots; his feet look enormous next to mine.

Jen rings me, just as I am about to lend him a hand by passing him a screw. 'It's Claire; she's just puked on the lounge carpet dying it Ribena red. Any ideas what will get the stain out?'

'White wine should do it.'

'There's no way I'm wasting alcohol on a sick stain. Not even Lambrusco. Perhaps nail varnish remover might work?'

'Doubt it, Jen. Have you got a rug?'

'Good idea. I'll be over tomorrow as planned – I've not forgotten. What's that banging?'

'It's Ollie. He's putting up some shelves for me.'

'Be good! See you tomorrow.'

I understand that Jen doesn't mind the stains on her carpet made by Claire's virus, just like Mum and Dad didn't mind the greasy handprints up the stairs, or orange Play-Doh embedded in the beige fibres of my bedroom carpet. Mum loved the marks up the door frame, pencil marks that showed my height and my age, starting at two.

I think about Adam's return – his eagerly anticipated entrance through the front door with his suitcase and his laptop bag, the overcoat he will hang in the hall. Later, the toothbrush he will put beside mine in the bathroom and the sidelight he will switch on in bed to read his magazine before he falls asleep.

'That should do it,' Ollie says, interrupting my reverie. He tests the shelves' strength by pushing down on them; there are three, which will be more than enough for my books and a few ornaments.

'Thanks, Ollie. Fancy a coffee?'

He puts his screwdriver in his pocket and looks at his chunky plastic watch. 'Just a quick one. Any biscuits? I'm starving.'

I laugh because it seems he is hungry most of the time. 'I can make you a bacon sandwich, if you like. My thanks for putting up the shelves.'

'Lovely. Where are your books? I might as well make myself useful.'

'Ah, they're in the garage. It's open.'

'With the Land Rover in there? I'd lock it, if I were you.'

'The main garage door is locked, it's the side door I leave open because I'm in and out for logs.'

'Righto.'

While I cook the bacon, Ollie fetches the books from the garage. 'Bit of a bookworm, I see,' he says, joining me at the table. 'I'm more a magazine man myself. *Lonely Planet*.' Within minutes, he demolishes his bacon sandwich and then gives me his infectious smile. 'Delicious, Maple Rachel.'

'You're easily pleased!'

'The simple things in life are the best.' He takes his dirty plate and mug over to the sink and washes his greasy hands. 'You've got clocks everywhere,' he says, gesturing at the enormous wall clock on the kitchen wall. He must have spotted the ones in the lounge and hall as well.

'Adam always likes to know what time it is.'

Ollie raises his eyebrows. He is a man who happily spends hours fishing, so I can see why time isn't a priority for him. I've wondered what it would be like to sit beside him with a rod on a slow afternoon.

'Are you doing anything on Sunday? I'm taking a delivery to Tarporley Manor. The owner, Mr Hunt, is a top man. I think you'd love his garden, even at this time of year.'

'Yes, I'd like that.' I grab a blue biro and make a note on the calendar. The image for December is a photograph of snowdrops, with mist rising from the landscape like smoke.

Ollie leans over, watching me. I blush because my stomach flips at his nearness. The twenty-third of December has a large cross on it to mark Adam's return. 'Old-fashioned, isn't it, having a wall calendar?' I say. 'I do use my phone, but it's not the same. My best friend uses her phone and has a wall calendar, and she still jumbles up dates. But she's got three children, a husband and a fourth child on the way, so it's no wonder. I have no excuse.'

After Ollie leaves, I place a photograph of my parents on one of the new shelves. The frame, made from driftwood painted white, was bought on a seaside holiday in Devon.

I load the shelves with the rest of my books and immediately feel more at home. I run my finger across the spines, anticipating their worlds, knowing some have illegible scribble in their margins.

Is this nesting? Dad kept his hen's nesting box clean. It was an upturned milk crate. He'd talk to the hens the whole time when he was in there, like a stream of consciousness.

On the top shelf, I place a few trinkets: a silver chicken, two lavender candles, a lily in a purple pot, a postcard Jen sent me from a weekend trip to York. Adam thinks most of my knick-knacks are junk, but I couldn't live in a space, however fancy, without them. They mean something. Perhaps, with more time, they will mean something to Adam.

Ollie is right, I think: the simple things are the best. The free things, like walking in the woods, the view from the top of Peckforton Hill. I hardly know him, yet I feel very comfortable in his company.

The bed beckons me to lie on it to take a nap.

I see myself kneeling on the lawn where Dad took his life. With my bare hands, I scrape away the soil to make room for seeds and bulbs. The earth is crumbly and yields to my fingers, free from bones or ashes. I stare at my dirt-rimmed nails, unconcerned because Adam is away. Before I have time to stand up, vines and climbers break from the surface in a magical surge of growth, green and thick stemmed. They twist from the horizontal and surge to the vertical. Trees from the wood are stirring, moving closer, watching. I am too scared to get up from my knees.

The hands on my watch turn at speed, accelerating from one hour to the next, moving manically. I cannot keep up with the change. Nervously I push a loose strand of hair behind my ear and my touch makes it snap in my hand. It is grey in my palm, almost white and brittle with age.

Pain erupts in my abdomen, sending my arms clutching to my stomach. Between my legs, blood trickles and runs into the soil, chasing rivulets this way and that until the back lawn is entirely red. At first, I think I am menstruating until I see old wounds reopened and leaking.

In Dad's room, there are rows of rotten tomatoes, each one bursting, sending fragments of red flesh flying into the air. The stink of rotten flesh hits me. The rows of tomatoes merge into one expanse of blood as an intense hum from a swarm of flies fills the noxious space.

A mighty oak begins to rise from the ground. Its trunk is so thick I can't get my arms around its girth. The span of branches reaches out in all directions, rising into the sky until its uppermost leaves nestle in the clouds. Its elf-green foliage whispers to the clouds, something incoherent, secret, shielded by an ancient family of branches that push the wind away. One branch lifts like a strong arm; from it hangs a rope swing. It dangles at a great height, as if from heaven.

A little girl – four or five years old – swings back and fro, giggling. Her mother, with long luscious hair, pushes the little girl on the swing; her mother is human, except she has a hole for a mouth, a red cave from where no sound comes except a long, ceaseless moan. The mother pushes the child once, twice, three times, then she winds the rope swing around the little girl's neck and pulls. Hard.

The child flops like a rag doll, slithers off the swing onto the earth. Around the little crumpled body, upturned pink faces of the hydrangeas look on. Parts of their bloom have gone, bitten off by lots and lots of baby teeth. Pink petals drift in the wind and land like confetti on the dead girl. The leaves on the gladioli turn from emerald to brown and begin to rot and stink. The soil is parched, lined with cracks like an old inmate's face.

Ivy is stroking my neck. When I touch it, it wraps around my hand, locking it in place. I open my mouth, in a vain hope of screaming, but loose teeth fly out and nothing more.

A crow lands on my knees and gazes at the sculpture of myself.

8

'I'm almost there! Satnav says I'll be ten minutes,' Jen says with the tune of something like 'Baa-Baa Black Sheep' in the background and Will's voice singing along.

'Fuck!'

'Are you okay? You sound croaky.'

I jump out of bed, pull on yesterday's clothes, which are in a heap on the floor. My tummy is bloated because my period has started, and the hangover from the nightmare is difficult to shake. Are the two connected?

'My head's a bit boxed. Bad dream. Must be the move or something.'

As I open the front door, I hear music coming from Jen's purple people carrier. Two enormous furry dice dangling from the mirror come into view, bouncing around on the rough track. Yesterday's nightmare has left a sour taste in my mouth.

'No way, Rach – you look rough. What's the deal?'

'I had a horrible dream, that's all. Violent. I had a miscarriage, I think. Weird shit I don't fully understand. I'll get us something to drink.' I pat down my ruffled hair as Jen carries

Will in with one arm and a large bag in the other. 'Let me take that.'

'So, what happened in the dream? And it was just a dream, so don't sweat.'

'There was a child on a swing, and then a poplar tree turned into a pregnant woman. Swallows flew into her mouth, and I could see their wings beating inside her.'

'Grim. Do–'

'It gets worse. Dad's decayed head popped up from the soil and worms appeared from his eye sockets. The last thing I remember is a headless hen running at me.' I take a long slurp of black coffee.

'It's this place. You're bound to think about your dad's death, even subconsciously.'

'Yeah, I guess.' I don't say it, but I wonder if the garden will be my grave. It is the altar where Dad took his life to be with Mum, where his last hen died, where he stopped thinking about me. Perhaps I will end here, too.

'Come here.' Jen hugs me and I kiss her cheek. 'Are you going to show me around?'

She is appreciative of my home. 'Wow! It's just how I remember it. Your mum sewing there, and this hatch. Gosh, it's lovely.' She appraises my face. 'Is Adam still away?'

'Yes. Come on, I'll show you the Christmas tree. I've got something for the twins and Will.'

In the lounge, Jen fills me in on the children's infections, Jonny's plans to earn more money, and their annual summer holiday to his parents' caravan in Cornwall. I catch a whiff of sea air, the gritty feeling of sand between my teeth and the wonderful chaos children bring into parents' lives. She tells me it takes nearly a whole day to pack; she puts Post-it notes on the fridge, listing item after item.

I notice Will's outfit. He is two; he wears a single shoe, a yellow gingham top and matching trousers. He is an adorable bundle, soft and almond smelling.

'Time for a cuddle, Will! I'm coming to get you!'

He toddles around the room, an unsteady cargo on two legs. He teeters from the sofa to the coffee table, each step on the brink of a topple, then I whisk him into my arms. Eclipsed by the feel and smell of him, I don't notice Jen watching us until she takes a photo with her iPhone. Even when he is back in Jen's grasp, I can still feel his adorable body.

I open the present she has given me. It's an acorn pendant.

'It's a kind of moving-in and good-luck present in one,' she says.

'It's lovely; thank you.'

'You've kept my postcard!' She notices it on the shelves. 'Wish we could have a night away somewhere – get pissed like we used to when you came home from uni.'

Upstairs, Jen opens the wardrobe in our bedroom and descends into fits of laughter. I don't need to ask why: Adam owns a lot of shoes. What Jen doesn't know is that he spent most of his childhood in shoes several sizes too small. It is a little indulgence, now that he can afford it; the shoelaces are inextricably bound up with his past. The shoes are in pristine condition and there isn't a mud stain anywhere, unlike mine.

'Why is your side of the wardrobe almost empty and Adam's is full of designer stuff?'

I shrug. 'I'm not into clothes and shoes like Adam is. You know that. I've got plenty of earrings.' I open the dressing table drawer to show her my inexpensive but colourful collection.

Beside them is a card from Adam. It says: *Sorry. Forgive me. Love always, Adam*. He'd yanked one of my earrings out, ripping my ear, in a fury about the attention I'd received from someone at a party. I've kept the card because it reminds me not to wear earrings around him. Mum's thimble is in the drawer, too, beside the embroidered bookmark.

Jen admires the oriental rug and the dressing table with a gold-rimmed mirror from Laura Ashley. Adam bought them for me recently, after he broke my index finger. She doesn't know about that. 'This is Maple Mansion!' she says, half-jokingly. 'Has he got the Midas touch?'

'Just a good job. You know Adam, he loves money.'

'He spoils you! Or is it guilt for being a tool?'

'Jen!'

I remember dancing with Adam after our wedding ceremony in an upmarket cocktail bar with a pianist and a chandelier. I remember the way the light fell across our hopeful faces, my hair chasing after me with each turn. Then I felt I was precious, made from silver and gold, his loving gaze playing Midas tricks on my skin. That was before he hurt me.

Jen picks up his bedtime reading, placed beside his bed in eager readiness for his return by Rachel. She knows he likes his things just so. '*The Life and Times of Donald Trump. How to make money and become a millionaire*. What's it like sleeping with a work-obsessed capitalist?' She grins.

'He wants to retire at fifty. That dream I had–' I rub my temples. 'A child dies. It's the mother's fault. And the garden sort of eats itself. It was like a haunted pregnancy.'

Jen's face breaks into what she calls her emoji face. 'Just a stupid fucking dream. I tell you, we need to get hammered once my womb is empty. Dance around our handbags. Though you never had a handbag when you were a cool student. I did, though. Come on – a dream doesn't mean anything unless you let it.'

Peckforton Wood is reflected in the oval mirror; it softens the prison bars of the pine trees to colouring pencils. Jen sprays some of my perfume in the air and Will giggles as she walks through it, striking a pose like Madonna.

'Poo stink,' Will says.

'Handy having a wood on your doorstep for a quick game of hide and seek.' Jen throws me a sideways glance. 'This is a lovely room, Rach. It's you, you know what I mean?'

She and Will – they remind me of butterflies flitting in and out of lavender as they go from one room to another. I follow, enjoying the way she moves around the cottage, the comments she throws like skimming stones into a lake. Will is gazing at me over her shoulder: it's impossible not to smile. His mouth twitches into a grin as if he and I are the funniest people alive. I put my finger in his palm and he grabs it.

'Any plans to change anything?' Jen asks.

'Only in the garden.'

'I bet Adam will have something to say about that.'

'I don't see anything wrong with the place.'

'It's charming and rustic, so probably not to his taste. I bet he thinks it's a bit dated and wonky. He likes clean lines, modern, no?'

'Well, I like it how it is. It's not meant to be perfect. It's a country cottage.'

'Hey, Miss Defensive. I love it.'

'Sorry, I'm a bit nervous about Adam coming home, that's all. I want it to be perfect.'

While Will throws wooden spoons through the hatch, I make tea and toast with cheese and raspberry jam, and update Jen on my visit to the fertility clinic.

'When do you get the results?'

'Tomorrow. I'm seeing my old doctor. It means driving to Altrincham, but I'm comfortable talking to him. And with the move and everything, I haven't had the chance to transfer.'

'Do you want me to come with you?'

'Thanks, Jen, but I'll be fine once I'm there and get it over with.' I'd love her company, but she would have Will in tow and be carrying her baby bump. Depending on the outcome of the test, that might not be what I need.

She smiles sympathetically. 'When did he last hurt you?' she asks gently. 'Is that why you're nervous about him coming back?'

'It's only been the odd time.'

'It's never okay to hurt someone. You know deep down it's wrong.'

'It got worse when starting a family became a delicate subject. And that's my fault because I haven't fallen pregnant. Being here will help. It'll happen, and then he'll stop. Let's wait and see.'

'I know a couple who'd been trying for years. One day she got rid of all the clocks and watches in their house.' Jen pauses, then says, 'I guess if you're feeling stressed, it's got to be worse for Adam.'

'Why?'

'Because he's older than you. At thirty-five, he's getting on a bit. Not that I'm sympathetic – the opposite – but I get that time can be an enemy. *He* might be the bloody problem. Has that occurred to him? I bet it hasn't.'

It won't have occurred to Adam that he might be sterile: he thinks of himself as physically perfect because he takes great care of himself. 'No, it's not come up.'

'Doesn't surprise me,' Jen huffs.

He talks about conception as if it's another kind of business, a transaction, a monolith like the skyscrapers he flies over, the steel that is engineered and assembled in the lifts that take him to the top floor and the ergonomically designed chairs he swivels on. He sees conception as a purely female act, as mystical and removed as the moon. How could I tell him that it may not be my biology that's the problem?

'He runs, goes to the gym, eats a perfect diet, rarely drinks while he's working in China.'

'But you're fit, too. I know you like the odd glass of wine but– Sorry, I'll shut up. Get tomorrow out of the way, then you'll know where you are.'

I finger the acorn pendant around my neck while she tells me about their money worries that are being made worse by the fact she is pregnant again.

I smile at my best friend. Her pixie haircut and her face – once pixie too, but now bloated pixie. Her cheeks are full, ready for hibernation. She looks more of a woman than me. She has a sense of style and a confidence, she is wearing a kaftan and Doc Martins, her sensible tote bag bought for size but styled with a Union Jack. My appearance depends on the weather or what doesn't need washing.

'You'll cope. You're an amazing mum!' I reassure her.

'That's the thing: I'm not. We veer from one chaos to another. I'm not saying for a minute that I'd get rid of this baby, but Jonny was going to get sterilised. Seriously. But we're blessed with the twins and Will.' She strokes the toddler's hair as he sleeps on the sofa beside her. 'How does it feel to be back here?'

'Lots of good memories, and sad ones too. But it's home. It's mine. The other places we lived in were just bricks and mortar. I've unpacked everything and I'm going to stay organised for once. And the garden is going to be amazing.'

'You're serious, then, about this being your forever home?'

'I want it to be.' I hesitate. Part of me wants to tell her about the skulls, but the other part of me wants to forget about them. 'Books?' I ask.

As avid readers, it's our tradition to swap books. It makes birthdays and Christmas presents easy. Jen passes me a wonderfully heavy Tesco carrier bag full of paperbacks; I have a thick paperback to swap, which she pretends to baulk at when she sees the size and the romance genre.

'Are you going mushy? This isn't your usual. What happened to reading crime?'

'I'll read crime when Adam's in bed beside me. It's pretty isolated out here – I didn't want to give myself the willies!'

Sometime later, the purple people carrier bumps away. I don't know if she feels the same sadness that I feel when we part, but I think she might. It's not just goodbye to Jen; it is a goodbye to that version of me, the one that is only Rachel, not married, not teacher, not a slightly bruised daughter, or a wife with an older husband who sometimes gets angry.

As I watch her and Will go, I see myself standing in the same spot, a girl holding a string to a kite and watching it twist this way and that. I was twelve, in new shoes, and I believed that all dreams came true. Dreams then were about winning the school history prize, seeing a fox cub, finding an undiscovered path through Peckforton Woods with Dad. Now I dream about trees. I dream about babies. I dream about Dad.

I wash up the dirty crockery then tidy up the lounge. I turn on the radio for some background music. Will's plastic green-and-yellow tractor pokes its head from under the sofa, and it feels like he has poked me in the ribs.

9

I look at my watch for the fifth time in as many minutes. The informative posters on the waiting room about cancer should help to keep the significance of my fertility results in perspective. Glowing faces and the healthy, fit bodies in the magazine I glance at don't hold my interest.

I can vividly recall the day I went to the Manchester hospital for the fertility test at nine o'clock in the morning. It was a wet Thursday, and the traffic was awful. By the time I arrived in the obstetrics and gynaecology department, I was stressed and tearful. I was tempted to walk out again, but I kept going with the image of Will's smiling face in my mind. I made myself think of Jen and her family as I worked my way through a maze to reassure myself this was what I wanted, and that one day Adam and I would be a happy family.

Perhaps the posters of heavily pregnant women and thank-you cards were meant to be uplifting to patients in the waiting area, but they had the opposite effect on me. It seemed cruel to make potentially infertile women sit next to those who were eight months into pregnancy, or directly opposite the image of a swollen belly button.

Eventually I was ushered into a large, clinical room, where a nurse took blood to establish an anti-Müllerian hormone level. Then I was ushered into a changing cubicle to put on an open-backed gown.

'Over in a jiffy,' the bespectacled nurse offered by way of reassurance.

'What happens now?'

'The hysterosalpingogram is going to look at your fallopian tubes to see if there are any blockages. The dye will be injected into your vagina and X-rays taken. It won't take long.'

'Sounds painful.'

'Not at all. Just try to relax.'

Relax?

My doctor is a stocky man with wiry, dark hair. I've seen him a few times over the years. He leans towards me to appear friendly, but I'm so anxious I find it uncomfortable and an invasion of my space.

'Is Mr Jordan joining us today?' Doctor Abie asks. By reading his expression, I try to predict what he might say about my fertility test.

'Adam's working, unfortunately. He works in China a lot of the time.' I babble because I want him to tell me the results so I can get out of this place as quickly as possible. Small talk is the last thing I need right now.

I have a kind of stitch in one side of my body, and I wish I had some nails left to bite. Perhaps I should have asked Jen to join me.

'I see. That can make conception difficult. Is anyone else with you?'

I shake my head, and the enormity of the results punches me

in the stomach. Is he preparing me for bad news? I draw a sharp intake of breath while he consults his screen. I try to imagine the other men and women who have sat in this chair and waited for their fate.

'I know you and your husband have been trying for a baby for over twelve months, so I can understand why you wanted the tests.'

I nod inanely, urging him to continue.

'I have good news for you both, Rachel. Your anti-Müllerian hormone level is 28.8 pmol/l, which is the optimum fertility level. Well done!'

'Really?' I say incredulously, then sit back in my chair. 'I'm fertile?'

'Yes, yes. And there is nothing wrong with your fallopian tubes. You are a very fertile woman.' He smiles. 'You look very relieved.'

'I am.' Not least because I dread to think what Adam would do to me if I were infertile. 'Oh, that's good news. Thank God!' Suddenly I realise how exhausted I feel. I've been bottling up the fear of this moment for a long time. The relief is tremendous. I smile at him and tears spring to my eyes. 'Thank you.'

'Now, if you have any anxieties you must come back in six months, but I think that by then you'll be pregnant. I assume, of course, that your husband has also been tested?' He checks his records.

'No, he hasn't been.'

'He must. It takes two, of course.' He smiles, making me feel about three years old. My cheeks burn red. 'But you already know that. Do you have any questions?'

'Are there things I should or shouldn't be doing? I mean, drinking alcohol is bad. Is running all right? Gardening? Are there foods or supplements that you'd recommend? Herbs?

Perhaps acupuncture would help?'

'Nature will take its course, as long as you take care of yourself and your husband. Good food, plenty of sleep, gentle exercise, rest. Try not to worry about time. It says on your records that neither of you smokes, which is excellent. You know how to work out when you are ovulating, yes?'

'I do. What about positions? Is there an optimal position?'

'Have plenty of enjoyable sex. Try to stop thinking about pregnancy. Relax.'

Relax. That word again. If only he knew. 'If for some reason I don't get pregnant naturally, what are the options?'

'Well, there are several we could talk to you and Adam about. There is IVF.'

I would never have IVF because of the risk of multiples. A friend from university had IVF and gave birth to triplets. 'Are there other options?'

'Some couples decide to adopt, or use artificial insemination by a donor from a sperm bank. You don't need to consider these options at the moment, but be aware of them. I sense you are very keen to be a mother.'

'Yes, very. My husband won't consider adoption – his mother was adopted, and he thinks she was permanently scarred – mentally. He blames her coldness towards him on her loveless childhood.'

'As I say, you are blessed – you *are* fertile. Many women and men who come to see me don't get such wonderful news. Why do you look so worried?'

'I feel strongly against AI – whether it's Adam's sperm or, even worse, a donor's. Morally it feels wrong to me, like I'm an object and the child is a project of some kind. A commodity. So I'm worried that unless we conceive naturally, we won't be able to start a family.' My stomach churns at the possibility. Dad's friend, Roland, uses AI to fertilise his cows at Witton Farm. Even that seems wrong to me.

'I very much doubt I'll need to see you again but, in the unlikely event that nothing happens in the next six to nine months, or if you want to talk to me about any worries, please come back.'

'I will.' I pause. 'If I'm fertile, I suppose there's a chance Adam isn't.'

'Exactly. Mr Jordan needs to be tested.'

All the way home to Cheshire, there are three words on a continuous loop in my head: *I am fertile. I am fertile. I am fertile.* The news is good, so why am I frightened? What is causing the dead feeling in the pit of my stomach?

To pass the evening, I do some marking and preparation for the new term, then read one of the books that Jen brought me until my eyes are sore. I toss and turn in bed, continually checking the time to see how many hours are left before Adam's return.

I am fertile. I am fertile. I am fertile.

~

It is just after two o'clock in the morning when I wake up with a jolt. Automatically checking my phone, which sleeps next to me, I read a text from Adam to say he has landed at Gatwick. I think about replying but decide against it, in the hope I can get back to sleep. But silence suspends in the room like a chandelier. It's impossible not to listen, just as it is impossible not to rearrange the mangled duvet so that it covers my bare feet.

I hear a sound, indistinct and vague, like a finger brushing a drum, a sweep of a paintbrush. My mind wants to give it a shape so it can have a name. I return to being a child in a tent, sitting bolt upright till morning. Probably a badger, or a fox. Perhaps bats or an owl.

Except.

When light dawns, I see the glossy white skulls are back. This time they are laced with dew, placed carefully on the back lawn to spell an ugly word. It is a chilling word to read because it is true.

In my head, I expand on the theme: *whore, harlot, tart*. Yes, I've dreamed, imagined, thought about Ollie and his muscular back and his protective arms and his mouth. I've wondered what it's like to taste the salt on his neck. I have imagined – but only that.

'Slut,' I say aloud to myself and whoever else might be within earshot. 'Slut!' I say, louder still. I pull my dressing gown tighter around me as I march up to the skulls in my ridiculous slippers.

Death is following me wherever I go. First, Mum, then Dad; now my existence is communicated through death. Adam is in the UK, so is he to blame for this? If so, I am made of glass, and he wants to shatter me. It wouldn't be the first time he's taken pleasure from my fear.

I could put a thread through those eye sockets and hang the skulls as bunting in the garden as a welcome home to whoever it is that is haunting me. Would that please my enemy?

How lucky people are to be asleep, or shopping, or eating breakfast with the newspaper in front of them. I shake my head in shame and desperation. The trees in the wood look down on me without mercy. Right now, in their shadow, I wish I could pack them up and move them away.

I kick the skulls until they rearrange themselves into nothing but the remnants of death. One skull breaks into pieces, and the disintegration makes me feel fleetingly powerful. I step back and look at them like an objective person would, like Adam would. They can't harm me now: they have no hair, no teeth or tongue.

The breeze drifts in and out of their orifices, nothing more or less, but still I want to fall to my knees and cry.

The delicate objects don't have a human voice, but I do. 'Bastard,' I hiss. 'I hate you.'

I imagine my words rolling through the woods, echoing, rebounding far and wide like a thousand claps of thunder. My joy at being fertile will not be tainted by the person playing the Grim Reaper. These creatures are long dead but I am alive, and one day I will give birth to a beautiful, healthy child who will be safe for as long as I live.

10

The best bit about Adam working abroad so much lately is his return. It is anticipated. We are reborn as a novelty to each other, and passions run high. As soon as Adam walks through the door, he holds me so closely I can barely breathe. He has a whiff about him of airports, secondary smoke and coffee. He brings his long-haul journey into our country cottage like a foreign creature.

'I missed you, Mrs Jordan.'

He strokes my hair gently, then holds my face in his hands as carefully as a newborn. His dark eyes, so dark it seems there isn't a pupil in the iris, look deeply into mine as if for an answer.

'You're as intense as ever!' I giggle, half-joking. 'I missed you, too.'

'You smell of cherries,' Adam says, as he buries his mouth in my neck under my freshly washed hair.

I watch him hang his coat in the hall and leave his car keys on the window ledge in the kitchen. There is a duty-free carrier bag beside his suitcase and his hand luggage which holds his laptop. He leaves his phone in the middle of the kitchen table next to the poinsettia, then opens kitchen cupboards. Some of the handles are loose and the wood is dented and scratched in places.

'It's very lived in!' He laughs and bangs each cupboard door shut as if he hates them for their friendly lived-in faces. 'You've done a great job of moving us in. I assume the Aga has been working? I asked the removal men to check you had everything you need. You've not been cold?'

'Everything works, Adam. It was all checked or upgraded before the tenant could move in, and she's left it in good order. The men were great – I didn't lift a finger.'

'You know, we can make this place perfect for us,' he says excitedly. 'Do you want to show me around. Upstairs first. You've been busy – it looks like we've been here for ages.'

Our bedroom is tastefully furnished with our newest furniture. I love the lavender walls and our mauve duvet cover, of which Adam approves. He opens the wardrobe to the carefully arranged clothes and shoes.

'Fantastic!' He appraises his side of the wardrobe. 'We're organised at last!' He takes me in his arms and kisses me spontaneously.

'This is a lovely room. I told you it would be worth waiting for,' I say.

'I know. It's so light and spacious.'

We stand side by side at the window, looking out onto the back garden and the maple tree. The silence is louder now that Adam's home.

'I can't hear a thing! Have you been scared to sleep here alone?' he asks.

'Not really – well, a bit.'

'There's nothing but fields behind us. I can't see a single house or a car. You could scream blue murder and no one would hear.'

'Except Shirley,' I remind him.

'It's as well Nantwich is close by. I wouldn't want to be cut off completely. I like my tennis and clothes shops too much. I'll look into joining a gym.'

'What for? You can run along the paths in the woods. The Sandstone Trail will take you to Frodsham. Dad and I once walked it – over thirty miles.'

'Blimey, no thanks. It's thirty-four miles – I looked at the map. Not for me, especially in the rain and snow. That might be your idea of fun, but it's not mine.'

'Have you entered another marathon?'

'Not yet. I'll see how my diary looks in the new year. I want to run Manchester again, but I doubt I'll be fit for that in four months. Time here with you is precious.' He turns from the window to look at me. 'You haven't been running, have you?'

'No. I miss it, though.'

'I suppose you've been thinking about your parents more than ever?'

'In a good way.'

He kisses me lightly on the mouth. 'Do you want to show me my office.'

His abstract painting of a mountaineer ascending the Matterhorn is positioned above his glass-topped desk. The desk and leather chair look too big in the modest-sized room, a doll's house with the wrong-sized furniture. On his desk, I've organised his favourite objects: a magnifying glass he uses to study the shares and small print in broadsheets, a solid-silver letter opener, and the objects from China that Ollie had admired. It looks neat and tidy.

'Thank you. It'll do for now, until we extend.' He is less impressed by the old-fashioned bathroom, but I feel optimistic about his positive attitude to the house and our new start here. I start to relax a little. 'The removal firm did all the heavy lifting?'

'Of course. Your desk was the heaviest thing, that and the

sofa. We could do with more furniture. The house is bigger than our old place.'

'I agree. All in good time. We could hit the January sales.'

'Do you want anything to eat?'

'Just you.'

Adam takes my hand, opening my fingers out like a Chinese silk fan. I mentally take a snapshot of this moment and see myself carrying it between two fingers, one of which he broke not so long ago. I am more than ready for this moment.

He explores my skin like a map, finding his way to a destination that is ready and waiting for him. I am navigated in the best way but then, afterwards, I must remain still and prostrate as Adam's sperm dribbles out of me, gluing my thighs together. He says it improves my chances of conception.

'I can't see you from this angle!' I laugh at the ridiculousness of the routine.

'I want to christen every room and available space, Mrs Jordan.'

'Shall we go to bed first?'

'Not yet.' Suddenly he kisses my eyelids tenderly then slides into me again. His words are ringing in my ears. 'Stay there. I'll get us something to drink. I picked up our favourite – Châteauneuf-du-Pape. Just a small one for you.'

I take a large gulp, hoping I might feel less of a body bag.

'I prefer Shiraz, I think.' He sighs contentedly while stroking his abs, and quickly drinks his glass down. His cheeks flush from the alcohol. 'I've started working with a new agent who's a single mother. Most unusual. China is male-dominated because of the one-child policy – it's dreadful. Newborn girls were often killed or abandoned because their parents were desperate that their one permitted baby be a boy.' He tops up his glass. 'Which sex would you prefer?'

'A healthy one. I don't think I need to keep still any longer. It's not comfortable on this thin carpet.'

I stand up at last. Adam spots the carpet burn on my back and laughs.

'Adam, I had a fertility test. The results were positive. I'm fertile.'

'I'll drink to that!' He kisses me deeply and inserts his tongue into my mouth. It tastes of red wine.

We sip our drinks and chat, both knowing we want to sleep with each other again, but waiting just a little longer is a kind of foreplay.

I let Adam get ready for bed as I tidy up downstairs. I hear the toilet flush and the buzz of Adam's electric toothbrush, then the bed springs as he lands on his side of it with his usual thud. He is probably reading his *Tennis First* magazine as he waits for me. It is comforting to have him at home to hear his sounds.

As I climb the eighteen stairs to bed, I listen to him make a satisfied groaning sound from the bedroom. He is happy to be back in our marital bed.

11

We light a fire in the lounge, and the snow-spray on the windows catches the glow from the flames. There is an open book of mine on the rug, and discarded paper from the presents we have unwrapped. Adam has bought me new black silk lingerie, as well as paying for the garden of rooms. My gift to him – a Newton's cradle – is very modest but he seems pleased with it. Adam is often generous and thoughtful with his presents. I chose the Newton's Cradle for his desk because work defines him in a good way – he loves his job and is ambitious. I know when his work is going well by his libido, though that's rarely been an issue in the relatively short time we have been together.

The cold world is trapped outside, wrapped around skeletal trees with bony fingers that are gesturing for the storm to pass. A gale is blowing, rattling doors and the sash windows and lobbing branches from the trees. There is a menace in its wail, so Adam puts another log on the fire and we listen to it sizzle. His dark eyes look at me lovingly. Time has slowed, and this is worth waiting for. We snooze and cuddle with the firelight trickling into the room and the gale outside battering the roof.

'I like this lounge. There's lots of light in the day, and the view, and a real fireplace. I'll get some logs delivered for the winter. I didn't see a log store.'

'Dad put them in the garage.'

'You want a log store right by the house. I fancy a top-up.'

'I'm okay.' I'd like another glass of red but prefer not to cause aggravation. Compromise is the key to harmony, and it is days and evenings like this that fortify our marriage.

He returns with a full glass and inspects it. 'We'll have been married for three years soon,' he says and toasts my almost empty glass.

'Is that worth a new pair of wellies?' I joke.

'It's leather.'

'You're well informed.'

'It was in an article I read on the flight home. Leather for flexibility, durability, or a good spanking!'

'No way! I'm not into that.'

'Ah, Mrs Jordan. You prude. I'm sure a bit of pain would turn you on.'

I don't like where the conversation is going, so I put another log on the fire and switch on a sidelight. 'Do you fancy a mince pie?'

'Sure. It's Christmas. New gym routine starts soon.'

On the kitchen table are the remains of the turkey we prepared together. Adam has three signature dishes that he cooks when he's at home, which include a Sunday roast, but I tend to do the lion's share of cooking and domestic chores. Since being with Adam, I have become more organised. He has brought order to my somewhat haphazard habits of eating and cleaning, and reason to my somewhat subjective view of life.

I load up a plate with four mince pies. Before snuggling back beside Adam on the sofa, I look at the twinkling lights on the Christmas tree that is decorated with baubles Mum handed down, some of which I made at school with card and cottonwool. Above the hearth there is a mirror Adam and I bought from a market in Didsbury; to the side of it, there is a painting Mum and Dad used to have in the same spot of a pheasant with its distinctive red and green markings.

I look at the outline of our furniture in this room, the symmetry of window and ceiling, and the flickering flames on Adam's handsome face. It is a beautiful arrangement of new and old, of cherished memories made in this room and of ones to come. The burning fire joins us like an old friend.

'Am I going to see you in your new lingerie?' Adam asks amorously, his eyes on my breasts.

I put a hand on my stomach, which feels bloated from all the food I've eaten. 'I will, if you visit the fertility clinic.' I hear my watch tick. 'Then we know where we are.' I hold my breath. I figure I have nothing to lose.

It hasn't occurred to him that he might be the problem. Not only that, he's done such an excellent job of convincing me that I am that it didn't occur to me either, until I saw the doctor. Jen is right. Adam is older than me; he will feel under pressure, perhaps rightly so. It might help him to get tested to put both our minds at rest.

His hand moves to mine, and I flinch. He pats it. 'I wish you'd stop biting your bloody nails.'

'Bad habit.' I say bending my fingers so the bitten nails and cuticles, which look like a mouse has been at them, are out of sight.

'Fine. If they can fit me in before I need to leave for Hong Kong again, I'll go this month. I'll go private, then we can get this done and dusted once and for all.' He gazes at me longingly. 'So, a deal's a deal.'

I pick up the lingerie from the arm of the sofa. 'Are you going to help me?'

12

Nantwich is a market town that is often bustling with tourists, shoppers and market stalls. Its character alters dramatically when the funfair arrives during the festive season and summer months. The gargoyles on St Mary's Church must flush at the jerking, hurling rides and the screams of joy and the swarming notes of music over the rooftops of Jacobean and Victorian buildings. Fond memories return of being thrown around on rides after being egged on by friends and my boyfriend.

We regularly stole bags of pick 'n' mix sweets from the local sweet store after school. It was a dare worth quite a bit of kudos in our group; at the time that made it worth the risk of getting caught. The sweet shop has shut since then, and I can see why.

I've come full circle, but this time with a husband.

The fair is alive with twinkling lights and music. As Adam and I stroll between the rides, I think that it would make a perfect picture if it were to snow.

Adam spontaneously takes me in his arms and strokes my long butterscotch hair almost gently. His eyes are dark brown;

little lines at the edges form when he smiles. 'Have you missed me?' he asks.

'Of course!'

He tugs at my hand to go on the Ferris wheel, but I loathe heights and dig in my heels. 'I've missed you, Mrs Jordan. Come on.'

'I'll watch you.'

'Really?'

I am relieved that he accepts my fear of heights without rebuke for a change. He climbs into an empty passenger car shaped like a suicide pill. At the highest point, he holds his arms in the air, a spiritual healer lit by gaudy lights and flashing colours. I pretend to bow in worship to my God up there, surrounded and suspended by steel. From that height, I must look like a squashed ant. The Christmas songs blare out of the stands and rides, sometimes competing with one another, sometimes in harmony.

Screams and laughter from the giant wheel follow me to a wooden bench. Years ago, I sat on the same bench with Stephen, a boyfriend with the most amazing brown eyes. He was my first love. On this bench, a few months after having sex in the outhouse, he broke off with me. I'd experienced my first heartache as he abruptly ditched me for Lisa, a girl with bigger boobs and a bigger personality.

Adam strolls over to me, fizzing about the view from the top of the Ferris wheel. I'd sooner have the view from the top of Peckforton Hill. His appetite for speed, height, risk, takes him to two more rides while I anticipate the rest of the evening.

We mount the ghost train together. Adam laughs when the train plunges downwards and I scream. We drop into what could be a bottomless pit; a trail of cobwebs clings to my skin, hair and neck, and I duck when lurching eyes blink out of nowhere. The rational side of my brain has stopped working. Adam laughs at my shrieks as I cling tightly to the railing.

'Hall of mirrors next,' declares Adam as he pulls my hand. I feel like a dog on a lead, one desperate to go home to lay my head on the sofa. 'You'll love it. Trust me.'

It is much quieter in the hall of mirrors; the crowds aren't drawn to this space. Adam holds my hand and yanks me from convex to concave mirror. There is a whiff of onions from the hotdog stall outside, and I can hear the cries of people on the helter-skelter.

Adam smiles at himself then at me in the mirror. I stiffen at the strangeness of his face, the lines around his eyes and the unexpected glare from his eye socket. His grin is a snarl, but his hair is groomed and his familiar, expensive clothes are neat. I smile back and try to look relaxed.

'You look pregnant! At last!'

'Ha ha. Funny!'

We shrink and expand, morph and evolve, until we reach the end of the hall and stumble out under a dirty shadow of a sky. We have lost hours, it seems.

Adam is smiling, holding my hand protectively. Under the barrage of Christmas songs and the blunt sounds of contact made with coconuts and basketballs, he gives up trying to speak. He wins a Rubik's cube on the 'test your strength' high-striker, and fairy lights on the 'hook-the-duck'.

'Perfect!' I say, admiring the lights. 'Just what we need for the tree. Let's go on the dodgems.'

The man in charge of the dodgems strides the ride, spinning a dodgem as if he is dealing cards in a Las Vegas casino. Wearing his leather jacket loose on his shoulders, he winks at me as he gives our red dodgem an extra twist for good measure. His pink tongue slides to the left side of his mouth as we slide to the right. I feel like a beetle spinning on its back.

Adam's eyes are shining under the red lightbulbs. I can't hear what he is saying because of the volume of music, but it must be positive for him to grin and laugh so much. The lights flash in time with the music, moving across his tanned face while his mouth opens and closes hungrily, working at something. It reminds me of a crow's beak worrying at a carcass. But I don't worry about what he's saying because Adam is home and I am fertile, and everything is going to be perfect. Almost perfect.

Then the spinning and the music stop. Las Vegas Man leans into the microphone in the booth to tell us it's safe to exit. Adam's face is all eyes popping with joy and an all-American smile, while I feel slightly sick and grimy.

We eat our hotdogs, ketchup smudged around our mouths, and sip mulled wine from polystyrene cups. Adam buys us candy floss, and a pink cloud that I carry around until I find a bin I can dump it in. When he kisses me, there is candy floss on his breath.

We will make love tonight many times. He expects it, and I want it.

'How come you're eating rubbish?' I ask.

'It's Christmas!'

The younger children have left the fair with their parents, and an older crowd swarms over the rides and the stalls like a spooky wing. I know that underneath the wing there is green grass, an innocent park where I used to hang out with friends after school and make daisy chains. I remember snogging the new boy at school – a skateboarder – by the swings, feeling like a film star.

Suddenly two boys come pelting from nowhere, raining laughter, sprinting across the grass, legging it to the exit sign. The skinny one has a teddy bear held loosely in his hand by the scruff of its neck; the other is wearing a Puffa jacket. The skinny one catches my shoulder at speed, forcing me down to the ground. I cry out in shock and pain. I hear their feet hitting the ground hard, sprinting fast, laughter. Not stopping. Not caring.

Then I hear Adam shouting. 'Oy! Stop, you bastard!' He sprints after them as I rub my bruised shoulder and pick myself up from the ground. I feel shaky and self-conscious as heads turn.

I retrieve my handbag, thrusting it high on my shoulder as I try to regain my composure. Adam catches one boy – a teenager, perhaps fifteen – as he trips over a wire connecting the lights on the dodgems to a power generator. He grabs the boy's face as if it is a detachable object, grabs it so hard that it is squished up. I know how much that hurts.

I wince and chase after them. I see that some people are stopping and staring. 'Adam, let him go. I'm all right! It was an accident!' I yell.

The boy's arm is yanked behind his back, bent into the shape of an arrow. When he shrieks, I turn away. The ugly lopsidedness of the image makes me stagger as if I'm back in the mirror hall. The other teenager has vanished, leaving behind the sandy teddy bear. Perhaps it was a dare, a silly prank.

'Adam, let him go,' I plead, anxious for the boy now and self-conscious. 'He's just a boy. Let him go home.'

'Not until he says sorry to my wife.' He twists the boy's arms some more until a cry of pain jerks out of the kid's wet mouth. 'You prick.'

'Adam!'

The crowd are murmuring. My cheeks flush with embarrassment. There's a snarl on Adam's face, and the scar on his forehead is glowing with sweat. I think the lad looks familiar, but I can't place him. He is spotty, leery, buoyed up with too much energy and testosterone, but I also see his fear and, because of that, I am sorry this is happening.

'Sorry, missis.'

Then I am close up and, after several moments, I recognise the boy. It is Devina Duffy's eldest son, Ted. His limp mouse-brown hair needs a shampoo. His expression changes as he recognises me. His mouth crumples into a sneer.

'That's enough, Adam. It was an accident.'

'Watch where you're fucking going next time,' Adam says, then releases him into the night as if he is a wild animal.

Ted, in his white trainers, stares at me and Adam as if we are criminals. Maybe he is right.

13

'Morning, gorgeous wife,' Adam says the next day at breakfast. He is dressed in shabby clothes, which I prefer to his designer suits and sharp shirts although I don't say this and never would.

I insert a heaped spoon of corn flakes into my mouth as I daydream about the garden out there, but Adam's reflection in the glass window interferes with the view. The sky is blanched with white and grey cloud, and drizzle is flecking the window.

'I've been thinking about an extension, an extra room downstairs for my office, and perhaps a conservatory. My bonus will easily cover it, Rach.'

'What bonus?'

'I miss some of the things about our apartment in Altrincham. The power shower and the dimmer lighting. A modern kitchen.' He sits down beside me and rubs his temples. 'I need an office downstairs.'

'I love the cottage as it is. It's authentic. It wasn't built to be modern and expensive. Let's focus on other things. Why don't you invite Derek and Bryony over, or Chris, before you head back to China? They could stay over. I'll cook – okay, I won't cook. We could eat out in Nantwich or get a takeaway. Or there's a restaurant in Chester that Shirley recommended.'

'Derek won't come. Bryony's pregnant again. The eldest son has just started secondary school, plays competitive sport most weekends.' He drinks a glass of water down in one. 'All our friends and my colleagues have got children. Let's head into Manchester for the day. The sales are on. I want a new suit, and you could get something new for Shirley's party tonight. We'll stop at John Lewis to look at furniture.'

~

The silver moon isn't the only light tonight: glow-worm lights from Shirley's garden vie for attention. There is music coming from her garden as we walk briskly to the New Year's Eve party holding hands. I can smell Adam's expensive aftershave, which has notes of cinnamon and spice. Fairy lights strewn in the rhododendrons from the bottom to the top of the sweeping drive add to the magical atmosphere.

'There's some money here,' Adam says enviously at the sight of expensive cars parked in the drive, including a Bentley and a Maserati.

As we approach the front of the house, a group of men come into view. They are chatting and laughing loudly on the patio, where the lighting is bright and welcoming. A man with a distinguished face and smart jacket opens a bottle of champagne.

Shirley must have seen us approaching as she is hovering by the front door. 'Come in.' She kisses Adam on both cheeks, which flusters him. 'Lovely to see you both. You look positively radiant,' she says to me, her voice full of welcome as she kisses me, leaving a trace of Chanel No. 5. 'The wine's in here. Red?'

I nod and tell her just a small one, because the glasses are more like goblets fit for a medieval banquet and Adam will only nag me. Shirley gestures for us to sit on the sofa. There's a smell of polish in the room. Adam remarks on the dark antique wood that reminds me of autumn: conkers, chestnuts and gold-tipped leaves in amongst the red and burnt ochre. I agree, pleased he's being so charming to my friend.

Laughter floats in the air. Lights, lots of fairy lights, bounce off diamonds and white teeth, silver hair and crystal wine glasses.

'We should go to an antiques' fair, Rach,' Adam says. 'Could be a sound investment. Some of our furniture looks a bit modern at Maple. A few antique pieces would suit the place. Nothing was right at John Lewis.' He turns to Shirley. 'We were saying we need a bit more now we're in a bigger place.'

'There's an excellent auction house in Nantwich,' Shirley says. 'The list catalogue comes out three times a year. There's probably one in that pile of mail over there.'

I smile at her relaxed attitude. I like that she doesn't worry about what comes in the mail; everything happens at her pace.

'Did you have a romantic Christmas together?' she asks.

'We did,' I say. 'Thank you. Did you?'

'I have a friend in Chester who lost her husband a while back, so we went out for Christmas lunch together. It was delicious – a new place, along the Rows. Humphrey's. You should try it some time.'

'Thank you for the gift. I love chocolates!'

'Ah, you're welcome. How are you settling in, Adam?'

'The cottage is charming. Something of a culture shock after Altrincham and working in Hong Kong. And hearing gunfire from my living room is going to take a bit of getting used to. I damn well spilt a glass of wine the other afternoon, it made me jump so much. Rachel tells me the pheasant shooting goes on till February. I'm not happy about the noise.'

'You'll be away for most of it,' I say neutrally.

'So, the countryside is new to you. Well, you're in good hands with Rachel. How do you like to spend your time together when you're in the UK?' Shirley asks. 'I guess it's precious.'

'We don't do a lot of socialising, that's true,' Adam replies. 'We used to hop on the tram and head straight into Manchester, didn't we, love? For shopping or a meal out. It's all new at this stage.'

Shirley reaches to top up our glasses. Her cowl-necked top shimmers in the light like whitebait. 'Rachel told me about your romantic wedding. I love Venice. The Bridge of Sighs especially.'

'It was romantic, even if I say so myself.' Adam reaches for my hand. 'Just Rachel and me. Neither of us have parents, so it was the right thing to do. We'd only known each other a few months, but we just knew it was right.'

'I'm sure Rachel's parents would be delighted that you're living here, and that she's married such a hard-working young man.'

'Well, thanks – but at thirty-five I'm probably not that young! One has to be ambitious these days: it's a tough world. I meant to ask you about Devina Duffy, our old tenant. Rachel says she's living in Gospel Avenue in Nantwich now. What was she like?'

'A lovely woman. She has her hands full with two children to bring up on her own. Devina told me her son Ted has started doing better at school, getting in with a better crowd. He'd been something of a handful before – angry about his dad leaving for another woman. But they were charming neighbours.'

'That's not my impression. She removed the curtains from the house. We've got them back, but in my book you don't take things that aren't yours. Rachel thinks we ran into Ted at the funfair. He seems to be trouble.'

'There are no hard feelings,' I say to anyone who is listening.

'He's not a bad lad,' Shirley says. 'When they lived next door,

Ted kept roaming into my orchard to climb the trees, upsetting the birds and the nests. He was bored, you see. Devina let him roam, probably to give herself a breather. I asked her several times to tell the boy to stop trespassing, but he wouldn't listen to her or me – so I fired my air rifle. At the sky, just to frighten him.' She gives a wily smile. 'Did the trick, too. He soon started playing in the woods instead, where he could be as wild as he liked.'

Adam's phone rings. He looks to see who is calling and then puts it on mute. 'It's good you're here, Shirley. You can keep each other company when I'm in Hong Kong.'

'Do you work for Agents International? They have their main office in London and another one in Manchester?'

'Yes, that's right.'

'Jonathon Finley is here. You might know him. I believe he works in the London office for the most part.'

Adam takes a large swig of his wine. 'Small world.'

'I'll introduce you later.'

'I'm sure I'll recognise him if I see him.'

Later, I meet a lovely couple who live near the church in Peckforton. We sit together on the terrace. Rebecca owns the bakery in town that Shirley frequents, and Paul is a solicitor. We share our love of gardening, and tips on what grows well in the sandy soil. The moon seems close enough to touch. It is such a beautiful evening.

'If you need a gardener, I recommend Green Fingers. It's a little firm but has excellent staff. Two of the regular ones have been with us for years,' Rebecca offers helpfully.

'We have a gardener, don't we, Rach?' Adam says. 'Does all the dirty work.'

'Yes, Ollie from The Hollies,' I explain. 'He's been such a help to me, not just with planning the garden, but other things too.'

'I hear you're taking part in Open Garden Day,' Rebecca says to me.

'Yes – the first year of many, I hope. Shirley roped me in, but it's great to have a deadline to focus on. I hear you have an office in Nantwich, Paul.'

'Yes, and one in Manchester on Deansgate.'

'I know Deansgate well. I've run the Manchester marathon twice right down that street,' Adam boasts.

'Adam's very self-disciplined,' I say. 'He trained for months so he could run it in under four hours.'

'Well done. I couldn't run that far. Just to the bottom of the garden and back is enough for me,' Rebecca chuckles.

Adam excuses himself to get another drink. I wonder if he is bored with these nice, ordinary and contented people.

'Have you done much gardening, Rachel?' Rebecca asks me.

'Not for a while, because we've just moved from an apartment in Altrincham. It was handy for Adam to get to Manchester Airport. Space is at a premium in that area, so we didn't have a garden. I had pots and hanging baskets, that kind of thing. But when I lived at Maple Cottage with my parents, I spent a lot of time outdoors. Dad knew about plants. And gardening programmes are about the only thing I watch on TV.'

'You must be so excited to be living here again.'

'Oh, I am. It's a dream come true. And spring is only a few months away and I'll be able to get stuck in.'

'This is a beautiful part of the world to live in. We loved bringing the children here for picnics in the wood. It's an ideal place to start a family.'

Shirley comes over to join us. 'This is my favourite season by Vivaldi,' she says, referring to the background music. '"Spring".'

'Me too. I can't wait to see the bluebells in the wood. They used to be amazing.'

'They are,' Rebecca says.

'The trees look beautiful lit up at night, but I miss the birdsong,' Shirley muses. 'A tree is an empty vessel without birds, like a poet without words. I'd sooner hear songbirds than violins.'

'Dad told me that.'

'Yes, he did.' Shirley smiles fondly at the memory of Dad.

I sense someone is looking at me. When I look to the far end of the room, I see that Adam is watching me. I sense he has been there for a while. He holds his glass up and mouths '*Happy New Year*' with an expression on his face I prefer not to read.

Shortly after midnight, we head home. Halfway down the drive, he stops. 'Damn. I've forgotten my coat. I'll run back.'

'I'll keep walking – it's cold. See you at home.'

I see deep blues and grey hues that murmur darkness. The wood presses up against the lane and my kitten heels slow me down.

Home.

Is it my imagination, or is something stirring, watching, dripping? I think I smell smoke. 'Who's there?' I call.

When the wind chime at the back of the door tinkles, I walk quickly so as not to linger in the dark lane. Ten minutes later, I hear the front door opening and closing as I unfasten my hair. I hear Adam climb the stairs and expect him to come into our bedroom; instead, he goes into his office.

I watch his movements in my dressing table mirror; he is so preoccupied with whatever is on his mind that he doesn't sense I am watching. He removes a file from his desk and opens the top drawer; it makes a metallic sound as it slides open. I watch him place the file in the drawer, lock it and put the key under the leg of the desk. I tuck the observation away, doubting it will be useful, but my curiosity is pricked.

When morning comes, Adam gets up early for an induction at the C5 gym in Nantwich. I wait for the sound of the front door closing and his car engine fading into the distance. I count to ten, then launch myself into his office to find what is so important he must keep it under lock and key. Nothing else is locked away in that office of his.

I retrieve the key and unlock the top drawer.

It takes me several moments to process the significance of the document in the file. The sums of money are large. Much bigger than the last time I was aware he 'borrowed' money. It is obvious from the amounts and dates, he never paid the money back like he said he did. I read it again and again. It appears that Adam has been defrauding his employer on a significant scale for a long time. Does this explain the bonus he mentioned?

I store the information in a safe place in my mind. What other secrets does he keep? Was Shirley's mention of Jonathon Finley from Agents International enough to aggravate his conscience last night? Was that why he was so preoccupied?

I wonder what this new year will bring.

14

JANUARY 2019

'I'm thinking of going on a reality television show like *Big Brother*. They pay well, and it's all in – full board. The other participants would cook, of course. I could give up eating out of tins for a spell. Just load the dishwasher from time to time, make myself look presentable.' Shirley strokes her spare chin. 'I might lose a bit of weight if the wine isn't decent.'

We discuss the pros and cons as we walk across The Barony to the town centre in Nantwich. We're on a shopping trip but, because Shirley is feeling frugal after an expensive weekend away and I'm not interested in clothes: we are rummaging in charity shops, me for books and trinkets, Shirley for anything under £1. This particular charity shop doesn't smell too bad, plus there is a sense of order to the items for sale.

The clothes aren't organised by size but by colour. There is a large section of blue and purple ones that look pretty to me, but Shirley makes a beeline for the oranges and yellows. She grabs several long, floaty garments and heads for the changing room. From the gap under the curtain, I see she has taken off her clothes and shoes. I had no idea she was wearing so much: items start to spill carelessly from below the curtain.

She comes out of the changing room in an enormous kaftan the colour of tangerines and prunes, and wearing a strange pair of pale sandals. When she went into the changing room she was Shirley; the Mr Benn experience in there has not been a good one.

'No, definitely not. It clashes with your hair,' I say, knowing I can be reasonably honest with my friend. I don't go so far as to say it makes her ample figure look immense. If she were a house, she'd have gained a single-storey extension.

She makes a twirl and poses in the mirror. Customers glance her way. 'Elizabeth Taylor?' she says hopefully, placing a claw on her hip.

'Mrs Doubtfire on a trip to the seaside.'

She laughs loudly. 'What about the shoes? They're a bargain, and it's nearly summer.' She dangles one in the air.

They are open-toed sandals, once white leather before they crossed the jungle and the Sahara. And they are at least two sizes too small for her.

'It's January.' I shake my head, trying not to laugh. 'It's not quite spring yet, let alone summer.' If Adam knew I was in a charity shop looking at clothes and shoes, he'd have a fit. 'And your toes are sticking out over the end!'

'They're very comfortable. I might get them.'

Like the reality TV show, I'm not sure if she is serious or not. But she appears to be generating an audience in the store, so I immerse myself in the bookshelves to avoid further embarrassment. I try to think about titles for myself, for Jen and the twins, but my cheeks feel hot because of the attention Shirley is enjoying. Luckily, the books are arranged alphabetically and there is plenty of choice.

In the end, Shirley decides against the shoes and opts for a brooch in the shape of a beetle, which is fifty pence. She donates the change from a pound coin to the Dog's Trust. I pay for my two books and a brightly coloured bangle, wooden and hand-painted. I think Jen will love it and plan to post it to her with an 'I saw this and thought of you' note.

Shirley sees Devina on the other side of the pavement and crosses over hurriedly to speak to her. A car is about to drive by. I remain outside the charity shop, feeling like a child who's just lost hold of her mother's hand.

It is hard not to stare. Devina tilts her head from side to side as she talks seriously to Shirley, holding her undivided attention. I'm pleased to see more traffic so I can stay where I am to watch.

Either the weight of the carrier bag or the camber of the pavement appears to be making Devina lopsided. There's a lot of animation in her free hand and her head as Ted's name is mentioned several times.

Finally, the road is empty of traffic so I feel obliged to cross.

'Rachel!' Devina looks startled. I haven't interrupted them, but her expression says I have.

A woman pushing a pram makes us shimmy to one side of the pavement. Over our shuffling, her two children overtake making aeroplane noises.

'How are you settling into your new place?' I ask, noticing Devina's eyes are the colour of steel, rimmed by dark circles.

'Fine, thanks.' She avoids my gaze. I wonder if Ted has told her about bumping into Adam and me at the fair. 'Adam's back in the UK, then?'

'Yes, spending hours working out in the gym. He's convinced he's gained weight over Christmas.'

'Who cares?' Shirley says with a wave of her hand. 'Do you approve of my beetle?' she asks Devina, stroking the brooch that has miraculously landed on her lapel during their chat. I take a closer look to check it hasn't got wings that will fly.

'Beetles can live almost anywhere on the planet, you know,'

Devina says. 'Desert, beach, water.' She gives a low, nervous laugh and makes small talk with Shirley. As we turn to go our separate ways, I think about how she scarcely looked at me once.

Later that evening, Adam rolls into our bedroom carrying an empty bottle of Malbec after knocking back glass after glass over dinner at home. He said he was unwinding after the fertility test and because he hates having to wait for the results. When I think about it, he hates having to wait for anything. If I don't get in his car within minutes of him, he gets cross.

He lurches from one side of the room to the other as if he is on a ship in a rough sea, then drops himself like an anchor on top of the mauve duvet. Moments later, he is violently sick in the bin.

'Night then,' I mutter before switching off the light.

15

I'm excited about seeing Jen, Jonny and the rest of her family at Will's christening. I can't remember the last time I got dressed up. I'm looking forward to being with friends and socialising with Adam.

'You look good,' he says, helping me into his car. 'You've styled your hair nicely.'

He looks more refreshed than he has in a while; he is wearing a white shirt and smart navy jacket and is clean-shaven. He has recently had his Mercedes valeted, and it still holds the scent of leather polish as we drive to St Mary's Church in Nantwich. But, despite its luxury, I prefer my grubby Golf with soil in the footwells from the plants I've bought.

'Jen,' I say when we arrive, and we hug for a long time.

She has modified an outfit she bought for the twins' christening and looks lovely. She and Jonny are beaming as Will runs circles around their legs.

Jonny and Adam shake hands while Jen and I exchange bags: a gift for Will from us, and books from Jen. I know my friend is feeling like her old self again because she is wearing her favourite lip balm, a red-tinted one that smells weirdly of mango. She is radiant with happiness; looking at her makes me feel a hundred per cent certain I want to be a mum. She makes me think of sunsets and cocktails and the cheerful spires of lupins soaring into the sky above the earth, grass and worms.

'Hi, Adam.' Jen gives him a fleeting air kiss. She's not too fond of him.

'Congratulations,' he says stiffly. 'Though aren't christenings usually when they are a baby? Will must be nearly two.'

I give him a light pat. 'Tactful, dear.'

'It's all right, he's right. We just hadn't got around to it.' Jen's smile is tight-lipped. I know that expression. Money has been – and is – in short supply. But I would never reveal that to Adam.

We turn at the sound of Jonny laughing at something a man in an ill-fitting suit has said. I hold my handbag to my chest as if it were a child.

'The good news is that it's a short service followed by a swift drink in The Red Lion, if you fancy one, Rach,' Jen says. 'The bad news is that the church is crammed with restless children.'

'Perfect,' Adam says dryly.

'Auntie Rachel, do you love my frock?' Katie gives a twirl, sending her long hair spinning out. She has sherbet around her mouth.

I admire the frill on her white socks, which matches the frill on the hem of her pretty cream dress. She tells me in complete confidence that her verruca has gone. We giggle and hold hands, and I feel like I'm floating with happiness on her cloud of perfect innocence.

I whisper in her ear, 'You look like a princess.'

'You look like Rapunzel.' She skips to the church. Like a cuckoo clock, as she goes in Will appears in the porch, wearing a gold waistcoat with matching Converse trainers. He runs up to me and I whizz him round in my arms. He attempts to say 'Rachel', but it sounds more like 'Rack-ill'.

'Shall we go inside?' Adam says impatiently. He tugs me towards the church before I am ready to move. 'I want to sit at the back.'

Inside the church, several children are playing hide and seek. There are flashes of brightly coloured frocks and shirts in the pews; some of them bob their heads up from behind the seats in a pseudo Punch and Judy show. The stone walls are warmed by the sound of children's laughter and the speed of their movement, the whisking of pigtails and unselfconscious giggles.

Adam and I sit next to a couple we haven't met before who have a little boy, Stevie. He sits quietly through the service, playing happily with a John Deere tractor. In his imagination, he appears to be ploughing our pew. I turn to Adam to share in the joy of this lovely little boy. Why can't Adam smile? There's a faint upward twitch of one lip. Somewhere beneath his tight skin is the man I fell in love with.

Stevie's mum and I admire the generous pale-pink and blue flower arrangements, one on each side of the pulpit. Her husband mutters something to Adam about a hip replacement.

My heart swells when the vicar and family gather at the font. Jonny stands tall, a proud parent, while Jen's face radiates love. Love: the rainbow kind between a mum and a child that strides any distance and brightens the cloudiest of days. The godparents stand to one side, looking a little self-conscious. I think Jen has never looked more beautiful.

'On your christening day, William Simon, may God take care of you in every darkness and protect you from every evil.' The water is poured over Will's head. The sign of a new beginning.

Adam knocks my leg because I've started blubbing. He hates it when I cry in public. Steve's mum passes me a tissue; I could kiss her for showing kindness when my husband doesn't.

Afterwards, I can't keep up with Adam. He starts walking

quickly to the car even before I've said goodbye properly to Jen and Jonny. It's drizzling and I don't have an umbrella. I can tell by the slope of his shoulders that he's feeling stressed. He slams the car door so hard the car rocks.

'Adam...' From the passenger seat, I watch the three-cornered leek growing at the roadside disappear at speed as we hurtle towards home. Its sweet scent is lost on us. Tears form in the corners of my eyes as I recall the faces of the twins, Will, and tractor-loving Stevie.

'Not now. I need to concentrate on the road,' Adam barks.

I can't help but brake with my right foot because he negotiates a sharp right-hand bend far too quickly. The seat is so slippery I fight to stay upright. My bangles jingle with each sharp bend, which irritates him further. 'Take them off.'

A light drizzle quickly turns into heavy rain, hitting the windscreen with some force. The windscreen wipers fight it one way, then the other. Drops stream miserably down the pane of flawless glass. The unremitting rain, the speed, the white campion, make me close my eyes. The downpour makes itself heard on anything it can find on its way to the earth. It's the only thing that has something to say.

When we get home, I pour us each a large glass of white wine. It's Pinot Grigio, one of Adam's favourites. 'Are you going to tell me what all that was about?' I say, and collapse into the rocking chair.

Adam drinks his wine standing up. He sighs deeply. 'Sorry, I didn't handle that well.' He gulps wine. 'It's being around children. And Jen, pregnant again – it just rubs salt in the wound. I feel uncomfortable around them, that's all.'

'They're our friends. You made a bit of a scene by leaving so hastily.'

'Jen will understand. Can you text her, or something? Say I was feeling ill.' He runs a hand through his hair. His jaw is set.

'Yes, I'll ring her tomorrow. Come here.' I stand up and hold him. 'I feel it too. I love you. One day it will be our turn. One day.'

'I get the results soon, and then I'm back to China.' I stroke his back, sensing the stress beneath his expensive shirt. 'I love you more than anything. You know that, don't you?' He looks at me intently, his eyes so dark I can't see his pupils.

16

Adam's return is announced by the spray of gravel on the drive, the slamming of the front door behind him and then, 'In the kitchen. Now!'

The lustre of our happy time together fades.

My hands are trembling as I try to button up my blouse before going downstairs. In the end, I put a jumper over the top. I hear Adam pacing the kitchen as I tiptoe down the stairs. From the middle of the kitchen, he turns to face me. I know the test result before he opens his tight-lipped mouth.

'Sit there,' he says, pointing to a kitchen chair. From his pocket, he yanks out an envelope folded in two. 'Read this.'

The letter quivers in my hands as I read it. It's dated today from South Shropshire Private Hospital. Once I get to the end of the letter, I don't know how to react, so I say nothing. Seconds tick past then Adam's hand strikes my left cheek. My upper body sways to the left so swiftly that two legs of my chair lift from the floor. Too stunned to speak, I drop the letter, watch it fall to the floor.

'That's where it belongs. With the dirt,' he says bitterly.

Adam steps forward to put his black shoe on it like a

paperweight. Even without it, the news of his infertility would hold the moment in one fixed place. I keep my eyes on his shoe, noticing the contrast of the white paper and the black leather, the shine of it. My heart rate is soaring.

Suddenly, he grabs my hair to yank back my head. If it weren't for the smell of him, I could pretend to be at the hairdresser's, keeping my head at an awkward angle as the water drips off my hair. I could pretend the hairdresser has had to dash off to answer the phone, leaving me with my head in the basin. My throat is aching, and the muscles in my neck are tightening.

'I'm the man of this house. Now, this is what's going to happen–'

I forget how it feels to breathe without fear. The tears are streaming down my cheeks, running down my neck and under my blouse, a soft tragic wetness. I see dust motes floating to the ceiling from the unnatural angle of my gaze. I wonder what other husbands are doing right now, what Jonny might be doing.

'You've always been pathetic,' he says and tosses my head away. I want to rest my chin on my chest because my neck hurts but I dare not, so I focus my eyes straight ahead, keeping my posture upright. I think of Jen and the secret acorn pendant in the drawer of my dressing table and the note beside it which he sent – *Sorry*.

'If you tell anyone I'm infertile, you're dead – got that?'

I nod as I keep my eyes trained on my mother's curtains, breathing in and out as evenly as I can, wishing he would move from behind me so I could at least see him to know from which direction the next threat might come. My tongue feels fat and swollen in my mouth. I recognise familiar shapes in the room – the kitchen table, the rocking chair – but somehow they are fragments, individual pieces I can't connect to make a whole picture that has me in it. He moves closer and I flinch, wait for the first strike to fall.

'You think I'm going to hit you, don't you?' He laughs. 'You have no fucking idea how patient I've been with you these last few years. And now it's too fucking late to have our own fucking child because I've been waiting for you to get your shit together, and now I'm too fucking old. It's your fucking fault, Rachel!'

The strike, when it comes, knocks me off my chair.

'Get up.'

I do as he says, and he grabs me around the throat and pulls me inches away from his face. I can smell his coffee breath and the sour notes of body odour. He looks the same, the same fit, handsome, muscular man. He looks how he isn't, like the face that I saw in the hall of mirrors. The silence between us is thick and choking until he pushes strands of tear-soaked hair from my face. His now-gentle touch is still as cruel as a punch. Then he holds my throat like a glass between his hands. Can this be the touch of a husband?

My eyes begin to bulge. As the curtains blur, I think of my mum's gentle hands, schooled in needle and thread. She was so nimble with pegs as she hung out the washing, skilful at plaiting my long hair before school.

Air is a luxury now. I hear myself gagging in my own home. Thoughts come in fragments, tear from the canvas I'd created. Shred to pieces. This crime of the heart. His eyes and arms pin me to this moment. Even if I wanted to look away, even if I could begin to think of good things, he forbids it – this ugly, seething spotlight.

This man's hands are not my husband's; they belong to a murderer. I try to fight his hands away from my throat, but I have no strength. I feel myself slipping underwater into a bottomless pool. The light moves further away.

A sudden sound outside startles Adam. He lets go of my

neck and looks through the window. I draw an enormous breath and give a dry, brittle cough. My chest expands and I rub my sore throat, still unable to move from the chair, panting like a dog.

I look around me. My vision is no longer blurred, but I am shivering and my lips are as dry as bone. I see dew twinkling on the grass and on the spider's web that spans from one edge of the windowpane, swaying in the south-easterly breeze. I long for a drop of water.

Adam has his hands in his pockets as he watches Ollie. He is concealing the instruments he had planned to kill me with. A murder weapon in the pockets of his designer trousers.

Ollie finishes marking out the shape of the garden of rooms with string and pegs. He must suddenly sense us looking at him because he immediately stands up and waves. He drops his hands to his sides, his arms loose and bear-like. I wipe away my snot and tears, feeling hollow and empty. The day has turned to stone.

Before I can move and hide, Ollie is walking towards us. I am still shaking so uncontrollably that I don't think I can stand.

'Ollie! So nice to finally meet you,' Adam says cheerfully, and offers him a hand to shake, which Ollie does warmly. If only Ollie knew where that hand had been. 'Thanks for everything so far. Shall we stroll in the garden?' He manoeuvres Ollie away from the back door. I don't think Ollie even sensed I was in the kitchen. He might as well be a million miles away.

Moments later, through the window, I see them talking at the bottom of the garden, their heads bowed. I rub my neck, close my eyes for a second as Adam's violence and his infertility bang around inside my brain. That man – that husband of mine – he was going to kill me. I know then with absolute certainty that I cannot continue to be his wife. Whatever hope and promises I've been feeding myself, whatever love I might have had for him, it's gone.

I watch them standing side by side. Are they discussing Adam's room, what he wants in it? For months I assumed I might be infertile; I punished myself for it daily. Even when the test was positive, I still doubted myself. All the pointless self-flagellation, the excessive sex, the doom I felt with each period, the tears. And it was Adam all along, all this time.

Adam and Ollie's heads are still bowed like two conspirators, so I take the chance to go upstairs into the bathroom, to the door that I can lock. My legs are heavy from lack of oxygen and shock, so I use the walls to steady myself and crawl up the stairs, eighteen of them. I am shocked by the thought that only minutes earlier I had dressed and walked down these same stairs carrying an ounce of hope.

Now a thief has stolen my heart, my dreams, my faith. I imagine the fingers of the wood gesticulating at me as if I have done wrong. I have to be punished again and again. The enormity of the truth is beginning to sink in, the reality that we can't have our children and I have married a violent man whom I need to escape.

My back rests against the locked bathroom door as I cuddle my legs to my chest and rub my bruised throat. Sunlight barges into the room, making beams of yellow on the tiled floor. The colour feels dishonest. I wait and wait, expecting to hear Adam's tread on the stairs, to see the door handle turn, to hear him shout my name. But none of these things happen. Hour after hour there is nothing but silence, which my mind fills with the worst kind of imaginings.

The evening grows dark. The telephone rings. I think of the pleasure I usually take in drawing the curtains, lighting a fire, making the house feel homely, cosy. Energy eludes me; I am weary of deluding myself. When I try to stand up, my body is slack and loose as though my skeleton has crumbled. The bathroom walls are tiled from floor to ceiling and our towels are suspended on the towel rail, two lilac Egyptian cotton towels, the softest I have ever owned. In the bathroom mirror, I see the fingerprints of my husband on my neck in shades of blue, pink and red – his real signature.

Heaven has stopped falling but I cannot forget. How can I have been so naïve to imagine life here would be any different with Adam? I sob quietly for a long time and eventually nod off. I think it's thunder that wakes me until I feel the door rattling.

'Open the fucking door, Rachel. I'm not going to ask again.'

I feel the door move behind me, threatening with opening, threatening with splintering under his weight, his foot, his fist.

'Open the fucking door, will you!'

I feel a trickle of wee run down my leg. Between sobs, I manage to mouth, 'No!'

'You stupid bitch.'

I hear him in the bedroom, then his feet tear downstairs and outside. It's only when I hear gravel spattering and his car engine that I start to breathe more easily.

As I look out of the bathroom window, something bangs the glass. I jolt backwards. Was it a bat? I decide to risk it so unlock the bathroom door. Gingerly, I make my way downstairs into the kitchen, trailing my hand on the wall to steady myself. There is a note on the kitchen table.

I'll be in Hong Kong for a month or two. We'll talk about our future together when I return. You'd better keep the doors locked at night.

17

It's a relief when daylight comes. Lying awake listening for each sound was exhausting. I thought I heard the rocking chair creak, the back door open and close, but I am in one piece and some of the horror of what happened has faded in daylight. The bruised neck reflected in the mirror is an ugly reminder, though, so I wrap a cotton scarf around it and apply a touch of blusher to each cheek to help me believe that today is a better day than yesterday, and tomorrow will be better still.

In the middle of the night, with the indistinct sounds outside and the ivy of twisted sheets, I was reminded of camping in the garden here when I was about ten years old. I wanted to show Dad I was brave and not a 'girlie-girl' like some of my friends at school. At the time I was re-reading the Famous Five story about a camping trip. I liked George, the tomboy. I wasn't too fussed about having a spooky adventure because I was on my own, but the thought of snuggling into my sleeping bag with nothing but a tent between me and the stars appealed to my romantic idea of nature. It was fun – until it seemed to me that an owl was hooting my name, over and over again.

The Famous Five characters camped out on open moorland,

which was wild and deserted, but Dad said sleeping at the foot of the woods was just as unpredictable. He was right.

The memory lurches at this point, like an amateur video made in black and white. It skips to the moment when I was jolted wide awake by a shriek, a startling, frightening sound I couldn't place, which I immediately associated with pain, an attack of some kind. Too scared to move, I listened some more. Although the shrieking had stopped, the new sounds were worse: they were close by, indistinct rustles and scurrying sounds right outside my tent. A frightening universe existed inches away. Much, much closer than I ever thought an enemy existed.

Maybe it was a badger. An innocent creature. Not a violent man. Not an abusive husband. Not a murderer.

I spend the morning at the front of the house planting up pots and hanging baskets, and attaching a trellis to help the clematis and wisteria spread. I push away any thought of Adam as soon as he pops into my head.

It's impossible not to be nostalgic about my childhood, for my happy ignorance of the truly frightening things in life, of brutality from people you love – loved.

Opposite the kitchen and utility window, I create a long, thin border which I fill with bulbs that will be visible from the window above the kitchen sink. It seems that this house and garden are all I have.

A soiled spade rests its head against the mossy wall at the back of the house, and the garden hose is a mess of idle green coils. Carrying the spade, I hear the mellow call of a wood pigeon and the twittering sparrows, then I see the maple tree at the bottom of the garden. I screw up my eyes to look more clearly. The sky grows around it as I creep towards the tree, unsure how I will feel when I get closer or whether I should walk away.

The tree is a globe of health and vigour, an upturned fountain of pure green like something heaven-sent, cascading and shielding. It is a natural hiding place, a circle above fertile soil. I'm afraid to lift my gaze. Why must living death follow me around?

With horrified recognition, I see the mobile is suspended in the tree at an angle so the clouds and silver stars hang down as if it hangs from a bedroom ceiling. It hovers above nothing, belonging in another world. Not a baby, just soil, stones, fallen leaves. A burial site for hope.

The leaves sweep out, pushed across the earth by an invisible broom. The sadness lies still and heavy in the shade until a light breeze stirs it, a chorus singing a sad song to accompany my sobs. I steady myself by placing a hand on the tree's thick, twisty girth.

Tears stream down my face, falling this way and that as the foliage moves like a child's fringe. The rough grain of bark pushes against the skin on my forehead and damp cheek.

I yank at a branch, pull it, making the leaves rustle in protest. I push away images of a baby, a skull, my name written in bone. I yank the branch harder still, hating the sight of the mobile that is both goading and redundant. A thrush hops into the circle of shade then makes a panicked sound and flies out, as if alarmed by what it has seen.

I am glad of the dangling branches and the concealment they give me as I wail and tug pathetically. The branch snaps and the dislodged mobile tumbles to the earth, a spent object of little moons and silver stars. I kick soil at it, grab the spade and smash it to pieces. Its light-coloured fragments graffiti the soil.

But behind me are the woods. Omnipotent. I wonder where the secret roots that transfuse life and blood to the trees begin and end. The dark world in those woods feels closer than ever; some part of it has trespassed into my garden, been here where it does not belong. And it will not go away. Is Adam watching me? Is this his parting shot.

I feel as if there are hovering faces or grasping hands before me, waiting for me. I look up to Shirley's house and the sight of its sturdy old walls gives me some comfort. I know my friend isn't far away. But who has done this? Does the perpetrator know the painful symbolism of the mobile? Is Adam playing with me, or has an intruder been here?

This daily fear, a pipeline to death or insanity. It is bindweed; it is a tapeworm.

The remoteness of the location takes on a new complexion. I see the door to the garage is wide open, like a mouth caught in a clamp. It looks menacing, forbidding. The vacancy around me stretches out.

With sweat-ringed armpits, and grit grinding between my teeth, I wipe my hands on my dirty jeans and collapse, exhausted, as the grief of never being a mother overtakes me. My hair has come loose from its plait and it falls into my eyes. The shovel falls to the ground. I taste the dust in my mouth and feel satisfaction at my suffering.

Should I run from here? I look at the cottage, its familiar warm sandstone, its chimney. The windows look back at me. Is this my home? Home should be safe. Should I keep moving, board a train, a bus, go somewhere. Anywhere.

I kill the thought. It seems I belong here, no matter what or who frightens me. This cottage matters to me. I long to see shops, hear the thrum of a tram, the rise and fall of chat and the laughter of busy people, music and cash registers opening and closing in boutiques. But ultimately, I belong here.

I move back up the garden as slowly as a sunset. My shadow elongates on the lawn as I retreat to the safety of the indoors, and the vast sky looks down unforgivingly at me, keeping all its secrets to itself.

18

FEBRUARY 2019

I drive slowly, aware of road signs, shop signs and letters on the road. After a while they stop, and the hedgerows concentrate my gaze on the road ahead. I leave Peckforton Hill draped in pink-sorrel behind me and head into Nantwich, with a small detour past The Hollies.

I have never been into Ollie's room, which overlooks the roses, but I've imagined it more times than I care to remember. I think I see the skylight he mentioned. He has told me that the room is so small that he has a single bed and a coat stand for his clothes.

Does he think of me at night as I think of him? Ollie has become my bedside reading, with the light off. When I feel afraid, I think of him in his room.

A display of pansies and violas liven up the entrance to the garden centre. There are just three cars in the car park; February must be one of the quietest months for the nursery. I don't stop. It's taken only a short time for me to know I can trust him and he won't hurt me. I feel safe knowing he isn't far away.

At long last crocuses have pushed their way through the soil in the borders of St Mary's Church in Nantwich. The town centre is busy with shoppers; they are still wearing coats, but there is a faint warmth in the air. The dress shops display brightly coloured spring wear in anticipation of warm weather, which may or may not come as quickly as everyone would like.

I head to a quirky café bar for a coffee with Jen. The Shed is aptly named. We have been meeting here for years, often after a night out together during one of my visits out of term time. I take a table in the back corner; it lacks natural light, but is private and cosy. While the place aspires to be a cocktail bar, inside it has had an identity crisis. It sells real ale and pink gin side by side, dainty breadsticks with humus, and cheese and onion crisps. I take in the new fairy lights around a large mirror and catch the glitter of silver tinsel, a shred of it caught in the illuminations. Christmas has been and gone.

Background music starts. It's 'Nightswimming' by REM. Jen makes her entrance by doing the breaststroke and holding her nose as she joins me at the table. The bearded bartender shows his delight at seeing her by raising his shaggy eyebrows up and down in time with her strokes. She plonks herself on the sofa beside me and hugs me hard, until the delicious aroma of an Americano lures her away.

'How are you feeling?' I ask. She looks very heavy and tired.

She shrugs her shoulders. 'It doesn't matter how I am – he or she is on their way. I've never felt so ghastly. Must be age. First it was morning sickness like never before, and now I'm just a whale. The pendant looks nice.'

'Thanks.' I touch it, having forgotten I'd put it on. 'They are okay, though? The baby?'

'Yeah, just small.'

I start to relax and listen to Jen's description of their year so far and the usual new year's resolutions that only lasted a few days. 'How was your Christmas?' she asks. 'I didn't get to see much of you at Will's christening. Adam seemed very stressed.'

'It was good at first. We went to the funfair, which was okay, and to Shirley's for a New Year's Eve party.' I wonder if I should tell Jen about what happened but I know we will both get upset.

'Did he buy you a present?'

'He's paying for the garden of rooms. Ollie's getting paid for his labour and the plants. Oh, and he bought me lingerie.'

'That's good, Rach. A positive sign?'

'He... well, not really. It's got worse.' I swallow a sob and compose myself before sharing the tale. The coffee cups swim in and out of focus. 'Adam found out he's infertile. He went ballistic.' I rub my neck. Once I say it out loud, it becomes real. 'He frightened me this time, Jen. I thought he might–'

There is a pause; either Jen is processing what I've told her, or maybe she's composing herself in this public place. Her voice is breathless when she finally speaks. 'No! Fuck that! What did he do?'

I put my hands around my throat. 'He yanked my head back. I thought he was going to strangle me. If Ollie hadn't arrived, I dread to think–'

'The man's a monster. Do you want to move in with us? Shall I send Jonny over to threaten him? What–'

'No!' I hear the panic in her voice. 'I'm all right. He's in Hong Kong for a month or so. Says we'll talk when he gets back.'

'What's there to talk about, Rach? He's a monster, and he can't have kids. You need to get the fuck away from him.'

'I–'

She interrupts, urgency in her voice. 'If Adam's hurt you that badly once, he'll do it again. And each time it'll get worse, until it's so bad you'll either be too scared to get away or you won't be able to.' She takes a deep breath. 'I'm so sorry. You don't deserve this. No one does. What a bastard. God, I hate that man.'

'I've got time to work things out in my head,' I tell her, but she starts to cry. 'Please don't. You'll set me off.' My head starts spinning. The café is busier now; a couple have chosen a table close by. The man is in his fifties with a mane of thick grey hair. 'I need time to get things square.'

'Rach, are you listening? Now what? I mean, no kids? I know you're desperate. You can't stay with him. You know that, don't you?'

'Yeah. I do know it. I don't love him. But it's a lot to absorb in one go, Jen.' The sight of strangers smiling and chatting, and the smell and taste of coffee, bring me round. 'I thought it would be different at Maple Cottage. A fresh start for us both. I've been kidding myself. I mean, I can't leave. It's my home. He'll never leave me alone, Jen. I don't know–'

'Look, there's always a way. It's only natural to hope things will get better, but now you know for sure he's got a screw loose, he's got to be booted out of your life for good. Make a plan. I'll help you.'

I reach for her hand. 'There's been some weird things going on at the house, too.' I tell her about the skulls and the cigarette butt, the doormat turned the wrong way around, the mobile, my suspicion someone is watching me.

'Are you sure Adam's in China?'

'How can I be sure? When he first came back, it seemed like he'd just had a long flight. If it wasn't Adam, who else would want to hurt me?'

Jen shakes her head. 'I dunno. Weird locals? Old boyfriend? Listen, you only have to ring and Jonny or I will be round in a shot.'

'I know. Thank you.'

Jen's phone makes an audible ping. Unusually for her, she ignores it and stares gloomily at her empty coffee cup. 'I don't know what to say, Rach.' Her eye make-up has started to run. 'I feel sick he's messed you up. How could he do that?'

'I rushed into marrying him. You told me as much. There's

no prenuptial agreement, so if we divorce he'll take half the house – probably buy me out to spite me. There's no way I can lose Maple Cottage. That, and the garden of rooms, are the things that are keeping me going. It's all I've got. But then, Adam takes what he wants. A divorce or a prenup, he has no respect for the law.'

'What do you mean?'

'I found something in his office. Adam has embezzled a lot of money.'

She closes her eyes for a moment. 'Then blackmail the bastard. Or get some professional advice. God, he's such a fucking hypocrite, making out he's white as white and his shit doesn't stink. God, I'm mad!'

'How can I blackmail him? He'd throttle me. Or kill me.'

'Go to the police. Let's go now.'

'He might get a caution, which he'd ignore.'

I've never stood up to Adam, not once during the years of abuse, because he is stronger than I am and I used to think I couldn't cope without him. I kept a diary at my lowest point, thinking that writing it down might help. I used to read with disbelief my entries describing what he'd done or said; in the end, I doubted myself so much I even doubted what I'd written was the truth. I questioned my objectivity when the subjective was pouring out of me, undermining my judgement. So I stopped writing, found excuses to sweeten each day.

He didn't mean it. He didn't mean to. I brought it on myself. I should be in his shoes. It was an accident. He didn't mean it. He didn't mean to. I brought it on myself. I should be in his shoes. It was an accident. He didn't mean it. He didn't mean to. I brought it on myself. I should be in his shoes. It was an accident.

Suddenly Jen sits bolt upright. 'I need to collect Will from nursery! Sorry, I'm late!' It's as if she's suddenly read an important notice inside her head. She throws her phone in her bag and a beer mat – I'm not sure why she needs that particular coaster. 'Every day, I tell myself to be a better mother. Every day I fail.'

Jen is already standing up, her string bag over one shoulder bulging with the books I've given her. She has metamorphosised before my eyes into Mother-Jen, who is formidable. She wipes her eyes and runny nose with a tissue. 'God, I hate leaving you like this. I'll ring you. You ring me. Come over. Love you. Bye!'

I watch her bustle off with her purpose, her deadline, and the foetus in her womb. I turn and amble away, trying to avoid the cracks in the pavement, under clouds that seem no bigger than a baby's skull.

19

For teachers, staff meetings involve a lot of sitting on hard plastic chairs staring at PowerPoints. There is some variation to the theme this term, with a senior school briefing in one of the science labs. It has recently been revamped and, unlike a lot of the other classrooms, it looks pristine. But it reeks of hospital-smell.

The headmistress, Judith, cares deeply about Nantwich High School but she tends to speak to the staff like we are eleven years old. Just now she is giving the head of science a look that says 'put your phone away'. He obediently does as he's silently told.

Judith is standing at the front of the room, waiting for silence, wearing a neutral expression – a trick we all use in our classrooms with varying degrees of success.

I listen to her talk about data and distance travelled. My bright classroom, my students, seem like a foreign country because the normal parameters of my life have warped beyond belief. My colleagues think I am happily married, that on Valentine's Day I will share a romantic meal for two. What else can I say?

Lessons pass almost without incident, apart from a

misplaced history book about Nantwich containing the notes for the Tudor project that results in a hysterical child weeping during the break, and a fight between two new starters that leaves one with a nasty nosebleed.

I have a couple of bad days and barely leave my bedroom except to get more packets of biscuits, but I manage to maintain a facade of competence and happiness when I'm at work. I need my job. Adam sends me brief texts, which I immediately delete without reading.

Last night, the wind stampeded outside. I heard the topple of a garden chair and the mania of the wind chimes. I wanted to get out of the house, but I was afraid of the outside world as much as the inside one. But in daylight, Maple Cottage regains its smooth edges and soft carpets. I dress for work, and it could almost be a normal life.

Valentine's Day cards are on sale in shop windows, and some of my students speculate who might send them one. I listen to their romantic ideas, wistfully remembering that my kamikaze romance started to take a nosedive on Valentine's Day when we got engaged.

Sometimes it's possible not to think about my situation. Not forget – no – but distract. Work occupies time and energy, and I am glad of it.

One of my Year Eight students complimented me today on my earrings and my acorn necklace. 'You should wear them more often, miss. You look really pretty.'

Yes, I would if I could. I will, when I'm shot of Adam. 'Thank you. I get sore ears, though, if I wear them too often.' Which isn't a lie.

By one o'clock, I am home from work. I change out of my suit into jeans and a fleece and wait for Ollie to arrive. I want him to identify a few plants for Dad's room.

'Hello, Maple Rachel. You all set?'

'Yep. Gloves and all for the prickly stuff.'

Ollie is dressed in a blue T-shirt and a light fleece. I feel cold when the temperature drops beneath the pines. He hums a tune to himself, which irritates me a little, as do his energetic strides. He doesn't seem to have a care in the world.

We walk for a few miles without any real sense of purpose. Ollie chats about the weird and wonderful natural places he'd love to visit on the tour of Europe he's planning with the money Adam will pay him. I listen to him chatter away, feeling detached from his happy-go-lucky attitude to life.

He sees the mountain bike leaning up against the outhouse before I do. Even from ten feet away, I smell smoke which has a tinge more like marijuana than cigarettes. A smoke signal confirms that at least one person is inside. Letting Ollie dictate whether we investigate or steer clear, I slow my pace. I don't feel robust enough to deal with anything frightening or remotely threatening right now.

Ollie strides confidently towards the window and I follow in his long shadow. Underfoot there are a million pine needles, a million insects with a kingdom of their own. Inside the outhouse, there is a carpet of butt ends, broken skulls, cider cans, empty glass bottles and ferns, which crash into each other in a chaos of the natural and unnatural.

In the far corner of the dingy outhouse, Ted is smoking a joint. He grins when he sees us, then shoves his phone into his trouser pocket like that's his guilty secret. 'Well, well, if it isn't Mrs Jordan! Is this where you give me detention?' He smirks at me then blows an expert smoke ring. 'I know you,' he says to Ollie. 'Green Thumb.'

Ollie says, 'You should be at school, mate.' He looks at his watch. 'You've missed afternoon registration. Better get a move on.'

'What's it to you, Ollie?' Ted emphasises his name, clearly having just remembered it. 'I guess you were hanging out here while I was still in nappies.' He plays with his zippo lighter, throwing it up, catching it, between drags of the joint. 'Hardly climbed the dizzy heights of success mowing people's lawns, have we?'

'And you're gonna be the next prime minister, I suppose,' Ollie says sarcastically. 'You shouldn't be smoking weed, mate. It's a slippery slope to a class A.'

'I'm not your mate, and you don't know what you're talking about. Hey, it's my life, so sling it if you don't like it.'

Ted suddenly picks up a skull and throws it at the wall beneath the window. I am nowhere near the target but I still flinch and duck. Ollie doesn't recoil, which unsettles Ted.

A single magpie lands on a nearby branch to blink its black eyes at us. The sound of the ominous bird is harsh and raspy, which is enough to frighten me.

'Do that again, and you'll regret it,' Ollie says evenly.

I step away from the window and catch my foot on a thick branch that is nestled in a bed of mushrooms. Ollie goes to grab my arm to stop me falling but catches it too late. Ted's laughter sends birds out from the trees up into the cerulean sky. Twigs snap beneath me as I fall, exposing a network of scutch grass, disturbed ants and maggots.

My ankle smarts. I join the fallen branches and wriggle my foot out of the hole it's trapped in. Tears are close, so I swallow hard to stop them. Then, with Ollie's help, I stand up, feeling tearful and weak. Adam is always telling me how pathetic I am. He's right.

I dust myself off to the sound of Ted's laughter.

The distraction of Ollie reaching down to pick a mushroom distracts me. 'Don't! They're death-cap mushrooms. Poisonous,' I say.

Ollie looks at me in a mixture of surprise and alarm. 'Seriously?' He wipes his hands on his jeans.

I remember telling my best friend, Abbie, about the route to the outhouse, but she didn't believe me that the *Atropa belladonna* can take an adult life in minutes, or that there is no known antidote for *Ricinus communis*. She was too busy killing people in video games to care. Dad taught me about the beauty and the deadly nature of plants; he was adamant that one day I would be glad of the knowledge. Is today that day?

Ted suddenly stands up to face us at the broken window. His grey-and-navy school uniform is grubby, a shocking reminder of his youth. He's just a boy. He should be sitting behind a desk with a pen in his hand, an open book before him. 'Playing away, are we, Mrs Jordan? I thought you were married.'

'What I do is none of your business!' Rage grabs me. I'm tired and fragile. The last thing I need is Ted. 'Have you been trespassing in my garden? You've been a few times – that cigarette butt by the back door was you, wasn't it?'

He raises his hands in the air and smiles. 'Not me. You must be confusing me with somebody else leaving you a welcome-back present.' He bends down to retrieve a skull and holds it in the palm of his hand; a mole's skull most likely. 'It was him!' He laughs at his joke.

I walk away. Ollie follows. 'He's just a kid,' he says. 'We've all been there.'

'He's messing with me. I'm sure of it.' I'm angry with myself for not putting Ted in his place. 'Those skulls belonged to Dad, from his pest-control business. Ted's taken them out of the wheelie bin.'

I walk back to the window and have the advantage of standing while Ted is sitting on the floor again, his large white trainers pointing at opposite corners of the outhouse. 'Does your mum know you hang out here during school time?'

He stops scrolling on his iPhone, which Devina will be paying for. 'She don't and she won't.' He emphasises the 'won't' to threaten me. 'But then Mum thinks the sun shines out of my arse. She'll defend me whatever you say because we're family, see. That's how it works, ain't it? Loyalty, that's the word. But you wouldn't know about that.'

'You mean, "she doesn't" and "isn't it". Well, it's about time she got to know, you little shit.'

Ted scuffles into a standing position then lurches to the window. 'Don't you–'

Ollie appears from nowhere. He sticks his hands through the window and grabs Ted by the collar. Ted's tie moves comically to one side and his phone makes a pinging sound from the ground. Nobody moves.

'I get it,' Ted says to me, raising his arms in the air. 'You got yourself a guard dog.'

Ollie tightens his grip some more.

'Ouch! You're hurting me!'

'Listen to me very carefully, Ted. If I find you anywhere near this wood or Mrs Jordan or Maple Cottage, I will make your life very uncomfortable.' Ollie releases his grip then gently strokes the creases in Ted's shirt.

We walk away.

'He's not a bad lad, really,' Ollie says minutes later. 'Just lost his way. I was far from perfect at his age.'

I hear my shallow breath and our footsteps, and I'm so glad to be with Ollie. I focus on the smell of ferns, the damp earth beneath my boots and the sunlight filtering through the net of leaves up ahead because I want Ollie to hold me. It's wrong, but I crave it.

I stop. When Ollie sees the tears in my eyes, he wraps me in his arms. I can hear his heart beating through his T-shirt and smell pine scent on his neck.

When I pull away, he is smiling infectiously. 'Don't worry – Ted's got the message.' He steps back to look at my face. 'You all right? I can stay if you want?'

'I'm fine.' I smile back.

I thank Ollie and pretend I'm fine, but I can still hear Ted's hyena laugh ringing in my ears.

'Ring me any time. I've always got my mobile with me.' Ollie holds me by the shoulders, looks at me intently and then kisses me on the cheek. 'I mean it, Maple Rachel.'

20

MARCH 2019

A combination of tiredness and emotional strain has left me feeling chilled a lot of the time. There is a pair of Adam's cufflinks on my dressing table, but his toothbrush has gone from the bathroom; still, there is a kind of vacancy about the upstairs, as if it remembers him leaving with a suitcase. Or is it that he's barely been here at all?

His texts are frequent and often long, but I continue to delete them. I suspect there is a message on the landline from him, but I can't face listening to his voice. If I knew he wasn't coming back again, I could relax and benefit from a sense of freedom; instead, I have a persistent toothache, a feeling that he will reappear as the spring weather warms the landscape. I have a constant fear he might reappear in a room, behind a door, through a window at any moment – a horrible jack-in-a-box surprise.

But spring is finally here. The garden of rooms will begin to take shape and rise out of the ground in harmony with its surroundings. Surely that will help me to forget that ugly, frightening day of Adam's vice-like grip and the end to my dreams of being a family here.

After the shower during the night, puddles of water sit idly on the lawn and sparrows peck at the grass looking for worms. I watch a blackbird's yellow beak reel in a long thin worm. The hedgerows, threaded with heart-shaped ivy and the foam of cow parsley, tremble with pleasure from the repetitive attention of the chaffinches and yellow tits, pulse after pulse, shiver after shiver. From the patio I watch a ladybird disappear under the garden table; further away, little birds collect nesting material.

I pull on a thick pair of socks, resisting the urge to lie down on the bed and not get up again. My energy fades, so I give up on getting dressed and pull on my dressing gown.

Behind the cottage, the fields are turning bright yellow with spring rapeseed. I'm not sure if the red dots are in my eyes or if they are the generous blossoms of wild red poppies. I didn't get a lot of sleep last night, despite a long brisk walk in the woods and the joy of seeing the bluebells along the way. An unbroken night's sleep has become a luxury. Coffee will bring me round, once the kettle boils.

'Lovely morning,' Ollie says, then closes the back door behind him as if it's his house. 'I've been up since five, fishing. Thought I'd call in.'

The kitchen is a mess of unwashed crockery and mugs, and an empty tissue box is on the table. His six-foot frame steps confidently into the kitchen with a snatch of light and birdsong. I instinctively pull my dressing gown tighter and touch my neck. Seemingly oblivious to my self-consciousness, he twitters on. 'Adam asked me to see to a few things while he's away. You know, keep an eye. Just want to check if there's anything you need while I'm here?'

'Has he been in touch with you?'

'Yes, by text.'

'Oh. I see. No, I was just...' There is something disarming about the bulky size of him in the kitchen at this early hour and the familiar way he wears his jeans.

I take a deep breath. 'I was going to drive over to my friend's house.' I rearrange the tablecloth, so I don't have to meet his eyes. When I step away awkwardly, my hair has flopped over half of my face. It can stay there for all I care.

I fidget with an empty mug with the dregs of bitter coffee inside it. I wish I'd got dressed or had something on underneath my dressing gown.

'No worries.'

'I've got time for a quick walk up to Peckforton Hill and back. Just need to get changed.'

'Perfect.'

It's a steep climb to the top, but when we get there it takes my breath away. I stand tall above the Cheshire plains. The sky is an endless backdrop for the church, Maple Cottage with its protruding chimney, and Shirley's Bird House with its orchard. The ground drops precipitously away beneath our feet where there is a tangle of branches and fallen trees.

'It's beautiful,' he says and playfully pushes me.

The soil and stones beneath me move and tumble down the hill. My heart jumps into my mouth. 'Ollie!'

He laughs, surprised by my alarm and lack of good humour. 'I wouldn't let you fall!'

After taking in the glorious view, we jog and walk back. I return home feeling rejuvenated. He is as laid-back and happy as ever. It's hard for it not to rub off.

'Call me if you need anything. We've got a delivery tomorrow, and I think your lavender will arrive. It's going to be special.'

The mention of Mum's favourite plant brings a smile to my face. His goodbye feels a little strange, but he leaves without kissing me this time. I don't know if I'm relieved or disappointed.

My jubilant mood deflates when Adam rings me. I ignore the phone. My reflected face is wan and sad, so I pinch each cheek and watercolour pink suffuses my skin. I yank my hairbrush through several knots, which gives me the physical pain I need right now. It's time to grieve for my loss, get a plan and move on. Seeing a heavily pregnant Jen and her children isn't going to be easy, but she is a dear friend who needs me.

Jen starts crying almost as soon as we sit on the sofa in her living room. My arms reach round most of her. Despite her size, it is a Jen without her giant personality; she is doll sized. Eventually, she lets go of me and I hold her hand. I have never known her so quiet.

She smiles at me as I stroke the fringe away from her clammy forehead. I wish I could come up with a joke – that's what Jen would do if the tables were turned – but I can never remember any, so we sit in silence for a while. Then her words come, the gate to a sluice released.

She'd been worked to the bone, failing at everything, feeling endlessly tired and low. It is Mother Earth's monologue. Luckily, Jonny has taken the children swimming so she can unburden herself.

'...clearing up sweat and blood and shit and piss. Cleaning, shopping, spooning food, grafting...' She is sobbing, dribbling, everything is leaking. '...Warts...'

The machine of herself is broken, burnt out. She says no one is looking after her while she's heaving her big bump around, running the house and caring for three children. The baby inside her is small, very small, but she is bigger than ever and scared. Here in her house, the living room is trashed. There might be a carpet, but I can't be sure.

'I'll get you a drink,' I say. I feel the need for tea but, knowing she is hot and sweaty, I decide against it.

A whiff of stale food emanates from the kitchen. An ancient banana skin looks up at me from the floor, asking to be put in the bin. I run the tap and pour two glasses of water. There's a tooth carefully wrapped in a tissue on the kitchen window ledge. All the other surfaces are buried under dirty crockery and pans.

As we sip our drinks, I notice Jen's library of books, typically alphabetised, has huge chunks missing. Like hair yanked from a head, it is plain wrong to see this in her home. I can't do anything until the books are back in their rightful places. The world is on the wrong axis otherwise. I put my drink down and make a start.

'Don't bother. Will pulls them out because he knows it winds me up.'

'I have to. Keep talking. I'm listening.'

She makes a face then launches into another monologue, starting with a food fight with Coco Pops at breakfast. It is crisis time: no one is happy and, according to the children, nothing is fair. Most of her sentences began with 'I want...' – to use my brain, to throw the Hoover out of the window, to fit into my old clothes, to get wasted on cocktails, to have normal-sized breasts, to sleep for a week.

I listen and try to be a good friend by letting her talk and let off steam, but she veers from one subject to the other until I am giddy.

'We've never got enough money. Every month it's a strain... When will we be able to go on holiday again?'

I fetch chocolate and caramel biscuits and fresh strawberries. I don't see Jen eat them but the plates are suddenly empty, and she has red juice down her chin. This is a different Jen, off-balance and griping.

'When we got home after the three-month scan, the twins were throwing mud in the garden and Will was splashing barefoot in a puddle. He must have been in that puddle for some time, and in between got hungry, got cold, got adventurous, got tired, because his footprints were all over the fucking house. I cried.' Her pudgy shoulders are hunched around her chin and her neck has disappeared. 'And I've not really stopped.'

'Does Jonny feel the same way?'

'He's really worried about money. I was going to look for part-time hours, but there's no point now because the wage won't cover the cost of childcare. I wanted a boy because it's gonna have to share a bedroom with Will for the rest of its life.' She sounds bitter. 'We can't afford an extension, even if the drive or garden were big enough for one.'

I stroke her hand. She's always been able to stare out anyone with her navy-blue eyes. Now the stare is so blank; it's as if the person behind the eyes has gone on holiday. 'I feel so fat and useless...'

I feel small as I pass the envelope of money to her and put one finger to my lips. Our secret.

She shakes her head. 'Not this time. You need it.' She pushes the envelope back to me. I can't argue, knowing I need to get away from Adam.

There is so much to do to make the house habitable, let alone clean. From under the coffee table I remove a pink nightie smelling of pee, and there is a picnic under the cushions on the sofa. The stair carpet has quenched its thirst on floating debris. Every hook, hanger and shelf is empty.

'Why don't you have a nap while I clean up a bit.'

She nods obediently and sleepwalks up the stairs. I take her a hot-water bottle, a glass of Ribena and, because she insists, a tin of rice pudding for a snack should she need one. By the time I return to her bedroom with an extra pillow to put under some part of her anatomy, her swollen feet are poking out from under the duvet. She is a dam in the flow of the room. I wish the river of time could flow over or under her.

'Did you know that you're my knitted tea cosy? My life-support machine? If only you could see how see fat and disgusting I am underneath all this, and how waiflike and gorgeous you are. Sorry I'm so useless to you.'

'Jen–'

'Think of me as a frozen asset. A casserole in the freezer. I love you, Rach.'

There is a kind of graffiti in the house that shouts anarchy at me in every room. In the bathroom, Jonny's newspapers have taken over the space to the side of the toilet, which is where Will has chosen to pee. Only just out of nappies, the step he needs to reach the loo has been shoved behind the bath so he can't get to the toilet seat. I feel sad that Jen and her family have got in such a muddle, that it has gone so far before I came here to help.

I focus on tidying up the lounge first, which results in a pile of items for the children to take ownership of, including a fairy costume, a hunk of yellow Play-Doh and a stickman drawing. With each item, I try to imagine what it's like to live in a universe with children.

In the kitchen, it takes nearly an hour to return all of Jen's jars, pots and weird implements to suitable homes so that it is the wizard's kitchen it usually is. I'm about to mop the kitchen floor when the door opens. A stream of small people and noise follow.

'Auntie Rachel!' The twins wrap themselves around me like I'm a lamp post. Will looks up at me. I hope he doesn't think he's a dog and cock his leg. Jonny looks on, amused.

In the end, I stay for three days while Jen gets back on her feet. The girls bring me up to speed on their verrucas and warts, the empty knicker drawer, the chauffeuring they need so they can go swimming/dancing/shopping. Will tells me facts about wasps and rats. Claire can swim fifty metres and has the badge to prove it, while her twin sister, Katie, has the twenty-five-metre badge, which is 'incredible' because Katie is older than her (by about a minute).

By the second night, the shine on my little halo is starting to fade. I've fed and bathed them, washed up, read them a story, tucked them up for a second time. Then Ribena, warm milk, brushing of teeth again, then sleep so sudden you'd think I'd knocked them out with a frying pan.

By the time I leave I'm exhausted, but Jen has some of her strength back. She has stopped crying, and I am happy to watch her be the matriarch of her tribe. Forever patient, she tends to their needs, anticipating them before they know they have them. It is a special gift.

Seeing Jen with her children reminds me of how I took my mum for granted and how love comes out of a mother's heart like an endless ribbon. Mum tended to my nettle stings; she listened patiently to tales of electric shocks from fences; she washed my filthy clothes without complaint. I wish now that I hadn't taken all those things for granted. But I did – and so have thousands of others before me, I expect.

As Jen colours in a rainbow with her children, I remember Mum sitting under a lamp, her back upright, sewing all hours. I thought her life was the size of a coin. It was around the time I was twelve that she started nodding off in the rocking chair, dropping her sewing into her lap mid-stitch. I saw her then not just as Mum but as an ageing woman. I saw her smooth cheeks and the delicate bird-like hands that needed the firm branches of my father's arms to make her strong. At the time, I didn't know Mum had been diagnosed with bowel cancer.

Some time later, she told me that her best friend, Audrey, had died. She wept into a light-blue handkerchief. For days, I saw the handkerchief poking out from under her sleeve. I hadn't thought of Mum as having friends or experiencing loss. I thought only of me. I was entirely self-consumed. Selfish.

Jen has almost finished colouring in the yellow section of the rainbow when I say my goodbyes. Katie insists I take the rainbow with me 'for good luck'. The children have left me tokens in my car to remind me of them: mainly crumbs, the odd sweet wrapper and a tissue with something green in it.

My drive home to Maple Cottage feels alarmingly quiet, so much so that, uncharacteristically I turn on the radio. Dad used to say there are 'quiets' and there are 'kind quiets'. This is a quiet, a falter between heartbeats.

Without those few days, I would have only known parenthood in the same way I have known war or murder, through an article, a report, a photograph taken by someone else, an image in colour. I realise I have been fed spools of joy through parents' propaganda, a *Big Brother* of procreation; the images of shit, tears and blood have been left on the cutting-room floor.

I am glad to be no longer so ignorant and for the distraction from my own problems. But do I still want a child? Do I want to feel a toddler's knees in the small of my back in the middle of the night when, at seven o'clock, we are spooned and perfectly bent in shape? Of course. I am human. I am a woman. I do. I do, desperately.

21

Inside the cottage, I make Ollie and myself a cold drink. At the window the new and emerging view makes me pause as I knock back almost a pint of water, glug after glug. Sweat trickles down my forehead and my hands are soil-covered, but I don't bother to wash them now that Adam isn't around to nag me about my nails. The bright-pink nail varnish he insists I wear has entirely vanished, save for the odd stain around the cuticles.

Now that Ollie is here with me, nature is responding to our touch; I feel a lightness opening up inside me. For once I am in control, and can nurture to my heart's content after feeling powerless and frustrated by my inability to conceive. The garden of rooms is bringing me out of the darkroom, and it so wants to grow that it is an inspiration to be strong and grateful for life.

'We're getting there,' Ollie says as he finishes his drink and we go outside again. 'It's amazing how quickly the plants take hold with good soil and water. And a decent budget, which means the plants have some size about them already.'

'The box hedging works brilliantly to give the rooms structure. That was a really good idea of yours.'

'Ah, brains and beauty,' and he toasts his empty pint glass.

Nearby, a jackdaw swoops onto the bird feeders. Seed spews from the mouth of the dispenser as it prises its black beak into the dangling orifice. A nervous robin pecks at the birdseed that falls from the rich man's table. Above it, the jackdaw's beak rocks the feeder like a hand on a cradle. Its pale eyes blink in time with each swing. A flap of its silver-black wings startles the robin away to the washing line, where it watches and warbles enviously.

Sweat drips down Ollie's face but he doesn't seem to notice. He looks at home, with the endless sky as his backdrop and his fingers grubby from working.

'Any thoughts on what you want in Adam's room? We can order in most things.'

'Still thinking about that one. Sorry.'

'He expects a room of his own as he's paying for the lot.'

'I know.' Adam can have his room if it means Ollie is here with me, but I don't know what should be in it. I've thought about topiary but I don't appreciate its rigid, controlling form, though it would be apt. 'Just need a bit of inspiration from somewhere. Adam's from the city – I think that might be why.' And I have no desire to look at anything which reminds me of him right now.

'I know. Well, think on.'

I bend over the border to look at the forked soil more closely. My nipples are standing out like stalks, but it is moments later when I realise they are in the centre of Ollie's gaze. Forgetting I am revealing my bra and cleavage, I remain bent down, with the soil spilling through my fingers.

Ollie bends down beside me, puts his hand lightly on my exposed arm. He gazes at me, leaving me feeling undressed and thankful Adam is not in the house. Goosebumps march up and down my arms. I can hear light birdsong as if it belongs in another world. Ollie touches the side of my face then traces the line down from my ear to my neck to the clavicle. I feel a kind of passion and a self-loathing twisted and plaited into one. He takes my long thick plait, wraps it around my neck then gently places it on my back.

His kiss is gentle and searching. 'You look well-rested for once,' he says, and moves away.

The intermittent buzz of an insect fills the silence. The swallows are playing and chasing, heralding the start of spring, wheeling high in the sky above our heads. A flock of chaffinches chat merrily next door on Shirley's silver birch. The intimacy comes and goes, almost dream-like.

~

For the next few weeks we work in companionable silence, preparing the soil, measuring out the rooms then planting the box hedges. Watching the foundations and the walls of a house go up in a few days is astonishing. I stand back to look at what is rising out of the ground; it is a kind of reincarnation.

'Shall we celebrate?' I say, when the walls are up. 'Ginger beer, beer, wine...'

'No, thanks. I'll head home once this edge is done.'

Then Ollie is walking away, a slow-moving picture, and I try not to feel disappointed. He is gathering his tools, his jacket. He parks the wheelbarrow where he found it. He'll deliver the next lot of plants as soon as they're in stock. I can't think of anything to say that might prolong his stay. He hesitates at the back door, where he has left his keys and phone. 'I think it's going to be something special. Like you, Maple Rachel.'

I smile and feel grateful for his words. I shouldn't follow him but I can't stop myself. 'We've achieved loads. Thank you so much, Ollie.'

'The pleasure's all mine.' He holds my gaze so firmly I can't look away, and then he lightly pushes a strand of hair away from my face, kisses my neck, my mouth, and leaves me longing for more. More.

'I'll be back soon. Lupins next.'

After he's gone, I sit on the garden chair on the patio and wait for the sound of stones being moved by tyres. I imagine the plume of dust that follows him down the lane. I touch my neck where his lips lingered and close my eyes as I recall his hard body against mine, his ribs jutting into mine. I sigh and release more than oxygen.

Then my phone rings. It's Adam. I press mute.

22

APRIL 2019

It is a Saturday morning and the weather is warm enough to dry a small load of washing. Dressed in a nightie, I pull on my wellingtons and go out with my washing basket through the back door. On the mat, there is a dead bird, a jay. It looks alive in every way except for its stillness, its vacant staring eyes and the angle of its speckled head. Poor thing. It must have collided with the door. I decide to bury it later.

To have a washing line in my back garden is a pleasure. At our apartment in Altrincham, I used a washer-drier because we didn't have the outdoor space. I have memories of Mum hanging out her washing with brightly coloured pegs, taking time to pin each garment carefully so it dried properly and the creases hung out. I loved the smell of the lavender washing powder and seeing the wind tugging the garments this way and that, knowing they would never fall off. Safe.

Like Mum, I keep my pegs in a bag which I hang on the line. Like Mum, I carry my washing basket at chest height and hug it a little. The routine of carrying my washing out in a white basket and pegging it to the line is one of the few domestic chores I enjoy.

Except when I get outside, I see there are objects already suspended from the washing line.

Black. Lots of black. Oily and black.

Moving closer, I see crows, or ravens, blue jays or whatever blackbird has been shot, ten times or more. All hanging by their claws, their beaks dangling, pointing to the earth, their wings silent and still, save for the breeze which flicks a feather despondently.

I drop the basket, and the clothes and knickers tumble onto the lawn. As I stagger, a blue top gets caught under my welly and is dragged along. I mustn't fall.

I hear the angry swarm of flies disturbed by something – me? As I bend down to retrieve the fallen garments and the basket, I see an unfamiliar object in my line of vision. The compost heap is larger than it was last time I looked. It should be shrinking, not growing. The stench hits me first as I move closer, then I hear the incessant buzz and menace of flies.

Two badgers. One still grinning.

A squirrel with an eye missing.

The remains of a cat with a protruding pink tongue.

On and on. One on top of the other. Stinking and rotting. Feathers, fur, entrails, claws, paws, unseeing eyes and teeth. Beaks.

Roadkill.

There's so much death near me that I am glad to hear and feel myself breathe. I realise I've been holding my breath. Thank goodness I don't have a child to see such horrors in her garden. I see a warped mind in the frozen terror of the badger's face. I see a terrible face emerging from the twisted skeletons and sinew. I see human lasciviousness in the pink tongue.

Has someone scoured the country lanes for roadkill? Stopped, pulled over, peeled them from the tarmac, the grass verges, and hauled them into a car boot? Then carried them here, his oozing loot, the prizes someone wants to share with me?

If I don't bury these creatures, the flies and vermin and possible disease will spread. I can't call my husband out from the kitchen to lend a hand. Is there a magic number to call for someone to do this job? Firstly, I photograph the evidence and resolve to report the incident to the police. Adam was careful not to harm me so severely that hospital treatment was required so he could keep our distorted domestic life a secret. Still, these pictures are another kind of destruction, a mark of cruelty.

I hate my vulnerability, so I take the spade in my hands and dig.

I won't be trapped inside my own home. Bit by bit, I dig and bury the creatures. It takes me the rest of the day. By four o'clock, the washing line is bare, the compost heap is inoffensive, and the clothes I carried out in my basket at the beginning of the day are back in the washing machine. Soon they will smell of lavender.

I won't be frightened out of my home.

I won't be beaten down.

23

Ollie is dressed in shorts and his usual brown boots; the laces are double knotted, as they always are. There is something touching about the way his socks protrude from his boots. His calves are heavyset with muscles, and the hairs on them are bleached blond. The Easter egg he brought me is on the kitchen table because he will probably eat more of it than I will. He's been hard at work for a few hours. We are both early risers.

I knock on the kitchen window and shout, 'Breakfast?'

He gives me a thumbs up, so I make us both a bacon sandwich. He makes walking look like arduous work with his heavyset legs and pendulous arms – he is a bear of a man. I wonder if he could sprint if he had to. He devours half of his bacon sandwich before I have sat down to eat mine.

'Rather than planting brugmansia in your dad's room, I suggest you use containers.'

'Okay. I texted Jen a couple of photos of her room. She says it looks amazing.' I think it does too. What better way to show love for a friend than with pulsatilla, orange dahlias, magenta, scarlet and yellow tulips, and a flutter of pink lupins – the hues of sunsets, summer holidays, cocktails. The riot of colour is Jen: it is fun, garish and jangling.

'You know, you can tell it's good soil just by touching and smelling it. You won't be able to tell in a pair of gardening gloves!'

'Habit. Ad–' I was about to mention Adam's disdain for grubby, chipped fingernails, then think better of it.

'I love bacon.' Ollie licks his grubby fingers. 'Great buttie. Thanks.'

The warm weather and the spade in the soil call him back outside. I know that feeling and smile.

Outside, I remove my polka-dot gloves and toss them to the ground as if they aren't mine, but they land so close to my wellingtons there is no mistaking they are a matching pair. I feel strangely self-conscious for someone who rarely cares about her appearance. The soil is fine and warm to the touch, alive as living skin.

Ollie and I push the wheelbarrows of debris to the bottom of the garden to dispose of. Suddenly he bends down to pick up an injured bird. It is a starling and looks horribly mauled. Feathers poke out at odd angles from its body and wing, and its beak opens and closes beseechingly without song or sound. I watch Ollie stroke its belly softly, then he passes it to me.

'I'd break its neck, put it out of its misery, but I'll leave it up to you.' The primal look in his eye catches my breath as he gives the grim diagnosis. The bird is tiny and fragile in the palm of my hand. It returns horrible memories of the roadkill and the blue jay I found by the back door. 'I'd guess a cat's been playing with it. It's kinder.' He looks at me. 'You all right?'

The swallows are playing and chasing, wheeling above our heads high in the sky as if life is a game. 'I can't do it!' I hastily pass the bird back to Ollie, who breaks its neck in one swift movement. I watch his shoulders arch over the hawthorn hedge as he tosses the dead bird into the undergrowth like an apple core.

'Nature isn't always pretty.'

'I know that.'

I tell Ollie about the roadkill, and he hugs me. The sound of a car and disturbed gravel pulls us apart. Moments later a policeman appears in the back garden. 'Mrs Jordan?'

I wave. 'Yes, hang on a mo!' I drop the wheelbarrow and walk briskly over to join him.

'I just need to take a look round, if that's all right.'

'Yes, the officer on the phone said you might. Be my guest.'

'Shouldn't take long. A list of acquaintances, enemies – if any – and tradesmen that come and go would be useful at this stage. It is probably a one-off, but it's better to provide a complete picture.'

'I can do that.'

'It could be kids messing about. Your father's death might have attracted the wrong kind of attention with your return. Keep your valuables locked away. It's a pretty remote spot.'

'Dad's suicide isn't new.'

'*You* are new. This is rural Cheshire. Some people are parochial, they resist newcomers. I'm only speculating. The important thing is to report any activity that concerns you, however small.'

'Oh, I will. All the evidence of this visit is buried under there, but you have the photos.'

~

Apart from Adam's room and the fifth room, the rest of the garden is almost complete and utterly radiant. I have something to show the locals on Open Garden Day. I'm glad to support Shirley's efforts with the initiative by participating, even though

I'm nervous about having local people here. Shirley reassures me that Dad is remembered fondly and they won't come to gossip.

Just as Ollie climbs into his van, Adam rings me yet again. This time I decide to speak to him. Ollie has texted him photos of the garden, which he has responded to positively, much to Ollie's relief.

Adam's voice sounds strange. I try to decide if it sounds far away, as if he is in China, or not. His gentle voice is at odds with my memory of a monster.

'I won't keep you long. I get the message – you don't want to talk to me. I just wanted to say sorry about leaving like that.'

'Sorry? You–'

'You understand what I'm dealing with? As a man? The way to deal with it is to keep working, move on. It won't beat me.'

'I don't have anything to say right now.' I hang up.

I wish I could climb in the van with Ollie and disappear for a while.

24

MAY 2019

I lie very still on top of the duvet in my dressing gown, barely breathing. I toss and turn for hours. The clock says 3.24, which isn't a relief because there are more hours to wait before the dawn chorus.

Something is outside. I can hear it beneath my window. I listen intently for a footfall. In my mind's eye, a figure is moving as stealthily as a fox across the lawn. My bladder aches so badly, but I'm too scared to move from the island of my bed to go to the bathroom. I wish the morning would come.

The sound is too close. Someone is outside. Despite what Adam once said about me imagining things, not being able to trust my judgement, being 'over-emotional', I am sure something or someone is outside. I don't know who to call because Shirley is away, staying overnight at a friend's house, and poor Jen and Jonny have enough to cope with. I feel uncomfortable about burdening Jen with my worries.

I know that in Shirley's orchard the branches shoot up to the sky with apples and plums. I know Dad's room is dotted with wild poppies. I know that, in a converted loft above the office at The Hollies, Ollie sleeps in a single bed with a window that overlooks more rose bushes than I could dream of. But all these places and all these faces seem very far away. I know my spade is covered in rich soil when it should be muck.

The jostle of the trams into Manchester, the empty ones when the stark white lights pick out the late hour, are a world away from here, from me. A place which exists under orange lights, where the dew dries on the tarmac before anyone can see it. I've walked the block from our old apartment at all hours: I know.

There is no place like Maple Cottage. It is where I belong; I am sure of that as the scream of the empty tram car into the hollow tunnel of the night. Moss and sandstone here might suffocate screams from Peckforton Woods, but it is still home. Whatever is out there.

Tomorrow Ollie is going to stay for dinner. I want to celebrate the garden with good food and wine. I close my eyes and imagine the taste of the meat, the wine, and the tension begins to fade.

The flicker of flames from the open fire catches the light on my wedding ring, but the man on the sofa watching me place another log on the fire is not my husband. Ollie is in his dirty work clothes, so I have put a throw over the sofa. He looks at home, nestled into the cushions with his long legs outstretched before him and a glass of wine in his hand.

'Here's to the garden of rooms!'

We toast and sip, smiling at one another. Ollie sips until the glass is empty and then puts the glass down without once taking his eyes off me. I put my glass down, and he pulls the fabric of my top over my head. He pushes me onto the rug beside the fire and inscribes his initials on my flat stomach. His broad shoulders are taut under his T-shirt. He kisses my stomach and moves up to my mouth.

'God, I want you,' he says again and again, until he covers me with his body and I surrender myself, every inch, to him.

I feel mad for him. I am bound by gravity, not by vows.

After we make love a second time, I cup his stubbly chin in my hand. He takes my hand in his. We lie side by side beside the dying embers of the fire with the throw over us for warmth. The light fades from the room. I listen to the rhythm of Ollie's breathing change as he falls into a deep sleep beside me.

~

When I wake up, Ollie has gone. There are three text messages and a missed call from Adam on my iPhone.

I realise there's a lot of my life I can't remember. Memorable moments are either happy, defining, special moments, or horrible, frightening times. I am lucky to have both kinds; some people don't. It seems that lately I've had more frightening moments than good ones, but there is still time to address the balance.

Catching sight of the time, I throw back the cover and dress hastily for work with a fat grin on my face.

25

From the kitchen window, I watch Ollie push a wheelbarrow of leaves to the bottom of the garden. I hope the cheerful sight of him will help me decide on a plan to be free of Adam.

The shape of my fear of Adam morphs with the quality and type of light, preventing me from using reason and judgement. Some nights in bed, ants seem to march up and down my limbs, over my forehead. In the early morning, it is fog sneaking through a crack in the door, then a menacing face in the clouds following me wherever I go. No deadbolt can keep out fear. I hate Adam for that. There's no end. Is there? Just because an abuser isn't physically present, the sense of fear doesn't end. There are all those endless possibilities, some chance, others contrived; a corner turned, a curtain opened, a door left ajar. Thief. He has stolen my peace of mind.

Twiddling the gold stud in my ear, I think about my permanent scars. The rest of my wounded skin has healed and seemingly forgiven him. Even my earlobe looks normal even though he yanked a dangly earring straight through it, tearing it into two. The scar on my wrist is from a mouth-shaped burn; it is just as red, even now, several years later. I prefer not to dwell on the other scar.

There are luminous yellow fields behind me and I think I must keep on forever, nurture this plot even when the birds are startled into the sky by something I cannot see, even when a thousand rooks take flight, and their dark wings are portentous.

I join Ollie in the garden to help plant out the lupins. I need to keep busy.

'You look tired,' he says.

Feeling self-conscious, I drop my head and inspect a stone. 'I didn't sleep that well.'

'What kept you awake?'

The memory of his skin and my longing makes me blush. 'I did get some sleep – but I thought I heard something. Nothing has been damaged as far as I can see. I'm probably just nervy.'

'It's no good you being scared like this. I guess in Altrincham you had neighbours around you. Just ring me if you're worried. Any time, Maple Rachel.' He grins, and I feel some of the tension in my shoulders ease. Ollie has no idea how cruel Adam can be, or how frightened I am of him.

The ground is bursting with colour. The growth is rampant and beautiful, something which cannot be stopped. The plants want to survive and will do whatever they can to do so: grow twisted for more light where there is competition; limit growth to parts of a flower if the rest isn't strong enough after the frost has attacked it. I should follow their example.

I feel happier up to my elbows in soil, groping to remove stones, pleased to see worms aerating the soil, seeing a future in the brown earth. I have spent the morning with the perennials, the spires of lupins, and listening to restless bees flying in and out of foxgloves, exploding syllables of colour and sound. My parents live on. There is no hard work in carving out this garden of rooms; the spade and the trowel are happily soiled with earth and grass. Petal by petal, leaf by leaf and stem by stem, the seasons will be marked and life will go on and on. I'll find a way to be free of Adam for good.

'Where have you gone?' Ollie asks, catching me daydreaming as I gaze down the lawn and imagine a child running, hiding under the maple tree, playing peek-a-boo with me. I imagine a child blowing bubbles with the wood as a backdrop, the rainbow orbs punctured by a friendly branch. I hear happy shrieks and giggles.

'Daydreaming. Bad habit.'

'Nothing wrong with that.'

The wood is now a background to my garden of rooms, and I feel less of a pull to roam its paths while the cottage holds me gently in place each day. Ollie and I sit on the grass, sipping from a glass of water. I lie down and watch the clouds drift and reform. The seasons have changed around me from winter through to spring. In the heat of the morning, I sense more change ahead.

'Have you made your mind up about the fifth room yet?'

'Yes, I'm going to remove the box hedging.'

'Pity,' he says thoughtfully.

Outside, there is the sound of a cuckoo and welcome warmth in the sun. After so much work, I've stopped worrying about opening the place up to the public on Open Garden Day, even though the fifth room is still blank. Rightly so, because its emptiness reflects the barrenness of my relationship with Adam.

I see the space as an empty cot. I regret planting the box hedging for it, but in other rooms my roots are digging deeper and further with every heartbeat. The place is alive.

'There are three beautiful ones – soon there will be four.'

I've gone through a bedtime routine including a drink of hot milk, a bath and reading in bed by a sidelight. To me, it makes sense to have a decent night's sleep after lots of fresh air and exercise in the garden.

Ollie put the tools away in the garage and locked it before he left because the weather is due to turn stormy. He was in the garage for a long time, sitting in the Land Rover, fantasising, I think, about driving the vehicle he covets.

My phone is on the bedside table if I need it. Finally, at eleven o'clock, I turn off the light and close my eyes on the soundless dark pressing against my face.

When will Adam return, and what then? I can find no answers. He leaves voice messages, sends texts and emails, but it's all hieroglyphics which I have no compulsion to interpret after what he did to me.

Leaving his return ticket to Maple Cottage open-ended is a smart way to leave the door on terror open. Each time I sit in the kitchen chair Adam almost strangled me in, I am reminded of his protruding tendons, veins and muscles as he squeezed tighter and tighter. I recall the sensation of bulging eyes fading in and out of light then, once free of his vice-like grip, I remember panting like a dog.

The very sight of that kitchen chair reminds me of what I have lost – a marriage, my hope of being a happy family, my dream of being safe each and every night beside my husband. Sleep evades me because a low hum of anxiety is permanently beneath the surface of my consciousness. The alarm clock tells me more than two hours have passed since I switched off the light.

It starts whistling at first, then the wind gathers momentum and force, seeking entry under cracks, between doors, rattling manically for a way inside the house. Something crashes and bangs making a harsh, metallic sound I can't place.

The only local contact in my phone is Ollie, so impulsively I dial his number. 'You're awake. Thank God. Can you come? I think there's someone outside.'

'Stay where you are. I'm on my way.'

It seems that hours pass before I hear an engine on our lane, then Ollie's feet on the stones walking round the perimeter of the house and garden and inside the garage. I switch on the hall and landing light before opening the door. I'm so pleased to see him. I hug him, forgetting I'm not wearing anything under my dressing gown.

'Just badgers. There's a latrine by the compost heap. They'll have cubs at this time of year.'

'Are you sure?'

'Positive. You must have heard me arrive. I've been out there for twenty minutes or more. If someone was there, they're not there now. What did you hear exactly?'

I run a hand through my hair. 'I don't know – it was vague but close, right under my window. It sounded–'

'Trust me, I'd put money on badgers. They're out feeding. You've got pots under your bedroom window. They were probably snuffling around there.'

'Oh God, you must think I'm such a fool. A complete wimp.' I wipe my eyes. 'I just wish I could bloody sleep.'

I try to collect myself. Ollie puts his hand lightly on my hair. 'Relax. It's okay – I'm here.' He gazes at me directly, leaving me feeling undressed and aroused. He touches the side of my face so lightly I could be imagining it, then traces the line down from my ear to my neck and my breast.

We make it onto the lounge carpet and we christen almost every room in the house.

26

Now Ollie has left, an unstoppable desire to clean the house overcomes me, leading me to yank at the sheets on the bed so roughly that I fall backwards. Feverish, lying on the carpet, I see my old olive-green parka shoved under the bed. I pull it out and stroke it as it lies on my lap. It is covered in dust; a couple of spiders have died and got lodged in the lining. I put my hand in a side pocket and pull out the white envelope.

Even before I open it, I sense this moment has been a long time coming. At long last, I am ready. I am ready to face whatever it has to say. I feel nauseous. The envelope is addressed in Mum's handwriting and my name is written in faded blue ink. I can hear her voice as I read my name, which puts fresh blood in my veins. I sniff the paper. There isn't a lavender scent anymore but I bet there was once.

I take a few deep breaths. My chest still feels tight. I look around me at the imperfect walls and the latticed windowpane. This house – this is where my mother raised me. Her hands were gentle and kind. She lit candles and kept me inside when the moon was out.

Throughout my childhood, it was her face that I saw first

and last thing each day until cancer took her away. The transformation was terrible, painful, and then sudden.

Maple Cottage

My dear Rachel,

It's time for me to put my house in order and so this is a very special letter from me to you. I won't pretend it's easy to write. To you, it probably seems like I just disappeared. It wasn't a vanishing trick that I chose. Let me explain.

When we met at the pub in Leeds during your final year at university, I had planned to tell you I had a few weeks to live. I planned to say goodbye, but when I saw you looking so happy and carefree, and with your finals on your mind, I backed out. I am sorry.

My mother fell ill with cancer when she was in her thirties, and I became her carer until she died. Although I was lucky to meet your dad and have you late in our lives, I missed out on a lot while I nursed Mum. When I was diagnosed with bowel cancer when you were thirteen, your dad and I decided to keep as much of my illness as secret as possible because we wanted you to lead a normal, happy life. Then your dad got busy with helping you to be independent and strong. I mollycoddled you a bit when you were little, smothered you with all the love I had in my heart. Your dad helped me to let you find your own way, so you could be your own person when we are gone. I am sure that, as you read this letter, you are a strong woman, unafraid to tackle the challenges that life has a habit of throwing at us.

We both love you with all our hearts. I only wish that I could be around to mother you a little longer, to see you grow into a beautiful young woman. I do hope you will be happy.

I've been writing to you a lot lately. Shirley has my letters to you. Your dad promises to pass this one to you, and with it, I hope, the understanding of the love I have for you in my heart. The biggest love is a love that lets you go. It is the hardest and the kindest thing a parent can do – a hard lesson for us all.

We all have to die, and the fact that you are reading this means I have had my time.

I have been so lucky to know you and your dad, and to lead a happy life at Maple Cottage. One day the house will be yours. It is a special home. I have known contentment leading a simple life, and that is worth a lot. I have many happy memories of us there. Motherhood has been the most wonderful thing. Perhaps one day you will understand what I mean.

You are forever in my thoughts, and God bless.

Love always, Mum xxxx

Her hands were always gentle and kind. I was everything to her for all of her time.

The relief and the love wash over me in a warm wave. I read the letter again and again until I can quote chunks of it by heart.

Elated, I run around to Shirley's. I knock and let myself in. 'Shirley?' I call, panting.

She is perched on the window seat; the room feels incredibly quiet and still. 'My chicks have flown the nests. It's so quiet.'

'I came for my letters.'

Suddenly Shirley stands up as if a spike of electricity has charged through her body. She smiles, then pats her knees in a mini-celebration dance. 'Bingo!' Now her eyes are on me, and I feel someone is seeing me properly for the first time in a long time. 'I thought you'd never ask! Come here, my friend!'

We embrace. Shirley goes to the sideboard that I've looked at countless times in recent months where her post generally lies idle. She gingerly bends down to open a drawer. 'They've been in here all this time. Your mum said to wait until you asked for them. It's been quite a secret to keep, this last year especially.'

'How many?' I ask impatiently. 'A few?'

There is a bundle of letters in blue, white and yellow envelopes, wrapped in a lavender satin ribbon. I put my hand to my mouth to stifle a gasp.

When Shirley passes them to me, she gently touches my hand then wipes away a tear. 'Your mum and I were close friends in the end. She was a lovely woman.'

I spend the rest of the day reading, laughing, weeping. Hours and hours in the rocking chair, forgetting to eat or drink, so happy to see Mum's handwriting, to read her words, let them put shape and colour back into my life, make me feel whole. The feelings of sadness and self-pity I've harboured since her death ebb away, further and further out to sea until they are just a dot on the horizon.

I read until I can't see Mum's lavender swaying in the breeze through the window. It doesn't matter that it is shrouded in darkness; she is here. She is with me always, and neither she nor I will ever leave this house, this garden of rooms.

27

As the breeze from the open window crashes into the bedroom and rearranges Ollie's fine strands of hair on the pillow, his muscular shoulders peek above the line of the duvet. I remove my clothes for him very, very slowly and climb into bed beside him. The first time is fast and furious. We make love a second time in the lounge, and it is lazy, slow sex after the passion and urgency he showed me before. Moving around the house naked, not drawing the blinds or curtains, I want to laugh as I follow Ollie upstairs for a shower, his tackle dangling between his legs and his bare, muscular behind close to my face. The image replaces old memories of reluctantly following Mum to bed at seven o'clock on a school night.

'I'll be back later.' He kisses me passionately before gathering his shirt and socks from various corners of the bedroom. 'Any plans for today?' he asks as he gets dressed.

'I'm going to call in on Shirley, take her some flowers to thank her for the letters and everything.'

'See you around six.'

I see everything at home a little bit differently. To begin with, I light one of Mum's scented candles in my bedroom, then imagine her creams and perfumes on my dressing table, her hairbrush. I remember her before the chemotherapy – her neat bun, the pretty clasp to keep her hair in place.

The lilac softness of the room aches for her return and so do I. I would have nursed her. I would have willingly given up my freedom to take care of her in her final few months, irrespective of finals.

I bury my face in the pillow then climb under the duvet and pull it over my head. The smell of detergent fills my nostrils. I feel a strange wash of happiness and sadness and contentment I've not known before, which I owe to Shirley. The thought pushes me out of bed and round to The Bird House.

'Just a thank you – for being a friend to Mum and me.'

'They're beautiful lilies, Rachel. You didn't need to.' Shirley smells the white and pink lilies wrapped in whispers of sugar paper. From a kitchen cupboard, she removes a delicate cut-glass vase in which to put them, then places the arrangement on the kitchen window. She looks lovely with the flowers beside her.

'I'll make us some tea.'

'Did Dad say anything to you about wanting to take his life?'

Shirley stops the elaborate process of making tea to steer me to a comfortable seat in the lounge. I surmise that the question is unexpected but not unforeseen.

'What do you remember about your mum's funeral?' she asks.

There was a nasty bright sun. Dad wore the one smart jacket he owned, and he had cut his chin shaving. I ran out of tissues during the service, so I blew my nose on my cardigan. I remember we sang a long hymn and lavender-scented candles stood on the lid of Mum's coffin. Dad cried.

'It was the first time I ever saw Dad cry.'

Dad's tears had come as a downpour, with spit and snot,

and his hands were balled up into fists to wipe the giant tears away. Those tears came from the well of his stomach, a child's. He had cried so hard that he hiccupped. I was scared he might die of a heart attack and drop to the ground. He sounded as if his insides were burning, as if his clothes might tear into shreds.

He had put his hand in his pocket when we were in the car on the way to the church and pulled out a shopping list written in Mum's neat hand.

Washing-up liquid.
Fruit.
Veg.
Prescription.

It made it worse. Dad screwed it into a ball and it landed in the footwell of the Land Rover. Roland was driving. Dad howled.

'I remember some of the things Dad said about Mum during the service. The reading about there being many rooms in God's house...' I say slowly.

'After the funeral – maybe a week later – I helped your dad sort through your mum's things. He'd got into the habit of sleeping in the single bed in the lounge by then, where your mum slept when she was too ill to get upstairs. He was adamant that the only thing he wanted to keep was her hairbrush – it was still matted with her soft brown hair. The chemotherapy had taken the rest. Do you remember her neat bun? She had lovely hair.'

Shirley describes the bonfire Dad lit; in the hours he stood watching the dying flames, he seemed to age before her eyes. He wanted to climb in the coffin beside Mum.

'The only thing he was waiting for – was living for – was seeing you to give you Dilly's letter. I know you're angry and hurt that he chose to die, but he was tortured. He was a broken man, Rachel. The last few weeks were hell for him and your mum.'

'Why didn't he give me the letter at Mum's funeral?'

Shirley looks at me. 'He was grieving. Nothing else was on his mind then except laying your mum's body to rest. The day you came to visit him on his birthday, he had the letter then to give to you.'

'But why not let me help him? Why not wait for me–'

'It was his time. Your dad believed in nature, it was his–' she searches for the right word '–philosophy. In his mind, there was no way he was meant to see another spring or summer without your mum.'

'It's not–'

'Listen, when you're a parent – and I'm sure you will be one day – you'll understand.'

'I keep wondering why I didn't open the letter straight away. I mean, how would my life have been different if I had? Instead of being sad and angry, and pushing it into my stupid coat pocket all those years ago – not feeling brave enough to deal with it. Would I have got married?'

'What ifs – what's the point in wondering? You've come home, surely that's what matters? And if you and Adam aren't meant to be, then split up.'

'It's not that simple.' I take a deep breath.

'It never is, but that doesn't mean there isn't a way. I've sensed you're unhappy with him. When is Adam due back? It's been a few months.'

'That's the thing; I don't know.'

'Come to The Olive Tree with me tonight?'

I blush. 'I'd love to, only I can't tonight.'

Shirley smiles at me. 'Another time then.'

28

The graveyard where Mum is buried is only a couple of miles away. Ordinarily I would enjoy walking there, but I feel short of energy. As Adam isn't at home right now, he's not around to complain about the waste of petrol or the unnecessary mileage the journey is putting on 'his' car – even though he said the car was a gift to me. I hop in and drive to the village church, happy to know Ollie will be calling round later to keep me company.

Local people speculated that Dad took his life because of financial difficulties. He'd barely been working, I suppose, which is where that idea came from. But if those gossipmongers visited the grave, they'd see no expense spared.

IN LOVING MEMORY OF DILLY ASHWORTH, 1955–2015 WIFE AND MOTHER, SORELY MISSED, LOVED ETERNALLY.

There is a small kingdom here of insects and birds breathing around me. The wind ripples the grass. A gentleman nods his head to acknowledge me and we carry on, respectful of each other's privacy.

'Hello Mum, it's Rachel. I've been thinking about you a lot lately, especially since moving here. Your curtains are still up, and the embroidery you made is hanging on the wall. I painted the main bedroom lavender, and you have your own lavender room in the garden. I miss you.

'I haven't chosen so well, Mum. Adam isn't like Dad. I'm not sure what I'm going to do. Adam can't make children, and that might have been the one thing that could have made him a better person and a better husband. He hurts me, Mum.

'I read your letters, all of them. Sorry it took me so long. It means everything to me to know you loved me until the day you died. Shirley is here, looking out for me. We talk about you and Dad. She still loves her birds.

'I know it's wrong, but I fell for someone and we slept together. He's a big, placid man like Dad. He loves the woods and plants, and I feel I'm at home with him. Safe. I hope you'll understand. I know you didn't approve of Shirley being with Russ. I judged too, and now I'm as bad, but it doesn't feel wrong. He's helped me create this amazing garden of rooms, a room for you and Dad and my best friend, Jen.

'There's so much colour and life in the garden. The maple tree has finally got a rival for beauty. I wish you could see it. The long wait to move back home was worth it. I'm not far away anymore, and I've kept your thimble, though I don't sew unless I have to.

'Dad's ashes are in the woods, Mum, up on the top of Peckforton Hill so he can look down on Maple Cottage and the church and see you, see me.

'I should go. Thank you so much for your letters. Love you, Mum.'

I'm halfway through removing the box hedging for the fifth room when Ollie arrives and leads me under the maple tree. 'Leave that,' he says.

The familiar sight of my spade and fork fades away; the lavender blurs. On the ground, with Ollie on top of me, his finger traces the shape of my lips, then my breasts through my blouse. I undo the buttons on his shirt as quickly as I can until his broad chest is exposed. He pulls up my blouse and pushes up my bra. Our bare chests meet, and he kisses me deeply and slowly. I feel the curve of his spine and watch the fragile fan of his eyelashes pinned to his eyes. The smallest movement of his hand sends a tidal wave through me.

After it is over, he lies on top of me for a long time then he rests on his elbows to gaze down at me. He is too close to be in focus. My fantasy of making love under the maple tree is fulfilled. Once he moves to lie beside me, I can see the rise and fall of his chest and a rainbow of colour in the background.

Ollie and I must seize every opportunity to sleep together. Is the beauty of what Ollie and I are sharing born from the constant threat of time? I think how sometimes his arrival is a vandal ransacking the cottage, my body. The muscular size of him, moving with such urgency under the low ceilings, fills me with fear and desire at the same time. I don't want another ending.

29

When my mobile rings, I assume it will be Adam or Ollie, but the caller is Jonny. Before I can speak a voice tells me, 'It's a girl! A beautiful baby girl.' Down the phone, his voice is full of emotion and excitement.

I feel tearful and so happy for them that it's difficult to drive safely, so I pull over. 'Already! Gosh, she's early! Oh, but that's wonderful news. How are Jen and the baby? Are they all right?'

'The baby's in an incubator. She's only five pounds, but she's all right. Jen's asking for you, Rachel. When can you come over? They want to keep her in for a few days.'

'I've just left work. I'm on my way.' I am already turning the car in the opposite direction towards Leighton Hospital, wondering if I have enough money with me for parking and gifts. 'Does she have a name yet?'

'Milly May Rachel.'

'Oh! I can't wait to meet her. Send my love to Jen. And congratulations!'

When I get to the hospital, I find Jen looking exhausted, radiant and triumphant all at the same time. She is on a maternity ward with six other mothers. Her face is a sunflower of joy; she looks beautiful. As she holds my hand, she cries a little and tells me that even though it is her fourth baby, the magic and the wonder of giving birth are just as strong as the first time.

'Can I see her?'

'Not today. Come here.' She kisses me. 'I've only known Milly for a few hours, but I love her so much. It's mad! Are those sweets?'

'For the children!' I pull up a chair beside her.

'Not anymore!'

We devour them, eat three bags of sticky sweets without the slightest twinge of guilt, suck on sherbet lollies, try to speak with gobstoppers in our mouths. It seems like the right way to celebrate Milly's entry to the world.

'I'm so relieved she's all right. She's small but she's going to be fine, the doctor said. We're so lucky, you know. This is our last.'

I stroke Jen's brow. 'You are amazing. Honestly, I'm so proud of you.'

'Me? God, don't be. Tell me more about Ollie.'

'He's all the things Adam is not – gentle, contented, calm. And he doesn't care about money or clothes, and he makes me feel safe.'

'So it's more than just passionate, excessive sex?'

'All I know is I've been a hypocrite. I judged Shirley when she was sleeping with someone's husband, but now I am the one having an affair and I don't want it to end. I do feel guilty but–'

'Not enough to end it?'

'Exactly. When something feels right, can it be wrong?'

'Adam would say so. If he finds out, there'll be a shitstorm.'

'I don't want to talk about him. I've stopped trying to stop myself and instead I luxuriate in it.' I think how I keep feeling unfed. If anything, like the plants in my soil, my desire to see Ollie is growing roots. 'Hope got Adam and me so far, hoping and wondering, dreaming too. Now I see it more as deluding myself. I've stopped hoping for a normal marriage. I love my home, but it hasn't changed who Adam is.'

After a while, Jen starts to fade. I tiptoe to the door and blow her a kiss goodbye. Her face is still a smiling sunflower, even in sleep.

I call in on Shirley to tell her Jen's news. On my walk back, I don't at first notice Ted wearing his school uniform like a shield because I am so wrapped up in my thoughts and excitement. But I soon realise he is in a bad temper and is pleased to see me to take it out on. I cross over to the other side of the lane and keep moving slowly in the direction of Maple Cottage. It isn't far, but with him blocking the road it might as well be miles away.

'Ted,' I acknowledge, giving in to his intimidating presence. I feel myself stiffen. 'What brings you here?'

He is standing quite close to me now, so I can see he has a black eye. His school blazer is several sizes too small in an ill-fitting way, which makes me think it's second-hand rather than last year's. 'That looks nasty.'

'That's the pecking order, that's what that is. New kid, hanging out in places he don't belong. Getting bollocked by Adam in front of my mates. I'm bottom of the fucking ladder being the new boy in town. Funny that. There's quite a bit of violence about at the moment, following Adam around, though you'd know that already.'

I let his words fatten in my mind while starting to fear for my safety. My palms feel sweaty. The lane is a dead-end, with the woods on one side and Ted blocking the way out into Peckforton. I could make a run for the house. As if he can read my mind, he moves closer towards me.

'Them skulls were only meant to be a bit of fun. I didn't hurt anyone. Something to look at while you're hanging out your washin' and dancin' around with the butterflies in your fancy clothes, while we ain't got two pennies to rub together.'

'Ted, I'm sorry–'

'Mum was happy here. We were a normal family, getting along – and Tommy quit crying all the time. Then you and that twat Adam turfed us out, and he battered Mum.'

'Adam hurt your mum?' There's a bad taste forming in my mouth, as sour as old milk.

'Don't pretend you didn't know, Lady Rachel. He's been an' knocked her black and blue. She won't leave the bloody house, that's what.'

'Oh, God, I didn't know. I'll see her. What can I do to help? Really, Ted, I didn't know.'

Ted falls silent. He kicks a stone with his shoe.

'I suppose you'll take her some of your fancy flowers, won't ya? A fat lot of good they'll do. You tell Adam to stay away from us or I'll– I'll...' He swallows quickly, fighting the tears.

'Has your mum been to the police?'

'Adam threatened her. She won't go because she's too scared to leave the house or make contact. He said he'd–'

'Get in the car with me, Ted. I'll take you home.'

I am struck how Devina's terraced house is an incongruously spotless place floating on the debris the neighbours leave willy-nilly in back and front gardens, even on the pavement where I park my car. Ted doesn't seem to notice the broken pram as he walks around it. The wheels are spinning ridiculously in mid-air.

When the door opens, I'm not prepared for Devina's injuries and she isn't prepared to see me.

'What do *you* want?' Devina says with a white-hot stare as we enter her living room.

Her chin is lifted a little defiantly, but her face is a bruised poppy. I swallow my shock at the sight of her battered skin, at the spectacular technicolour of the bruising to her cheeks and forehead, at the twisted pansies in yellow, red and purple that contrast horribly with her slender lily neck. If I try, I can tell myself the blue and purple shades around her eyes are eyeshadow.

I take a deep breath before I speak. 'I gave Ted a lift home and I– I wanted to say how sorry I am. Ted told me it was Adam who did this to you. Is that true?'

Ted hovers by his mother, who is lying on the sofa. I perch on the end of a chair so I can make a swift move if I need to. There is a small football trophy on the mantelpiece. Tommy is crying.

'I'll get him,' Ted says with a jaded look.

The crying goes on, octaves of despair, rising to a falsetto rage. It pins Devina and me to the spot until it rebounds around the room; the thin carpet does nothing to dampen the carrying sound. Minutes pass, and the volume drops. The room starts to warm up, feel better, and as Tommy's final sobs echo, I hear Ted's bitter and frightened words in my head.

'Can you tell me what happened?'

Devina's fingers play with the throw she has covered herself with. It is tiring to watch the fingers scrunching and unscrunching the material, like she is handwashing in air. 'He barged in here and hurt me in my own home.'

'Adam?'

'Ted is pretty confident he recognised him from the funfair.'

'When was this? He's supposed to be in China.'

She gingerly touches her eye. The bruises and cuts are fresh, recent. 'I don't know what I've ever done to the man – or you, for that matter, and that's all I can tell you. I think I took a beating for Ted.'

I look away in shame and horror. 'What can I do to help? Do you need anything?'

'Your husband's a violent man.' She levels her gaze at me; a languageless connection traverses the distance between us. I think she can see the scars on me. I see a frightened woman looking straight at another one. I see her pity.

'Please, go to the police. Tell them everything. I wish I had before.'

'Has he hurt you, too?' she asks.

I nod. 'It's complicated. I don't expect anything from you – only please, report him.'

'You're as scared as I am.'

All the way home I see the fear in Devina's eyes, the haunted stare when I first entered the lounge, and the horror of her battering that is still unfaded in every move and word she makes. Her verdict – *your husband's a violent man* – roars in my ears when I stop for a red light. It rumbles around as I drive down the lane to our house.

Your husband's a violent man.

She's right. I am as scared as she is. And Adam must be in the UK.

30

We've walked miles along the Shropshire Union Canal and arrived at his flat thirsty and hungry, but food and water doesn't satiate us. I feel Ollie's need for me, as he does mine.

I put my finger to his lips and made a slow 'sssssshhhh' sound. The only thing I want to speak is his hands. Trembling beside him, and more aware of my skin than I have ever been, it seems like currents are running through me. There is desire in my hair, nails, teeth, in my ears, hands and the fluid trickling into my knickers.

I undo his belt buckle and peel off his sweat-stained T-shirt, exposing the broadness of his chest and the lightly tanned hairs that I dream of touching, licking. We are both breathing quickly and trying not to. He peels my clothes off so slowly that I ache.

I take his hand and place it on my breast, down my torso and inside my knickers. I feel his fingers and my wetness, and he gasps, but the corners of my mind start to char. Something is building inside me, an urgency, something fierce and fine and wonderful, but the paper edges of my mind are on fire now, the flame is going to spread. I try to dampen the paper down as his fingers probe deeper and my mouth moans in hunger, but the fire spreads and licks its way into the centre of my mind, and I come long and loud. His fists uncurl as a primal groan escapes his mouth and his body becomes slack.

After my shower, I creep back into the bedroom. Ollie has curled himself into a question mark, and his breath is a far-away train. I tenderly trace his shape with my eyes. I look at his face; knowing self-consciousness will steal me away when he stirs, I savour the last few moments of him this way. I touch his thigh down to his knee, tracing a route on a map only I can see. There are hundreds of routes. They run everywhere, all over his flesh and back to me.

I think about my friend Tom, who was an alcoholic by the time I met him in my final year at university. He was the thinnest person I'd ever seen. He told me how his life wasn't his own anymore because every thought of every hour was about the drinking – either getting it, recovering from it, hating it or loving it. If Adam were away indefinitely, perhaps my desire wouldn't be insatiable. Or am I addicted to this bear of a man who surprises me with his tenderness? I know it isn't love, but I feel a longing in my belly and sometimes wonder if – But what's the point in wondering when you are married, and married to a man like Adam? How can I be free of him to start again?

Ollie's hands are always dirty, ingrained with soil even after he's scrubbed them because the soil is within the epidermis and part of him. His shop window, he says.

The light is fading from the room, tiptoeing back through the skylight where it came from. Ollie smiles as soon as he opens his eyes. He sees me looking at him and immediately sits upright. 'We should probably get up.'

I sense he feels uncomfortable. Guilt. I am not infected with it. Should I be? I have fantasised about making love under this remarkable tree. At Maple Cottage sometimes I think my mum is watching and her voice is disguised as birds in the maple tree. I hear footsteps after Ollie has gone; they follow me around for a while. But not here.

I rub my arms, suddenly feeling cold, and dress hurriedly but only because I sense Ollie wants me to. It makes me think of our other times together – we rarely sleep all night long. I wish he stayed more often but when he does, the sun gate-crashes the room and there is an abandoned sense of coming around together. He jump-starts to something: the shower, the garden, or back to work.

'I have to call in at the supermarket,' I say. 'Do you need anything?'

'No, thanks.' He yanks his top over his head, leaving his hair standing to attention. 'Adam phoned me. I've got to meet him when he gets back. He wants to see the garden of rooms before he makes the final payment.'

There is a sick feeling in the pit of my stomach; something feels wrong. There is a clot forming in my chest. Ollie's blond hair juts out in all directions so endearingly.

I watch a moth circle the room before battering the closed window. I open the window and it leaves. 'What else did he say?'

He looks away from me into the distance, seeing something in his memory that I cannot see. 'He mainly wanted to know about progress with the garden of rooms. I told him about the weird stuff happening, and he seems to think Devina's responsible.'

'Devina?'

'Yeah, he got pretty angry actually. I didn't know he had a short fuse.'

'He does.'

'What, with you?' he asks forcefully, staring at me with wide eyes.

'Me and Devina. If you hadn't turned up that day when

Adam and I were in the kitchen, I think he might have killed me. He had his hands around my throat.' The words sound brittle as they leave my mouth but they still don't convey the agony of that moment. It was a day defined by endings. 'Adam and I can't have children. He found out that day. The fifth room – it was meant to be for our firstborn.'

'You're not telling me anything I hadn't figured out already, Rachel.' Ollie's face is pale. He shakes his head.

'Devina told me that Adam attacked her. He's already back in the UK.'

'It's best if we don't see each other for a while. I haven't been in this situation before. You're his wife, Rach – I can't keep seeing you while he's sleeping beside you at night, especially a man who is prepared to hurt women.' He hastily pulls on his T-shirt and socks. 'God only knows what he'd do if he saw us together.'

I glance anxiously around Ollie's tiny bedroom, the unmade bed a relic to our lovemaking. The sheets are as knotted as my stomach. Eventually I shake my head. 'I understand, but I want to keep seeing you. I don't love Adam anymore.'

'I'm just trying to tell you I can't see you for a little while. Please don't make this any harder than it already is. You're beautiful, Maple Rachel.' He strokes my cheek and holds my hand. He looks troubled. 'But we can't.'

A peculiar feeling of apprehension fills my lungs. Watching him, I feel a terrible sense of doom. I fear something terrible might happen to him and I will never see him again. 'Is there someone else, Ollie?'

He hesitates and raises his head. I feel his gaze lock onto mine while he lets go of my hand. 'No, of course not. There's only – only you. If Adam lays one hand on you, you ring me right away.'

I shiver with fear and yank my tousled hair into a ponytail. I force myself to move, to grab my bag, the odd pieces of clothing and spare toothbrush I've left at this flat.

The thought of Adam's return to the country and *my* home has suddenly become all too real. I wish I could blink and wish Adam away. Life has been so good; it's been like living in another universe for the last few months with this gorgeous, gentle man.

Outside, the swallows are playing and chasing, wheeling above our heads high in the sky. The plants and flowers at the garden centre are awash with the colour of sadness; blue and runny watercolours, dripping and splashing as if clouds have exploded jugs of water, doused the petals and the leaves until every living plant is weeping, weeping.

'Don't go!' I grab Ollie's hand and pull him close. His breathing is fast but then he takes a hasty step back from me and looks me straight in the eye. I reach out to touch him but he moves away. The softness of his gaze has vanished.

'It's time,' he says heartlessly with his fists clenched at his sides.

'What do you mean?' With my hand on my chest, I am scorched as if by the African sun. 'You–'

'I mean the garden of rooms is planted out, save for the fifth room. Pretty soon I think you'll feel different about that. You can't be here – Adam's back now.'

'But–'

'Leave it.' His voice is raised, a tone and volume I haven't heard before. I hear the space between his words and it is painful to listen to. The familiar sight of his loose-fitting jeans, his broad shoulders, make my stomach flip. Did I say something wrong? Should I have confessed my feelings for him? Hands have seemingly grabbed him around the collar and yanked him through a mirror.

Adam. If only there were no Adam. Thief.

I shiver unexpectedly.

Goodbye, Ollie. Again. Goodbye.

Does he watch me drive away? I feel myself miss him, this quiet, calm man even before the traffic lights have changed. That first night with him was a kind of death of my fidelity to Adam, but the sound of my name on Ollie's lips, gently at first then swilled and barrelled and full-blown, will forever be imprinted like a tattoo. A magpie tattoo.

My hands feel numb on the steering wheel as I drive home. It seems very quiet for a long time afterwards. I wonder if I will feel Ollie's bare skin again or if he is nearing extinction. There is a fist of air slamming into me. It could be a premonition.

31

JUNE 2019

Under the bleach of the strip lights, the large glass windows and the uniformity of the aisles in the supermarket, life feels normal.

I think of Dad in the fruit and veg aisle, surprised at how similar blackberries are to the fruit of deadly nightshade, and the similarity between button mushrooms and death-cap mushrooms. These foods have grown quietly, discreetly, until picked and packaged and shelved. I love the ruby damsons and the sombre aubergines.

In the cake aisle, I think of Shirley; in the sweet and biscuit aisles, I think of Jen. I avoid the baby aisle and the whiff of talc and baby wipes that goes with it, the smudginess of nappies and the marketing of all those baby faces and bottoms and perfect peach skin.

In the meat aisle, I think of Ollie when I see a rack of ribs and smoked bacon rinds. The roast beef brings back memories of Mum's Sunday dinners. I buy a packet of icing sugar, not because I can be bothered to make and ice a cake, but because it reminds me of Mum's baking days and my attempts at icing one as a child.

There is a small selection of earrings for sale that remind me of Adam. As much as I'd like to look, I don't bother because I think of all the pretty earrings in the drawer in my dressing table that I'm too scared to wear when he is around.

I savour the low din; not one voice dominates. There's a lot of browsing and pausing and moving along, unhurried shuffling. I want to join them, I really do. Many of these people here will return to their suburban homes and their normal lives and I envy their normality. Some are gaining weight; some are stocking up the fridge with wine; others spend time deciding on a new paperback. Maybe some are shoplifting. I don't care. I want to join these people with their ordinary lives and their routines and existences, where fear only comes on TV or in a book.

I go back to the fruit and vegetable aisle and look again at the berries and grapes that could have travelled from Peckforton Woods. I am struck by the similarity in their appearance to toxic plants. They seem to watch me inquisitively. I buy a large portion of berries.

As I push my trolley towards the checkout, I realise that fear owns me. I pick each item out from the trolley and place it to be scanned, and in each item I am more certain of my fortune. My ill-fortune, unless I do something about it.

My marriage is the clipped wings of Dad's hens that renders them trapped and doomed. One day I'll be mauled and killed, too.

When I get home, the landline rings. I know it's Adam because it goes on for so long. It is tempting to ignore it, but he will ring and ring until he speaks to me. I picture him in his smart, respectable suit, perhaps taking a drink in a hotel lobby somewhere near here, his expensive leather briefcase by the side of his polished shoes. Time has hardened the miles between us to a permanent distance.

'Is everything all right there, Rachel?' Adam asks.

'Fine.'

'You sound out of breath.'

'I've just got back from the supermarket. Why are you ringing me now? Are you in the UK?'

There is a beat when the silence lasts longer than it should for a telephone conversation. 'I wanted to hear your voice.'

'Everything is fine here, Adam. Except you left before we had a chance to talk.' I see myself hiding in the bathroom, my back against the door, wondering what will come next. I look out of the window anxiously. Is he watching me? Are the trees providing cover for his surveillance? Is someone looking at me now as I talk on the phone?

'You understand how important fatherhood is to me. And I know how much you want to be a mother.'

'Adam, you were the one who said not to run away from your problems.'

'I'm not running. I'm working. Wheels are turning.'

'What's that supposed to mean?'

'That life is carrying on. I'm not licking my wounds. You know I love you and I'd do anything for you. That garden of rooms of yours – I'm so happy I can buy it for you. It's my gift. I'm working so we can make Maple Cottage our dream palace. What have you planted in my room? Something poisonous?' he says jokingly.

'You hurt me, Adam, last time you were here. There isn't much else to say.'

'We share the same dream of the future and that's what's important. Let's forget the past. Start again. We'll talk properly when I get home.'

'I don't know about that.' I recall Adam's rabid face and the choking sound I made in his throttling hands.

'I promise I won't hurt you,' he says softly.

'You've said that before.'

'I love you. I'll do anything for you.'

'I feel safer without you. I wouldn't dare to say that to your face. Do you understand what I'm saying?'

'You've been coping without me. You've thrown yourself into the gardening project that I'm funding, but that's not long-term, it's not real. You and me are.'

'I won't be talked around this time,' I say. 'I've wiped away the blood from a split lip and a ripped ear. I've set my broken finger. I've used make-up to conceal bruises. Do you hear me? I don't love you anymore.' And I put down the phone.

Tears come then, seemingly from the bottom of my stomach, a place a long way down where they've been stored, like an opaque water tank. They pour silently from my eyes, nose. The wetness drips down onto my ribs and curls around my lower back, it dribbles down my neck and behind my ear. I purge myself until I'm empty.

My appetite and motivation to cook dinner have gone. The sight of the entrails of a pepper and dirty kitchen implements on the slab of the chopping board grieves me. '*We share the same dream of the future and that's what's important. Let's forget the past. Start again.*'

His unfaltering confidence in us continuing as before is deluded and disturbing. He tells me he loves me unconditionally. His words are empty shells.

I take a long bath after dinner and I find myself thinking longingly about Ollie again. Lying on the bed, having rehearsed what I will say, I dial his number. The line is engaged. I fidget with the duvet. Should I leave a voicemail? It is 7pm, and I wonder who he is talking to, what he is doing. Should I drive to the nursery?

Because time is precious, I want what I have never tried before. I am reminded of my request to Ollie to make love to me on Adam's desk – it is as big as a single bed. I want us to be everywhere in this house, the garden, to spread far and wide from the landing to the hall to the maple tree, so we can reach each other in each room. I hated seeing his hesitation as he looked at the glass-topped desk. I knew it and willed it away, but then he tugged my hand and led me into the shower instead.

I see my reflection in the mirrored wardrobe, and it stops my train of thought. The red dressing gown I'm wearing is silk, bought by Adam in China. It is something that I rarely wear. I look like a concubine. I am a concubine. Am I?

The night passes slowly. I switch off my phone in an attempt to switch off my thoughts of Adam and Ollie.

This fear is invisible. It is inescapable because it lives within, only it fattens on itself, parasitical. It can't be escaped, not even in sleep. Nightmares come and go and the morning merges with the dreams.

This fear is more than just a splinter in my finger or a stitch in my side; it is louder than a creaking floorboard, and it tastes as sour as vinegar. Adam has a key to the front and back door. Countless times I think I hear a key turn in the lock.

Tick tock.

32

There are only a couple of vehicles in the car park at The Hollies. I've been thinking about calling in for a while but haven't had the courage. Ollie hasn't phoned me and it's got to the stage where a text doesn't feel right.

The Hollies' vans are parked up by the trellis and garden canes. The sight of Ollie's van makes my heart race. I pretend to browse, looking this way and that along the path and through the middle of the greenhouses, but I know the shape and size of him isn't at the nursery. Something stirs in me; it's a feeling I can't name, but I don't like it.

'Hi!' I say a little too brightly to an assistant with a shiny name badge. Ali. She is young, pretty. 'Is Ollie here? He's been doing a bit of work for us.'

The face frowns. 'Ollie? No, he's abroad.'

'Abroad?' I exclaim.

'Spain. I'm covering his job. Can I help?'

'Oh, I see.' I touch the side of a large planter to collect myself. The wood is smooth and damp. 'Is he coming back?'

'Yes, he's back in a few days. Who should I say called?' The girl lurches towards me then takes my arm before I land in a heap. 'Here, sit down. I'll get you a glass of water.'

'I skipped lunch,' I mumble as she hurries away. My head is spinning. The pots of tulips and hydrangeas zoom in and out of focus as if they are on the dodgems.

By the time she returns, I am driving out of the car park as fast as I dare. He's gone, without saying goodbye – not a single word.

Slut.

That's what I am.

Slut.

Perhaps his conscience got the better of him. Why didn't he say he was going away? He told me he'd planned a trip to Europe with Adam's money, but why take off without a word? A sob erupts from my mouth.

When I have to stop at the junction on Canal Street, a pedestrian halts on the pavement mid-stride then peers in at me in a way which makes me feel scrutinised. Does she know I'm an adulteress? She is younger than me. Her face is pale and blemish-free. I wish she would look away.

I pull out, narrowly missing a passing car. As its horn sounds, I cry even louder.

I think back to the last day I saw Ollie. Should I have heard the sirens of an ambulance? I've replayed the memory to look for a sign of sadness or a reluctance to leave – a lingering sense of there being more to say – but I am sure there wasn't.

Did I imagine our connection? Why did he decide the affair was over at that moment? Or am I overreacting? If he wants a few days away, that's his business. He's talked about Spain often enough. He loves sea fishing with his dad out there.

Back home, I stand in the middle of the garden. The spade Ollie uses is still standing upright in the garden of rooms where he left it. I can't bring myself to put it away. The image of the white skulls on the green grass flashes before me. The holes for eyes seem forever seeing.

Slut.

In my mind, I still see the word spelt out on the grass.

Slut.

Shirley appears some time later, looking elegant and cool in a pale summer dress and straw hat. 'The garden looks beautiful,' she says, as she smells the lavender. 'I thought I'd find you here. Why do you look so glum?'

'We've finished the planting, Ollie and me. The garden of rooms is more or less complete, save for the fifth room.'

'And you're sad because–'

'I am a horrible fraud.'

She cocks her head to one side.

'I've been sleeping with Ollie,' I blurt out.

'Well, I'd already worked that out for myself!' She laughs, and the sun catches her eyes.

I smile at her candidness. 'I loved being with him – the sex and the garden – we shared things in common. The wood.' Shirley's face is alight with interest. 'It was wonderful. And terrible. Adam hurts me. I'm scared of him, but I don't know what to do. He's coming back. I feel too tired all the time to even think about doing something about it...'

'Slow down.' Shirley smiles at me and strokes my arm.

'Ollie's made me so happy and Adam is–' My voice breaks. I put my head in my hands. 'I feel guilty about Ollie, but I don't love Adam anymore. He hurts me, Shirley. I'm frightened of him.'

She takes me in her arms and I smell her Chanel No. 5. 'My poor lamb. I never liked him, I must say.'

Her honesty makes me laugh out loud. I wipe the snot from my nose on my sleeve before telling her the rest of my story.

33

I am glad to get to work to occupy my mind and be in the company of familiar faces. Even the crisp sound of the bell to signal the beginning of the lesson is welcome. The focus in class is revision, a lot of drilling, building confidence through over-learning. It is a bit tedious, but it works. My Year Eleven class have their first GCSE examination for History on Thursday; they are the middle set who find the subject quite tricky, so they are nervous. I spend my lunchtime with students that want to stay because I'm not always around with my part-time hours. Eventually I get time for a coffee and a biscuit before my last lesson of the afternoon. I feel exhausted and famished, but I finish teaching at 2.30pm and get home half an hour later.

Shirley is waiting for me. 'Get your things. I've been thinking about what you told me, and you can't stay here if Adam's going to turn up. I won't allow him to hurt you. The man is a low-life. I wish you'd told me before.' Her silver earrings swing back and forth; she is shaking her head as she speaks quickly. She reminds me of the headmistress.

'I wanted to tell you. I just hoped that coming here would

make things better. I've buried my head in the sand the last few months while he was in China, but I can't sleep, I can't stop–'

'Come on, let's get a few things packed. I've got plenty of space. You don't look well to me.'

I don't argue; it's a relief to have company and a place to hide. Shirley helps me pack a few items from the wardrobe and dressing table. Suddenly she stops and appraises me with a wry smile. 'Ollie will be in his prime. Virile. You're not pregnant, are you?'

'Don't be ridiculous. We can't–' Then the words stop. In the gap there is a silence, and in that silence the dawning realisation that at no time did Ollie and I use contraception. I haven't had a period for more than a month – two months or so. The subject of contraception had never come up; it had never once entered my head.

How could I have been so thoughtless?

I look at Shirley. 'I might be.'

~

Alan Ward offering 10 per cent discount on furniture. I delete the text. I don't know why I bother carrying my phone around with me. Ollie hasn't been in touch and it feels like weeks, not days.

I thrust my phone back into my coat pocket as I buy two pregnancy tests from the local supermarket. Shirley understands I want to be in my own home when I use them.

I've seen enough TV commercials and advertisements in magazines to envisage the happy moment, the man and woman looking at the blue line with expressions of joy and wonderment. Their doll-faces bathed in soft lighting, their glowing skin, the spotlessly clean bathroom. It wasn't that long ago when I locked myself in the bathroom to protect myself from Adam's anger.

I see the second blue line and I am sick in the loo. 'I'm pregnant,' I say to myself. 'Oh, gosh.'

I place one hand over my mouth. I look at myself in the little mirror above the sink and say 'I am pregnant' again, expecting it to sink in. Stupidly I ask myself '*How did that happen?*' If the moment could be stroked, I would stroke it like the flank of a horse, the smooth ear of a dog. I have imagined the weight and feel of my baby as many as a thousand times.

I place a hand on my tummy. 'You are a tiny life I have longed for. I can't wait to gaze at your little face, study the bow shape of your mouth and your chin. I can't wait to be needed, depended upon, and to give. I have so much I want to give you. You make me feel blessed.'

And powerless and conflicted.

When I open the bathroom door, fear is in the pit of my stomach. I tiptoe to the landing and down the stairs. For a short while, I had almost forgotten what I needed to run from. How quickly perspective changes; now I have an unborn child to protect.

I tell myself I might be alone, but I know that Adam is no longer thousands of miles away. It's only when I am through the front door and I see there isn't a silver Mercedes on the drive that I breathe more easily.

The walk to Shirley's house is short but I am disorientated by the spellbinding news and my thoughts seem to add miles to my journey. With every step I pray I won't hear a car engine, I won't see silver metallic paint, I won't see Adam returning. Returning.

I walk, feeling joy mixed with trepidation about what the future might hold. I already feel love for the person growing inside me, but I can't quite process the big changes to come. Mum would be so happy for me. Will my baby have green eyes like Mum and me, or blue ones like Ollie? A baby, a fifth room in the garden of rooms. At last.

I think about all the times I cried when my period came, the guilt I carried around month after month, thinking that I had let Adam down. I will never again think I have let him down. Never.

Unusually, I pick my way where the lane is uneven and potholes could make me fall. I am carrying precious cargo now. There is suddenly so much to look forward to, and I can't wait to tell Ollie, Jen and my colleagues at work. I've got Shirley and Jen to help me out with the pregnancy and birth, though I can't think as far ahead as giving birth and having a child for the rest of my life. What will Ollie say?

My stomach is still quite flat, but I put a hand on it to urge it to grow. Mum and Dad would have loved to be grandparents.

I think about the fifth room – I've only removed some of the box hedging of its walls. I can easily replant that. What should his or her room be like?

I think of the hook in the ceiling where Tommy's mobile hung in the spare room at Maple Cottage. I think of all the stories I want to read to our baby while he or she snoozes in the cot.

34

From my bedroom window at The Bird House, I see that the dandelions in my garden are at the floaty stage. Dad's room is brimming with daisies and buttercups, the best kind of weeds. The silken eyes of foxgloves look boldly at me; I still have mixed feelings about them, but not the bees which love them so much. The delicate wings of cabbage butterflies pay Mum's lavender a fleeting visit. I love June for the promise of the summer holidays that are just around the corner and the long, warm hours of daylight.

Jen has just called me. She and Milly are home with the rest of the family; despite the lack of sleep and the feeding, Jen is coping and happy. The twins and Will are delighted to have a baby to play with – so far! Jen has been true to her word and kept my situation with Adam from Jonny; we both know he isn't good at keeping secrets and he would act impulsively if he sees Adam.

Both Jen and Shirley are sworn to secrecy about my pregnancy and are both quietly delighted for me. Jen says that now I am a mother-to-be I need a new hairstyle. My hair is still as long as it was at school; I am twenty-eight, and it still spends most of its time in a ponytail. I remember Mum plaited my hair before I caught the bus to school. Sometimes fine strands got caught up, which she pulled like puppet strings, and my mouth worked to make an 'ouch' sound. I wish she were here.

But I am not a little girl anymore.

My bedroom at Shirley's house is spacious, and the floral pattern on the wallpaper and duvet remind me of Mum. It isn't home, but it is a sanctuary. Shirley told me she used to use the room for yoga until her back gave way doing the bird-dog. She took up charity work instead and has raised thousands for Macmillan and the RSPB through coffee mornings and events at the village hall. For a woman in her seventies, she's got plenty of energy – more than me at the moment. Last night she was at a Conservative club meeting and then up early for a power walk, though only to the bottom of the lane and back.

The clouds in the sky are wispy. I think back to the day Adam told me he was infertile; the sky looked like it had been torn in two. The day was the end of oxygen and blood to our relationship – a cardiac arrest.

I look at my watch. Adam is due any minute. Shirley has planned it for me. She will be in the lounge reading *Cheshire Life*, a magazine that she aims to feature in at least one more time before she dies, in a position where she can see the patio on which Adam and I will sit and talk.

Shirley thinks I need to keep the evidence of his fraudulent activity under my hat while we gauge his reaction to my news of an affair and pregnancy. I want him to leave me and the baby and Maple Cottage alone. She says she will help me financially and has already made me a beneficiary in her will. I don't know what I'd do without her.

I am reasonably sure Adam arrived at Maple Cottage

yesterday afternoon, but where he was before that I don't know. He will have been shocked to read the curt note on the kitchen table telling him where I am staying.

My heart rate quickens at the thought of being near him again. My stomach makes waves and I take a deep breath. I'm not showing, and yet I feel like I look different. He might guess before I have a chance to tell him.

I answer the door to my husband. He is punctual at least.

'Why are you staying here? Is Shirley ill?' He looks straight at her through the window.

She has given me the confidence to do this. She's even made me laugh at imaginary episodes where he lashes out and she flattens him. Shirley's red hair and her red temper will save me.

'Adam, sit here.' I gesture at a chair.

As he sits down, he scrutinises my face, pins me with his eyes. They search me like a spotlight and I immediately feel dirty, guilty. I finger the acorn pendant around my neck.

'Your hair has grown and you've caught the sun,' he states. I wriggle under the microscope. He looks pristine, his hair too neat, his outfit too coordinated, his shoes spotless as always. How can such a neat, respectable-looking man be such a vicious bastard?

'I'm staying here because the last time I saw you I thought you were going to kill me.'

'Don't be melodramatic. It doesn't suit you.' He tuts. 'You know I was under a lot of stress. But I've done a lot of soul-searching while I've been away in China. It's a busy place and that helped to put things in perspective. I can't deny that I feel a sense of injustice and grief at my loss, but I won't act like that again. And God knows why you think I'd ever kill you. So listen, this last trip has been excellent for me and the business and–'

'Everything is different now.'

'The garden of rooms certainly has changed,' he says. 'I see you've named the rooms: Dilly; Goliath; Sunset. Mine hasn't been christened, so to speak.'

'It will be,' I say confidently. The Bullion Room will be its name when the earth is transformed into a block of gold for the man who worships money. I don't want to spoil the surprise just yet. The significance of the plant choices in the other rooms are probably lost on him, so I'm not worried he'll read the sub-text of the colour of his room when it blooms.

'That and other things have changed.'

'Meaning?'

'I don't love you anymore.'

'I can live with that.'

'I can't.'

For all the beauty of the garden and the elegant garden furniture, the atmosphere between us is airless and grey. A thrush sings its heart out. It is a startling sound, almost indecent in its proximity to our gloom. I hope I have the strength to bring things to a crisis point.

Does he know I slept with Ollie? Is my guilt evident? It feels like a bone protruding through my skin. Can I go through with this? When my resolve falters, I think of my unborn child, the treasure I must protect no matter what.

Shirley gives Adam an imperious wave from her wingback chair. A pigeon lands a few inches from our table and makes a soothing, cooing sound. Its jutting head lunges for a runaway crumb of cake that Shirley must have dropped yesterday. Lemon drizzle, probably. She'd had a few friends over.

'When did you get back from China?' I watch his face carefully, ready for a twinge of muscle, a blink, some indication of a lie.

'Yesterday. I expect you saw my car arrive.'

'I can't say I've been watching,' I lie.

He raises an eyebrow. Nothing in his expression suggests he is not telling me the truth, but there is no mistaking the bruises on Devina's face. Do I trust them more than my husband? Yes, I do.

'What are you thinking, Rachel?'

I push a strand of hair behind an ear.

'You're wearing earrings.'

The involuntary movement of my hand to ear to protect it is unmistakable, and I am glad of the jolt to my memory. It gives me courage. 'I always wear earrings when you aren't around.'

His face doesn't change. I want to stick an earring in his eye.

Will he hit me when I tell him about the baby? His infertility is a weeping sore. I know how it feels to look at children longingly, but I do not pity him. If I tell him I'm pregnant, will he tear at my skin? Will my face look like Devina's tomorrow?

I turn to check Shirley is still there and she gives me a friendly wave.

There is silence for a while. I sense Adam is calm, which encourages me to speak. I lean forward in my seat to close the distance between us. My cheeks feel hot but I tell myself to keep my nerve. I clear my throat and summon every ounce of courage I have. 'Adam, there isn't an easy way to say this, especially after...' I clear my throat. My watch ticks. 'I'm going to come straight out with it.'

'Well? What is it? Spit it out.'

'I had an affair.'

His eyes explore my face and I wonder what he is looking for. He doesn't lash out, so I continue. 'I'm pregnant.'

He doesn't say anything at first, which makes me wonder if I need to repeat myself, but then he comes to life. He moves forward to the edge of the seat. 'Are you sure? Are you positive you're pregnant? I mean, have you had a test or a scan?'

I don't say anything because I'm not sure which version of Adam I am talking to. His questions are such a surprise that it takes me a few moments to respond. Of all the reactions I'd anticipated, this wasn't one of them.

'I took two pregnancy tests. I'm sure. The first scan is at twelve weeks.'

'How many weeks gone are you?' he says hurriedly, but still there is no edge in his voice to hint at violence.

'About eight.' I stare at him incredulously, desperate to read his face. I put a hand on my tummy as if something is moving.

His eyes rake my body. His dirty gaze seems to work over my underwear, my flesh. Calculating, watching. I don't see my husband: I see the hollow, lost eyes in the skulls strewn on my lawn, then fussed over by soft wet noses of rabbits and foxes. Will he utter 'slut'?

No, he stands up and takes me in his arms. 'Oh, Rachel, that's wonderful!' His eyes are wet. He swallows and a tear rolls down his cheek. 'That's amazing!'

I gently extricate myself from his arms. It's a nasty surprise to be held by him; it's been so long. It feels repellent. More tears roll down his cheeks as he gazes at me in wonder while I look at him in disgust.

'Adam–' I feel ashamed that I'm staring at him with such incredulity and horror, but it's impossible to understand his warm, loving reaction. It is grotesque – another kind of violence.

'A baby.' He smiles, and his teeth have never looked whiter. 'Do you feel well? I mean, do you feel healthy enough to carry it to term?'

I nod inanely while my eyes flicker.

His eyes move over me again, then he puts a hand gently on my tummy. It takes all my strength not to bat it away like a dirty fly. 'At last,' he says triumphantly.

'The father doesn't know. I haven't been able to speak to him.'

He waves his hand in the air imperiously, dismissively. 'He won't care. Let's face it – he's been an effective sperm donor.'

'Adam...'

'What?' he laughs. 'Just kidding.'

'I thought you'd be angry about my affair. It wasn't just a one-off. We–'

He holds his hand up. 'I don't need to know. It happened and you're pregnant, which makes up for everything. You can't imagine how much I want to be a father.' He leans over to kiss me but I move away, sickened.

'It's all going to work out. You, me, the baby, Maple Cottage, money in the bank. You can give up work and be a full-time mum. I'll have to be away some of the time, but maybe once the baby is older you could both come out with me to China. I could speak to Derek. We could even move out there. You know Hong Kong.' He stops. 'Are you all right? You don't look so well.'

'This isn't how I thought you'd react,' I say.

'Shirley!' Adam says, and immediately stands up like he's scalded his backside.

Shirley blusters over. She is wearing a tangerine and black skirt and a black top. She reminds me of a red admiral again. I lean back in my chair.

'Adam.' She appraises him, then helps me out of my chair. 'Rachel and I have an appointment now. Perhaps you and I will catch up another time, but we really must be going.'

'No!' He reaches for my arm. 'This is my wife. You don't tell me what she's doing.'

'Sit down, Adam,' she orders. 'You'll scare away the birds. I'm sure I don't need to remind you whose property you are on.'

'Where are you taking my wife?'

'Oh, get over yourself, Adam. You don't own her. Do you

think you need to get checked over for schizophrenia? You're acting delusional for a man whose wife has left him.'

Something close to a growl comes from his mouth. The fists he's made have turned his knuckles white and I know Shirley has spotted them too. 'You're looking old, frail even, Shirley,' he says. 'Mind how you go.'

'It's true – I am too old for child's play. Come on, dear.' She extends her hand to me.

'It's not over. It's just beginning,' Adam spits.

'Goodbye. You know the way back to wherever it is you crawled from.'

As Shirley and I make our way arm in arm inside the house, Adam sends the garden chair toppling backwards. The few steps to the house seem like miles. Once the door is closed and locked, I break down. Shirley holds me as I sob.

'He's pleased! Oh my God, the man is pleased I'm pregnant with someone else's child. He's insane! I thought he'd be angry, demand a divorce on the spot. Shirley, what am I going to do?'

'To paraphrase, the best-laid plans of mice and men often go awry. He could be playing games.'

'Games?'

'Have a rest upstairs and then we'll go out for lunch, come up with a plan. It's all going to be fine once you've got your strength back. And tomorrow it's Open Garden Day, so let's focus on that. What time is Jen arriving?'

'Early, hopefully. What if Adam does something to the house or garden?'

'That can easily be repaired. You can't.'

'I've made a mess of everything.'

'The forecast is good, and so many of your parents' friends are looking forward to seeing you and the garden of rooms. Come on, lean on me. I'll help you up the stairs.'

'Oh, God.'

'Come on. You can get through this. You know, I feel like getting wasted.'

I laugh, despite everything, and hold her arm a little tighter because she is precious to me.

35

Adam's face breaks into a smile, but it freezes over again when he sees Jen behind me. The kitchen smells of bacon and eggs, his breakfast. Dressed in whites for a tennis match, he looks too fit and healthy for comfort.

I feel satisfaction that I have managed to wipe the greasy smile off his face. I have slept well. With Shirley and Jen behind me, I can deal with the day.

'Morning, Adam,' Jen says as she puts the kettle on. 'Lucky with the weather.'

'Mmmm. Why not make yourself at home?'

'Thanks, I will.' She helps herself to a fig roll from the biscuit tin and eats it with her mouth open to annoy him.

'You'll have a handful now – four kids in that shoebox of a house. I don't know how Jonny stands it – but then, he's only a low-paid painter and decorator, so what do you expect?'

'I've never liked you either.' She grins. 'But I must say the garden looks amazing.'

'I paid for it.'

'My Christmas present,' I say, like December was a hundred years ago.

'You should be bloody grateful, Rachel. And to be frank, I don't want people snooping here, so remember that.'

Jen looks theatrically at her watch. 'Bit late for reservations now. People are probably on their way as we chat so nicely to one another.'

Adam turns away from us to look out of the window at the garden. Jen gives him the bird behind his back. 'Look what can be achieved in such a short time with the help of an expert,' he says. 'Money really can buy anything. Ollie's work is amazing – plus it tells your story. Anyone who comes here will see that.'

'I'm proud of it,' I say simply, keen for him to leave. He is such a pompous prick. Whatever did I see in him?

'Let people see it this one time. I've got a tennis tournament, but I expect this village event will be done and dusted by the time I'm back.' He looks me up and down. 'You should smarten yourself up a bit, especially with people coming. All I see you in are jeans and bloody wellingtons. You could at least wipe them once in a while.'

My wellies are dirty, but that's what they're meant to be. Why clean them when they'll get dirty again? I like mud; I love its smell. And it reminds me of Ollie. Yet I say none of this.

After Adam leaves, Jen and I stand side by side in the kitchen drinking tea. She rubs my back. My shoulders are around my ears. 'Don't let him spoil today. He's got a tennis tournament,' she mimics imperiously, and we laugh.

I take a deep breath and feel myself relaxing. 'It's the thought of strangers roaming the garden, sticking their noses into my flowers and my memories, that bothers me. The stories are private.'

'The visitors will enjoy the colours and shapes. They aren't into deep and meaningful like you. Have we got time to cut up Adam's suits?' she asks, half-jokingly.

'Jen!'

'Okay. Bad idea.'

'Come on. I've got a few jobs to do.'

'I'm ready and willing. Got wellies, got chocolate, got a sense of humour, got a child-free day. I've got all the essentials.'

Outside, a tiara of dew is caught in the fine strands of a cobweb; at the centre of a peony, there is a large diamond raindrop. There is so much beauty around that it lifts my mood – until I look at Jen's room.

'Oh my God,' Jen says.

'No!' I yell and run to the vandalised room, which is a chaos of broken stems, fallen petals and holes in the soil where whole plants have been plucked and discarded. Orange and yellow petals, as cherished as fallen stars, are scattered to the ground. The once pert, smiling faces of dahlias and tulips have been stamped on by a large foot, judging by the footprint in the soil. The room looks blankly back at me as if in shock.

'Adam really doesn't like me, does he?' Jen says without emotion. 'What a complete cock.'

My hand is clasped to my mouth. The stalks are bent and broken; it's futile, but I can't help myself from trying to make them stand again. The four-foot sunflowers have been snapped in two. Their faces still smile, but on broken necks. Jen's neck is broken.

'Rach!' She grabs me before I collapse and helps me into a chair. I still can't move my hand from my mouth. I am still in shock. All the hours that Ollie and I spent planting, weeding, watering; all the thought, the planning.

'Who did this?' I say, still incredulous. Even after the battering, it's hard to accept that Adam could be so hateful.

'Oh, come on. It's fuck-face. Gucci Adam. Of course, it bloody is, Rach! See the light.'

He wants to cause me pain. What better way? There's no need to set traps, to gouge eyes out with beaks, to claw at the skin. He has destroyed what I have created. What better way to injure me?

He is a serpent in the Garden of Eden, low to the ground, previously hidden from view. Adam. There is no mistaking it: a human hand has done the damage to Jen's room during the night. The wind, disease or an animal could not uproot and disembowel on such a scale in such a short time. Jen's right. It has to be Adam.

The room. What's next? Me?

'How long till the guests arrive?' Jen demands.

'Two hours.'

'Where's your phone?'

She walks briskly into the kitchen and returns with my phone. She scrolls through my contacts.

'Who are you ringing?' I ask.

'Ollie.'

'Ollie? But I–'

She waves me into silence. 'Hello, Ollie, this is Jen, Rachel's friend. Yeah, well, the timing's bad. Yes... Today... Someone's vandalised my room in Rach's garden. It's a mess. Can you help?... Adam's not here. You will? That's brilliant. Thank you.' She hangs up and smiles. 'He's on his way with plants.'

'How did he sound?'

'Normal. Friendly. Bit sexy, actually.'

I look at the devastation and recall Adam's pristine white attire. He must have left feeling smug, leaving the vandalised garden to look straight back at me after he'd showered, hidden his dirty clothes, his dirty boots. His dirty mind, his dirty soul.

Ollie's arrival can't come soon enough. I'm not sure if it's the sight of The Hollies' van or him walking towards me with his loping stride, but I immediately feel better and worse at the same time. I want to run into his arms but sense from his posture and blank expression that this is the wrong thing to do.

His familiar form breaks something in me that had barely healed from the last tear of parting. The scar tissue is as fragile as wet paper. His gait, the movement of his hands and feet, his gestures, the alignment of his vertebrae under his T-shirt, are all tattooed on my mind, so achingly familiar.

Jen makes herself scarce while we sift through the plants in his van before unloading. He tells me to go inside while he plants out. Although I'm happy to obey, to get away from the ugly scene of the crime, I linger in the hope he will at least make small talk with me and we can clear the stuffy air between us.

'Thanks for coming,' I say lamely. 'How was Spain?'

'Good.'

He is reticent, immersed in his task. I have to accept that he is here to do a job; he has no spare time to talk to me. I can't pretend it doesn't sting that a distance has opened up between us for reasons I don't understand. Perhaps he is worried that Adam will return.

'Adam's got a tennis match. He's–'

'It won't take me long to plant this out. You get yourself ready.' He doesn't look up from his work. He is intent on removing the plants from their pots and loosening the roots before burying them in the soil.

The room is slowly resuscitated with hues of orange and yellow. It lifts my mood to see it, just as it does when I see Jen. Even so, I wish Ollie would look at me, just once. I feel invisible.

'Do you think many will come today?' I ask.

'Couldn't say.'

I remember the way I once put my finger to his lips and made a slow 'sssssshhhh' sound because the only thing I wanted to speak was his hands. I look at him now, kneeling in the garden of rooms, and I dream of him like that, sharing my prayer. I dream of the rain soaking his hair, dripping down onto his chin, and my lips tasting the drops away. I dream of the garden of rooms, our fifth room, when our baby comes.

'I'm pregnant.'

He looks up for a moment as if to speak, then picks up his trowel up and carries on with his work. 'Congratulations,' he says flatly.

There is a world outside this marriage. It is a vast, beautiful world of kindness. When I see Ollie here, I feel I can survive whatever misery Adam inflicts, like the delicate fuchsia through harrying frost.

Why won't Ollie look at me? See me? Hear me?

'I need to talk to you.'

'Not now. Please.'

'You're the father!'

He stops working and his head falls. 'I know. Please. Not now.'

I go inside the cottage for a bath. While Adam is out, I retrieve the document from his desk, the evidence of his fraudulent activity, and hide it in my bag.

By the time I re-emerge, the plants are in situ and Ollie has gone. Jen's room is restored. I sigh with relief and sadness as I meander to the bottom of the garden to sit under the maple tree. At two o'clock, the visitors will arrive. A distraction is the best thing.

Why is Ollie so detached and cold? Is he under pressure at work? Did he come here as a favour when he didn't have time?

Jen and I walk around the garden as the guests trickle in. I overhear snatches of laughter and smell a cocktail of perfume from visitors I've never met before. What would Mum think? When she was feeling chatty, she might have ventured outside, handed out delicious slices of cake or biscuits. Home-made, of course.

'What did Ollie say when you told him?' Jen asks.

'Nothing.'

A couple join us and entangle me in conversation about my parents. They are friends of Shirley and Roland, so I relax a little. I notice that Devina has arrived and is staring at the cottage.

Harry, an elderly gentleman in a cream linen jacket, steps forward to shake my hand. 'My wife was friends with your mother, Dilly. Audrey was her name. They loved to gossip.' I remember seeing him in the graveyard when I visited Mum.

'I wonder if the swallows returned this April,' he says. 'My wife, Audrey, used to tell me. You see the mud cups under the eaves.'

'They did, and I hope they'll be back next year.'

I can hear classical music from over the fence: Shirley will no doubt be pulling out all the stops to put on a good show. It paints a half-smile on my face.

More and more people arrive: I am delighted to see so many of them enjoying the stunning garden of rooms. It turns out it has become quite well known in local circles as a unique creation and a legacy to my lovely parents.

'The dahlias are cheerful, aren't they?' I say.

'Sunshine,' Harry says. 'Complete sunshine. You can't put a price on that!' He smiles at me and his silver hair glints in the sun. 'Thank you, Rachel. It's a pleasure to come here. See you next year!'

'You bet your life you will!'

Snatches of conversation and laughter float my way, lifting my spirits. I enjoy watching the way shoes move a few steps then stop, then move again in time with the wearer's appreciation of the garden. A mother shouts for her daughter to 'come here'.

This house loves lavender and autumn bonfires. It loves treacle tart and April showers. There's a thought of mine in each room, and there's a shade of my parents in the plants in the garden. Cream poured into a jug, like the dribble of slow-wave sleep. I feel contented; I am thrilled to share with my neighbours and my parents' friends.

A little girl frolics, dressed as an angel in chiffon which rustles with her every movement. A gentleman with soft grey hair lingers over the lavender. A surge of confident laughter from a group of people by Jen's repaired room surprises me because I hadn't noticed them arrive. My worries vanish, and the sun shines down on us.

Inside the house, I have half-drawn the blinds and curtains downstairs so the sanctity of the interior remains. I find the front door wide open. A wand of light has worked its way into the hall. Annoyed with myself for not locking up the house, I do it then and go out of the back door, locking it behind me.

Four o'clock comes so slowly. I sigh with relief and stand on the patio, smiling this way and that, receiving thanks from visitors like handfuls of confetti. They seem to leave in a slow-moving blur of colourful clothes and bags and shuffling shoes. A young woman with a child turns to wave goodbye, lured by Shirley's classical music. They are on their way there next, to enjoy her garden. She's serving champagne and canapés this year.

I watch Harry join another couple. Beside them is a tall, well-built man with a thatch of very blond hair. I screw my eyes, but he moves away with the crowd before I can see his face.

I enjoy some shade from the overhanging branches of the maple tree while Jen is in the kitchen preparing us a cold drink. I can make out beige sandals and a long white skirt or dress, something floaty and cool, just right for a warm summer's day. A pigeon's feather floats under the canopy. Suddenly, dainty feet advance towards my vantage point, then dark shoes step under it. It feels like they are stepping under my umbrella.

A face in the shade narrows its tragic eyes at me – a tight smile, then a tilting of a smart bob to the left. 'Rachel.'

'Devina!'

'Did you know you have a blob of sun cream on your cheek?' Devina reaches forward and rubs it in lightly. The sudden gentle movement passes before I can stop her. I blush involuntarily, feeling hot under my blue sundress despite the shade. Her bruises are concealed under a layer of make-up and a silk scarf. Her arms are in long sleeves.

'The view from the back windows needed it. The lawn was a bit drab. There's so much colour now. Amazing, in such a short time.' She speaks quickly, almost nervously. 'You've worked wonders.'

'It's been a pleasure to do. You all right?'

'I won't keep you. I just came to say I've reported Adam to the police.'

'You have? Gosh.'

'Such a beautiful spot here, isn't it? A little slice of heaven.'

A cabbage butterfly sweeps past my nose. 'You're brave to come here.'

'I knew he wouldn't be here.'

'How?'

'He's a selfish man. They all are. Men like Adam don't think about charity or community. He couldn't give a rat's ass about this garden. You okay?'

I nod and smile. Hearing Devina use slang so fluently is light relief. 'I don't know what to say.'

She looks at me sadly.

It suddenly feels tranquil, as if the birds are having a siesta. 'Thank you,' I say. 'You've done a brave thing.'

'Ted was angry about leaving this place and he did things he shouldn't have done. I hope we're even now.'

'We are. Completely. Thank you. I really am so grateful.'

'Men don't change – you know that, don't you? Once a bully, always a bully.'

'Yes,' I nod. 'I know that now.'

Shortly afterwards Shirley calls round, smelling of white wine and Chanel No. 5. The notes of Tchaikovsky's 'Waltz of the Flowers' still wafts over the fence. She ducks under the maple tree to join Jen and me; her dress is flamingo pink. Suddenly I feel underdressed in my blue summer dress.

'Did you do canapés?' Shirley asks.

'No, but the peanuts went down a storm,' Jen says, with a mouthful of fig biscuit.

'Went all right, then?' Shirley grins as she tosses a loose white scarf back over her shoulder in a theatrical gesture that reminds me a little of Jen.

'Fine. Probably about twenty-five or so visitors.'

'That's great. You should feel proud of what you've achieved here. It takes a lot of work to bring a blank canvas to life as you have. So far it looks like we've raised over £200. It's a drop in the ocean for Macmillan, but it's something for your mum's charity. This event plus the coffee mornings – we're close to a thousand pounds so far this year.'

'That's amazing! I heard your music and a lot of laughter earlier. Did you have a strip show in the garden?'

Shirley laughs. 'Excellent idea for next year. I love the idea of a hunk dressed in nothing but bunting. Perhaps Ollie would model for us for the right money? Just think how wonderful your garden of rooms will be this time next year.'

A year from now. Next June. How might our lives be different?

'You know, I feel rudderless now, after the event,' Shirley says. 'I need some Rossini and pink gin. Come and join me. I have elderflower-flavoured tonic and steak and kidney pie.'

'Tinned?'

'Of course. I appreciate the solution of tins. Jars are good too, except I can't open the damn things.' She holds up her bent, arthritic hands by way of explanation. 'Unless I get a man, of course, but I can't be bothered.'

We stroll around the garden. I feel happy to be out of shoes and back in my wellington boots. The air is cooling. All the guests have gone; only their footprints on the grass are left to remind me of them.

The maple tree looks eerie in the half-light; it has an unnerving, magical quality, as if goblins and fairies might sneak out to play tricks. I think Mum and Dad would be happy about the day, having their friends here, the beauty of the garden.

'Well done for today, Rach.' Jen kisses me and hugs me hard. 'I'll ring you tomorrow. Take good care of her, Shirley.'

'Oh, I will.'

Shirley waits for me in the lounge as I gather a few extra things from upstairs. My heart sinks when I hear Adam's car and the opening and closing of the front door, then Shirley's voice. Each creak sounds like an avalanche.

He runs upstairs and bursts into the bedroom before I can leave. 'There's no need to look like that. I'm not going to hurt you.'

I hear a creak. Shirley must be listening on the bottom stair.

'What's this?' I say, as he hands me a present wrapped in red paper.

I unwrap it, conscious of the movement of my hands and the sound of crumpled paper. I rush to get it open, to be away from him. 'It's a notepad,' I say flatly. Turning the first page, I feel the thickness of the off-white paper, the luxuriousness of its touch and smell. *LIFE PLANNER*.

'It's not just for you, it's for us – to work out our plans for the future. You, me and the baby. What we're working towards. What we want to achieve and share... There are lots of decisions to make. Names, schools–'

I look at the book in horror. 'You can't pretend everything is normal or good between us – it won't fix it. Nothing can.'

'It will work, Rachel, because you and I will make it work.' He sees my disregard; I see the curl of his lip. His eyes bore straight into mine. 'What have you got, Rachel? I earn the equivalent of your annual salary in a couple of months. Our baby will have the best of everything because I can provide it. You wouldn't survive without me. I won't let you.'

'I'm not staying.'

He looks away angrily, then closes the door behind him as he leaves. I count the eighteen stairs he descends before hurling the life planner across the room. It is even gold-coloured, the colour of money, chosen by the man who thinks money can buy and fix anything.

I hear Shirley shout something at him and then I run down the stairs with my bag.

36

JULY 2019

I've been staring at my phone for the last half hour. Ollie hasn't phoned or texted. The term is almost over and then there will be six long weeks of holiday. The weather has been kind to the garden of rooms so far.

Restlessly, I peer out of Shirley's spare bedroom window to Peckforton Wood. The ancient pines, the oaks and silver birch that shed their bark with love letters to nature. I recall the smell of living pine. I recall the dapples of sunlight through the leaves. The density of tree and bark and branch is still there, always watching. Is it a harbinger of doom or a protector, an educator?

I concede that the wood is less threatening now. The man I married is more frightening than anything there. If my parents hadn't lived here, things would have turned out differently. While our own lives were growing, twisted and bent like weak saplings, the wood remained steadfast, a giant on the landscape, a living monolith on the Cheshire plains.

I try to imagine leading my child through the paths, urging them to look and learn, to be a student of nature as I was. The wood has taught me how to deal with the hateful man I married. I just need to get a plan together.

I know where there is real wish-food; I know where wishes can be picked. I know food that makes death-wishes come true. My head is buzzing; it's a bees' nest of poisonous intent one moment, and anxious mother-to-be the next. I realise I will soon be a mother, a figure so central to my child's life that I am scared of the responsibility. I wish Mum was here to help me change a nappy, to feed a baby, to tell me what to do when I'm all out of options and the crying won't stop. Will I be a good mum?

I like the name Dilly, after my mum, or Russ if it's a boy.

I remember my friends at university speculating about the 'big' questions. Will you get a good husband? Will you have children? Will you be rich and fulfilled? Now the only question for me is whether there is hope for a happy, safe life. Hope, not a trick of the light, not willed amnesia, not delusion fed on wish-food. If it were, my baby and I would starve.

Perhaps Adam never loved me. Maybe I am just an incubator. How else can I explain his disregard for my infidelity? At least I am unharmed, and so is my unborn child. I never want to witness my child in Adam's arms.

I remember how sometimes I'd find grains of soil in the sheets after Ollie and I made love, but I didn't mind. Ollie's touch on my face was cherry blossom to the eye, to the nose; it seemed natural. I remember heady, all-consuming joy. One night in spring, the curtains billowed in and out when a storm whipped around the house, impatient to find something to move, to destroy. Luckily, it only found garden chairs and throttled the wind chime. He held me then, and we fell asleep until morning.

I miss feeling singed and exhausted by sex. Before Ollie, I was as parched as the soil in a heatwave. I miss the deep sleep after lovemaking, like a stone falling into a well. He once wrote his name on my tummy and my bare back with his fingertip. The memory makes my skin tingle.

I remember him helping me up from a fall in the wood, and him planting the lavender in my mum's room, and his body heat beside me through the quiet night.

Perhaps once Adam is out of my life, Ollie will show up again. He'll saunter through the door in his loose jeans with those loping big strides, with his knees mud or grass stained. It will be summer again: the hairy-bellied bees will be busy, and haymakers will be turning the land to gold. He'll grab me, like the wind grabbing a collar. There will be pink dog-rose and yellow pimpernel in the wood. Of course, the sun will boil in the sky; the garden chairs will be like hot iron. No matter, for he prefers to lie on the grass, to unfurl his long, chunky body and feel me and the earth beneath him.

Until now, I'd viewed my childhood through a pair of binoculars. I had tried unsuccessfully to push my past over the other side of a hill, to look at it from a high vantage point, but it didn't shrink with time. I was looking at it from the wrong angle. Now I am ready to take the lessons Dad taught me to save my unborn child so I can be the loving mother my mum was to me.

I hear my watch ticking, so loudly I can't hear anything else except for my thoughts, which are moving at the speed of the second hand.

From my window, the garden of rooms is still radiant. I watch the lavender moving in time with the breeze, but then the sound of metal pulls my gaze in the opposite direction. It is the sound of a heavy vehicle, an engine, gravel crunching and metal clanking, foreign sounds that remind me of a skip swinging on its chain.

In the caramel light of the afternoon, I watch my Golf being loaded onto the tow truck.

I open the window and shout. 'Wait! That's my car!'

I burst through the front door. The bloke looks at me nonplussed, then rummages in the pocket of his high-vis jacket for paperwork. He reads it out loud following the words with his finger. 'Says here Adam Jordan owns it. You don't look like an Adam to me, love.' He climbs into the truck.

I put my hand on the truck door to stop him from closing it. 'He bought it for me. It's mine.'

'Look, love, I'm not a relationship counsellor, I'm paid to take it away. The documentation is there. Mr Jordan owns this and he wants it removed. Sorry.'

I hear the bite of tyres and watch my car go, carried on the back of the tow truck like a piggyback. The vehicle drives down our lane at speed, sending plumes of dust into the air, and the magic trick is over. My car is gone. Abracadabra.

Incensed, I march round to Maple Cottage. How dare Adam take my car away? I need it to get to work and the hospital for my next scan. 'Adam!' I yell as soon as I open the front door. I am out of breath and red-faced with anger.

He appears from the lounge with a man I have never seen before.

'Rachel. Good of you to drop by. This is Geoff. He's going to project manage the extension.' Adam shakes Geoff's hand. 'Thanks for coming.'

'I'll be in touch.' The man closes the door behind him.

'If this is going to be where our child is raised, it needs work. You're sentimental about the place but it is very basic.'

Suddenly I burst into tears. I want to stop my mind from windmilling, to stop my heart from clenching. I want this man away from me. 'You're mad! I want a divorce. I want this to be over. My car, now this–'

Adam looks like he's swallowed sour medicine, then he laughs. 'I will contest the divorce until you're blue in the face. Or I might not bother – it doesn't change a thing as far as I'm concerned.' He smirks. 'You don't want unnecessary stress to jeopardise the health of our baby.' He reaches to touch my tummy but I bat his hand away.

'No! This house is as much mine as yours and I don't want anything to change. And I don't want *you* touching me ever again. Do you hear me?'

To me, my due date is an impending flight time illuminated on an airport screen. If only there could be a delay. The date is intertwined with a deadline for freedom, as well as a battle for my home.

'Or what?' He laughs.

'I'll go to the police about the money you've stolen from Boarding International.'

I have the document evidencing his fraud; I photocopied it at work. That is all I have as a possible passport. My eyes flicker to my schoolbag on the peg in the hall, mostly hidden under my winter coat, but he reads my face and looks at it. The penny drops.

'What's in that bag of yours?' he sneers.

His shape seems to get bigger before my eyes. He is enjoying the moment, seeing fear and a flicker of guilt in my eyes. He grabs the bag. 'You won't get rid of me, Rachel. Think again,' he says, matter-of-factly. 'In your state, you've got a lot to lose. Besides, your hormones are all over the place. Don't get irrational. And it's such a beautiful day.'

The moment stretches out before me as he rummages in my bag. He turns it upside down, spilling the contents onto the floor. My students' exercise books topple over each other. He finds the original document and the photocopy, and waves them in my face.

He lingers in front of me wearing a triumphant expression. There are frayed nerves, the pieces of marriage like broken china to step on to shred my emotions, cut deeply and embed pain. The house feels full of corners and edges.

'Did you think I wouldn't check? Did you really think you could take something from me and it would work out all right? So you were going to blackmail me into a divorce, leaving you alone, is that it? I've invested the last four years of my life in our relationship.'

'You've *invested*? For God's sake, Adam.' The disdain I feel fortifies me. 'You make me sick!'

His slap comes out of nowhere; a stinging, zinging sound full of heat.

'You're going to regret that, woman. Don't think Ollie will get involved with the baby. Our business arrangement is over. I hope you haven't been expecting him to call.'

A moan escapes my mouth and dizziness overcomes me so intensely it could be vertigo. 'How did you know it was Ollie?'

He doesn't answer, seeming to enjoy the moment for a long time. Silence sits between us like a fat, greasy toad that I want to stand on. Then he smiles a greasy smile. 'He needed money, we wanted a baby. You can stop feeling guilty about your little fling, if you want.'

The ceiling feels low and the walls close in. I feel like I'm breathing under water. I stare at Adam incredulously. It takes me a few seconds to process the revelation. How could he do such a thing to me?

'You engineered an affair so I'd get pregnant! Is that it? China. You stayed in China, knowing it was going on...' I falter, my voice quivering. 'You knew all along and let it happen. Made it happen!'

I shake my head, the horror of it sinking in and then the humiliation. I'd thought it was lust, desire. When Ollie said my name as he climaxed, was that for effect? When he lay on top of me and kept perfectly still after we made love, when he looked into my eyes and stroked my hair, was he thinking about getting me pregnant? 'You paid for my affair?'

Why didn't I guess he'd been put up to it? I put my head in my hands. I see Ollie's hand entangled in my hair on the pillow. It is too much. The tears come.

'Think of him as a sperm donor and yourself as a surrogate mother – only you get to keep our baby *some* of the time.'

He is smiling like a brilliant scholar, a mastermind. 'I'm the father, you see. Ollie was just a donor.' There is delight and triumph on Adam's face as he watches my heart break in front of him.

I avert my bruised eyes so he can't see them. Anger begins to replace my sadness. 'You paid Ollie to get me pregnant? I can't believe even you would do such a thing.'

'Yes, I paid him handsomely because I want a baby with you more than anything. And you made it clear that IVF or AI was out of the question. I did it because I want us to be a family. Why are you looking at me like that?'

The thought of being a commodity makes me feel ill. 'Are you mad?' I say. This tall, handsome man is an infantry of lies and I feel ambushed by them. 'You honestly thought I'd accept the arrangement you'd made and carry on being your wife? Like my child is a tribute to you?'

I have known loss before, but this time I will not mourn it, the loss of our marriage, of my faith in Adam and Ollie.

Adam's proximity makes me feel protective of my baby, as if even his presence might sully my child. What he says is a lie: I experienced lust and passion and, if I felt it, then it is real to me. But that was then. Ollie was just an affair.

I stand up, too angry to sit still.

Adam runs a hand through his hair. 'You, this house, us – it's all I want. I did it for us! Can't you see that? I was upset after the infertility test – but who wouldn't be? Now, we all win. I fixed our situation, don't you see?'

I shake my head, appalled by his delusional state. 'You're

sick. Did you think I could love you, forgive you, for playing God? While you were in China you carried on working, eating, sleeping, knowing I was sleeping with Ollie. You knew, and you didn't mind.'

'I did what had to be done to achieve our goal.' His voice rises then deepens. 'You have no idea what it's like to be a married man without a family. All my colleagues have children. They come to work brimming with stories of outings, holidays, family activities, and I have to listen and wonder why not us? Have you any idea how powerless infertility makes you feel? You've been so morose, so terribly fucking sad. But look–' he gestures to my stomach like a magician performing a magic trick '–I made this happen. For us.'

'You're a monster, that's what you are. A deluded monster.'

His face falls. So, not the hero, after all. My words are sinking in. I am appalled that he expects gratitude for his devilish ingenuity. Even his hair is sticking up like horns. Goosebumps form on my skin, skin that he has touched. I feel repulsed and want to wash, wash him away for good.

'This has to stop now, Adam. I cannot be near you.'

Can Adam be the legal father of my child? If so, how will I ever get him out of my life? I know this will end badly. There is no way out.

'I love you,' he says. 'I can provide for you, for the baby. Who are you to say I'm wrong and you're right? *You* are deluded.'

'For God's sake, it was wrong of me to sleep with Ollie but I was vulnerable. You both took advantage of that.' I look out of the window. How much time do I have left before my child is born to a life of fear?

'I am absolving you of your guilt. I know you felt it but now you know it wasn't passion you experienced, only Ollie's grubby hands getting hold of my money,' Adam says, smirking.

'This baby and this house are worth more than all the

money you have and will ever have. Money, Adam, isn't the same as value.'

'I'm the father of our child, whether you like it or not. Ollie signed away his paternity rights.'

'Get out, you despicable man!'

'I'll go. You are pregnant, after all. I'll do the decent thing and let you stay here. But I will come back. You won't know when. That's part of the fun!' His threat is a malign shadow. 'You don't know who you'll bump into in the woods, do you? Did you think you could play me, woman, without comeback? You live in a fantasy world. When that baby comes and you're a single mum, you'll have a double dose of reality.'

I think of Jen and her cramped house, her demanding family and her period of depression. I think of Devina, struggling and broke, raising children alone. Will I cope without Adam to provide for my baby and me?

Despite his threat and my fears, my lungs feel full of air. I remove my wedding ring and place it on the kitchen table. Miraculously, it is transformed into something small and insignificant like a washer left by a plumber. 'I don't need this anymore.'

This isn't the moment my marriage ends; that happened months ago. This is the moment I feel stronger than I have ever felt before. But I know this isn't the final battle.

I meet his eyes then hold them. Adam's head drops. If he hadn't frightened and threatened me, duped me, I might have felt a little pity or sadness but I don't. I hear only the unlocking of a prison door and I watch myself walk through it.

'Keep it,' he says nastily. 'You might need to pawn it for groceries when you get hungry.'

He goes upstairs to pack. He tosses a packed bag down into the hallway. The soundtrack to our history together is the opening and closing of drawers, the rummaging of impatient hands to find things that we haven't taken proper care of. I imagine the socks and pants I've washed countless times being thrown into his bag.

He packs up the office that he made in the spare room. He had wanted to extend, to refurbish, to remodel. Thank goodness it hasn't got that far. I hear the loud zipping noise of his laptop bag, and then he descends the stairs for the final time. I am saddened he has only packed the one bag.

These sounds – they aren't the final noises of him in this house.

I think of his gifts, his business trips, the fraud and his attack on Devina, and I wonder who Adam Jordan really is. I cannot bring myself to think about Ollie. I put my hand on my bump and stroke it gently. To comfort myself, I imagine the smell of lavender and the red berries on the holly in my dad's room in the garden.

Adam appears before me with flushed cheeks. He looks manic, angry, hungry for a fight. 'Rachel,' he says in an unsettling tone, 'I'll be in touch.' He looks at me with sick longing.

The hall is littered with his belongings. They are ugly reminders of time wasted with the wrong person. I want him and them gone. But I know it isn't over, every bone in my body knows it, but at least he will be out of my house and out of my sight.

'Thank you, Adam,' I say. A frown shows his confusion. I let the moment stretch out – a small victory.

'What for?' he asks, perplexed.

Smiling, I turn to look at him. I gesture through the window and say, 'For helping me have the garden and the baby I've always wanted. You even paid for it!'

His face is crestfallen, slack. A fake laugh emits from his

mouth like black smoke. He is fading now, just fragments, no symmetry of parts or wholeness.

Dad told me that everything perishes, even dangerous things. He said that nature is cruel in its survival instinct, that killing is brutal and merciless. His job was to control pests humanely. He said that sometimes people are predators, even though they aren't hungry. He spoke of genocide and the nefarious sides of even the most normal folk. At the time I didn't understand what he meant, but now I do. Adam is a predator, but now he is part of the backdrop to my life, as insignificant as an old snapshot or junk mail.

'You know how to reach me when you need me.'

'Goodbye, Adam.'

The hall is emptied of his detritus. The front door closes. He shrinks and, like magic, he disappears from view.

37

Ollie is knocking at the back door. Ridiculously, I look around for somewhere to hide. I look down at my tatty jeans and hoody; my hair is in a loose ponytail and I've chewed my fingernails to nothing. The blisters have healed after a break from gardening, and at least the hand lotion has softened my hands.

He tries to open the locked door before I have time to move.

My stomach is churning as I unlock the door. Ollie opens his arms to me, but I don't respond. I walk into the kitchen and stand by the window.

'You look like you hate me. You know, don't you?' he says.

I nod, frozen to the spot. I do hate him. The size of him makes the room smaller.

Ollie speaks again, his voice low and urgent. 'I've been lying low because Adam's a dangerous man – I know that now. If he sees me with you, we could both be dead. He's a businessman, and he expects me to honour our agreement. He had to be the one to tell you. I wanted to tell you–'

'Is that what we were? A business arrangement? A deal?'

'No. I wouldn't risk coming here if that was true. I've kept away to protect you.'

'I'm not flattered. What do you want?'

'You've every right to be angry with me. The way we– But I want to be with you. I haven't stopped thinking about you. If I give Adam back the money, would that make any difference?'

'Did you sign away your paternity rights?'

'I had to sign something. Adam said it was business, so I had to sign! If I'm honest, I only read some of it. The sum of money was at the top.'

I turn away, appalled by him.

He thrusts his hands into his pockets. 'I did a stupid thing. He talked me into pitying your situation, with you both wanting a child. And the truth is, I fancied you. So when he approached me to sleep with you for money, it was a no-brainer. I sensed you liked me too. If you hadn't wanted to, I would never have made you. It wasn't fake – none of it. I didn't know he was violent. I had no idea what kind of man he is.'

'You lied to me. I thought what we had was real.' I take a deep breath. 'It doesn't matter.'

'It *does* matter. Let's go to Spain. We can stay at my parents' house for a while. You can't live here safely, can you? Come away with me so we can spend some time together, just you and me, away from Adam. I want to keep you safe and I want to be with you, but I can't do that here.'

He moves closer towards me, and I step back. Hurt shows on his face. 'What can I do?'

'Tomorrow I have to get to the hospital for a scan and then go into work. I need that scan to be sure the baby is healthy, and I need to keep my job. Adam's had my car towed away. The only thing I want from you is to get the Land Rover running, then leave. For good.'

38

As I drive home from the hospital, I think about the kitchen at Maple Cottage. It was the family's peaceful oasis. Mum used to peep through the serving hatch, with its two little doors with shiny brass handles, cold to the touch. Dad used to say Mum had a 'cock-a-doodle-doo' face when she put her head through to surprise us with home-made cakes and biscuits, made with eggs laid by Dad's hens. She looked so happy. We *were* happy, the three of us eating meals on a checked tablecloth decorated with lines of light from the large window. Mum pouring the tea and sugaring each chunky mug; spreading soft butter on toast and spooning on raspberry jam. Dad took enormous bites out of his toast, like he was permanently ravenous or in a hurry. Sometimes the jam was home-made by Shirley as a gift for him putting up bird boxes in her paradise of a garden.

Will my baby and I sit at that same kitchen table?

The Land Rover drives like a dream. It feels like Dad helped me get to the hospital for my scan, where I saw my baby for the first time, a glow-worm inside me. Adam hasn't won. I'm still fighting and my baby, half the size of my thumb, is healthy.

Those perfect fingers, and the fingerprints forming on them, are growing inside me with each passing hour.

The joy doesn't last long. My face falls as soon as I get home and see the garden. *He* must have waited for me to go to work. Whoever it was that did it. I don't think for one minute Adam would do it himself. Why would he, when he can afford to pay people to do his dirty work?

Maple Cottage was named after the tree because its canopy of ruby foliage was beautiful. When winter came, the scarlet leaves fell to the ground, formed a circle around the trunk like a devil's mouth breathing fire. In the night sky the full moon would cast a ghostly glow over it.

The maple tree was my dad's and my favourite. We used to play hide and seek under there. Sometimes Dad's figure was absorbed into the trunk of the tree; if it hadn't been for the jangling of loose change in his pockets, I wouldn't have been able to find him and win a single game.

In the summer, its foliage was like a fountain of fire, a scorching red flame. To sit under it was a privilege. It was about fifteen metres tall, a page of history dating back twenty years or more, red and rooted right at the end of the garden. The place Ollie and I made love; the place I sat during Open Garden Day; the place Dad wept giant tears for Mum. The tree had been a friend: a place to dream and hope.

Strangely, trees are silent objects, yet when they vanish–

I sense the new quietness in the back garden before I see what has happened.

The maple tree has gone. Its shadow has vanished, too.

Beheaded.

The sun peeks into corners it never used to and it sees the stark reality. It mourns with me. The breeze has no one to play with, so it holds its breath.

An ugly bruised stump is all that remains, and even that has been defaced with red paint as if the tree and the leaves have poured blood, spilling its life forever. Is that my sad fate too?

I lift my arms to the sky and roar. A stray leaf lands by my feet like a splash of blood opening up a fresh tranche of grief. This ugly, knife-like language of Adam's.

'Bastard! Bastard! The police will know what you've done!'

39

I remember the day I found my father's dead body. Now I understand something of how Dad must have felt after Mum died. He hated spring and summer.

The front and the back door were open and so were many of the windows in Maple Cottage. 'Dad, where are you?' I called.

It was three months since I'd seen him last – and since he'd told me to leave. It was his birthday and he was expecting me. I'd bought him a present and even gift-wrapped it.

As soon as I entered the house, I knew something was wrong. Nature had moved in. A mouse was tucking into the mouldy remains of a loaf of bread, and there were slug trails across the carpet in the hall. The ants were always a problem when I was little, and now I saw red ants around the kitchen window and a spider's web festooned across the window frame. If Mum were alive, she would have been furious to see the house in such a state.

Judging by the debris, Dad had been living on Cup-a-Soup, eggs and bread. His favourite mug, with *Pest Control* printed boldly on it in thick black letters, was on the draining board with something brown and gooey inside it. The cupboard doors were open and the insides were bare. A bird had flown into the house and left a trail of white muck. There were maggots in the loaf of bread.

The single bed in the lounge was unmade. Footprints from muddy boots led me through the kitchen and back to the hall again.

'Dad? Are you upstairs?'

I decided to go up in case he was taking a nap, but his bed was empty. He couldn't have gone far because the doors and windows were open. I drew back the curtains and looked out. The lawn was overgrown.

I saw something like a scarecrow at the very bottom of the garden. I screwed up my eyes to try and focus but a riot of vegetation obscured my view.

I opened the window. 'Dad?' I called. 'Is that you? It's Rachel.'

I couldn't hear the hens. I couldn't hear them clucking and cooing. I saw feathers, lots of feathers, and then I ran downstairs, out of the back door and down the lawn. My mouth opened wider and wider as I got nearer and nearer to the scarecrow.

I heard the flies before I saw them. They were infuriated by my disturbance; some hit my face as they flew away.

'Dad?'

The iron fist of fear thumped me in the chest. A flick of its eye, and a rabbit sprinted for the undergrowth, making the nettles tremble in its wake.

Dad was asleep in his deckchair, the skin on his face so relaxed it was like melted wax. Despite the heat, he was dressed in his waxed jacket, the pockets brimming with mushrooms and flowers. His hair had not been cut or combed for some time, perhaps since I'd seen him last. I smiled at the shreds of bark and twigs in his hair, probably from his last bonfire or stroll. His face was tucked into his beard as if to find some warmth.

A dead hen lay beside his boot, as if dropped from his dangling hand when he nodded off; her claw-like feet were white and solid. Her head was missing and there was a space for maggots to feed. Eaten by a fox, presumably. It was his favourite, Lady. His best layer. Poor Dad, he'd be upset.

Lady was the last to go. Night after night, Dad must have forgotten to lock the hens up safely in their coop. If I closed my eyes, I could hear his hens singing and his low chat to them as he carried out his chores. A tractor rumbled past and beeped its horn: probably a 'hello' from Roland.

'Dad?'

I forced open his other hand, as lined as cracked willow. It was surprisingly cold to the touch. My eye rode over his skin; in his hand, there were dark, crumbly soil clots and something purple with a black berry inside. On his right hand he was wearing his wedding ring and, on his little finger, Mum's silver thimble.

From behind him, the breeze could almost have been stroking his salt-and-pepper hair.

Seventy-five years of age.

I touched his shoulder to wake him. 'Happy birthday, Dad.' I leaned in to kiss him on his cheek. Slugs nestled in his neck and the slime trail led my eyes to his mouth.

And then I accepted he was dead and I screamed. The horror of the poisonous object in his mouth. I yanked it free. There was spit and sick and a vile aroma. Now I saw his cheeks were shrivelled and his thin lips were blue from the poisonous berries, and perhaps from the cold.

'Oh, Dad. No.' I stroked his hair and dislodged a worm.

The secrets of his final days belong to nature, to the wood he visited for his final pilgrimage for a terrible banquet. The woods presided over his dead body like pillars, too tall, too shadowy. The clouds moved, as if leaning in for a closer look.

Even as he died, nature had come to him and the garden was teeming with life. His flesh had been there for insects to gnaw because nature's law is survival.

Nearby there was a flurry of eyes, tails, a chorus of loss, a swansong. There was disorder in the picture because Dad was gone; he was a sculpture of death. The bright sun mocked his pallid skin and I stroked his marble hand. Weeds were stillborn souls by his Goliath's feet.

Dad was dead and not a leaf had flinched; not a single cloud had moved out of view. The sun was playing hide and seek between the leaves. Nothing more.

His season was over. There wasn't the mournful sound of church bells, only the soft tinkling of a wind chime. Snail-trails led me back to the house where I rang for help.

From behind, Dad looked like he was sleeping in the sun in the garden on a beautiful summer's day, his birthday. I called an ambulance and my cries became one with the wail of the siren. Poisoned, I said. Suicide, I said.

At first, I thought it was just a foxglove eye in his hand, but then I remembered his warning about deadly nightshade and his careful handling of the purple-green bell-shaped flower and its nasty black berries. A malicious, poisonous plant but a fitting cause of death for this wanderer of woods and country lanes. A man who taught me the beauty and the deadly character of nature.

Once inside the house, I closed the windows one by one. It seemed like the right thing to do to contain what was left of him, of Mum, inside the place that they loved.

I see our old life through the eye of a needle. I see buttons and spools of cotton. I hear the kettle boiling for tea with a slice of home-made cake. Outside, I see my father as a giant of the evergreen, striding the landscape, whispering to the birds and animals, killing and controlling predators, succumbing only to the deepest and purest of emotions to bring him down. My invincible father, broken by grief. A man undone by loving his wife, forever faithful and devoted, unable to bear one more season without her.

40

A damp yellow light eases its way onto the pavement. For brief moments there is warmth in the sun. There is a shop window of prams, another displaying children's shoes and sandals, a third selling books promoting Beatrix Potter and Jacqueline Wilson. Here there is a portal into other worlds where there is kindness and beauty. Why objects, just fabric or paper or metal, bother me, I cannot fathom. The street feels like a jack-in-the-box where any moment an unexpected face could pop up right in front of me. Even here, in the town centre. *Am I going mad?*

I pause at a shop window to look at the baby clothes and bootees, the tiniest socks I've ever seen displayed next to a toy train and a soft toy. I see my exhausted face looking back at me between the blue, pink and yellow babygros. Fear doesn't work shifts; it never stops. It is a greased machine.

A whisper could push me over the edge right now, so I cling to suburbia, to strangers carrying shopping bags and neon signs. They provide artificial comfort and respite from silence. I dread the shops turning their signs to 'Closed' and the fading of natural light as another long evening commences when I am alone with my fear.

Here at least there are distractions; it is better than sitting, waiting, hiding. Here, there aren't floorboards that creak. Among these strangers, the day is more of a friend than an enemy. But still I look behind me to check bindweed isn't following me from my house.

I like the sound of chat, idle banter, the innocuous subject matter of the weather, sales, prices. I listen in to a couple of friends discussing their plans for dinner and I follow in their footsteps, hoping to regain my appetite which fear has stolen and replaced with the taste of vinegar.

The shops begin to close, drawing down their blinds and ending the welcome smile of the streets. I retreat to my car like an animal, docile and weak after hibernation. I rehearse what I want to say to Adam.

You prostituted your heart. You gave it away, sold it. I'm surprised you've lived this long without it.

The words return because they are lodged in my long-term memory, even the lilt of accent and accentuation appears to me in black loops and dots of distinctive handwriting. The words are an incessant camera flash in my eyes, leaving me temporarily blinded.

A piece of sick comes up into my mouth as I park the Land Rover on the drive because Adam is home. His immaculate Mercedes shines and winks at me as I tentatively open the front door to Maple Cottage. I watch him through the kitchen window, see the back of him dressed in a short-sleeved shirt and chinos. He is standing in the middle of Jen's room. I see the splash of urine landing on the petals and him readjusting his belt.

When he turns and sees me through the window, he grins.

I run outside. 'Get out of my garden!' I yell without thinking.

'Don't you dare tell me what to do.' He strikes me across the face. In the cold air, it stings. 'I was wondering when you'd get back.'

He grabs me by the hair and pushes me down into The Bullion. I land awkwardly on the roses and soil. The ground is hard after so much sun and very little rain. I moan with pain. The view from the ground is blunt and blurred, obscured by sheets and spires of purple foxgloves.

I remember Mum waving at me from the kitchen window as I played in the back garden with a kite. She was wearing her blue cardigan, her favourite one with a few missing buttons. Her hair was loose, framing her face. The lawn was long and full of daisies.

'The police didn't take Devina's complaint seriously. Someone like me doesn't go around hurting people like Devina Duffy, who's got a tearaway teenage son, a fatherless family in a rough part of Nantwich. Why would I have anything to do with them?'

The cheery yellow heads of the yellow rose bush nod their scented heads, a hardy variety chosen for its name of Anniversary Wishes for a nice twist of irony. They dance around me as Adam places a brogue on my stomach and presses down lightly.

'No! Don't!' I plead.

'For better, for worse, for richer, for poorer, in sickness and in health, to love, cherish, and obey, till death us do part. I take our vows seriously, Rachel. Pity you didn't show me the same devotion. You take the moral high ground, but you're an adulteress.'

My breath is coming fast now, and I try to keep calm for my unborn child. His lip curls slightly, suggesting repugnance – or is it satisfaction? I think of the roots tunnelled beneath me and I wonder if this is my ending, where I began. It is both tragic and neatly cyclical.

'We could have had it all – me, you, a family – but you've gone and messed all that up now. You and Ollie playing at happy families, are you? Do you think I haven't seen you together here, ferreting over what's mine? I warned him to stay away.' He inspects his nails. 'I hate it when people don't play fair. Business is business.'

There are tunnels through the long grass, trails where wild animals have trodden a familiar path or bedded down for the night. I wish I could follow their lead, get my legs wet with dew. It wouldn't hurt if they were scratched by thorns, stung by nettles. I wouldn't care.

'So you want to harm my baby? Is that it? Or harm me?'

'Not you,' he grins. 'I love you.'

My husband isn't a man; he's not even an animal. He was always part of the weeds, the thistles, the choking ivy, poison.

I imagine Adam as a skull, delicately papered with skin, smooth and colourless from brow to upturned chin. His eyes loll in his head from the poison I've fed him, and the serene hush between us is blissfully funereal. Regret nips at my throat: I wish I'd poisoned Adam.

Seeing the hate in my eyes, he pushes his foot down harder. I hear myself moan.

The lawn is flooded with white light. The sun is climbing slowly; she is not hurried. From the ground, a new landscape emerges. A new country. I fear a terrible truth is being revealed to me about where I will end.

I am cold, dehydrated and very disorientated. I want to sit up but Adam's foot pushes me down. His other brogue is planted squarely in the soil, where his footprint will stay.

He takes a sudden step back. Between the green stems and the bobbing yellow heads of the gorgeous roses, I take a sharp intake of breath to prepare myself for his kick.

There is a gunshot. Then another.

Adam staggers backwards in shock, and I roll over onto my side.

A figure appears and approaches with an air rifle in her hands. The sky is too big, too low. A crow perches on one of Shirley's trees, scratching the view with its ugly claws and ominous *caa-caa*. A spade rests in the soil. Can I reach it? It feels like I am moving, like the hedges are running.

'Get away. Now. I won't miss the next time.'

'You wouldn't dare.'

Shirley fires at Adam's knees.

'Fuck me!' Adam sprints to his car while Shirley fires another shot into the air.

Then it starts to get foggy. I look up at the sky to see the swirls of blue and white coming and going in and out of focus. Tugging at the frayed edges of my consciousness, Shirley leans over me. I feel her cool hand on my forehead. 'Rachel, can you hear me?'

I nod.

'You're going to be all right. He's gone.'

I look down between my legs, fearful there might be blood.

'Did he hurt you?'

'He pushed me over. If you hadn't arrived when you did, he was going to kick me – here.' I point at my belly.

Shirley shakes her head. 'I'm going to call for an ambulance. Stay there and keep still.' She puts her coat over me. 'Try to stay awake.'

In this dynasty of petals, the heads of dahlias nod like

queens and the geraniums and hydrangeas bow. Red and purple frocks dance around my head to the drone of insects. I think of Ollie, who helped me plant a garden in my heart, and I close my eyes and catch the scent of lavender. Only hatred for Adam keeps me awake.

I know there is a difference between killing and controlling; Dad said it was an important distinction to make in his line of work, which was all about controlling pests as humanely and efficiently as possible. That might mean traps, bullets, poison, depending on the species. I think of Dad as I move in and out of consciousness, wishing I'd been more attentive then, and procrastinated less now.

'Can you hear me?' the paramedic asks, and I nod.

A big vehicle, probably a tractor, rumbles along a lane. Large tyres bump over potholes. It could be Roland, Dad's old friend. I think how close Peckforton Church is, a place of goodness, kindness, a house of prayer. Is my unborn child going to be buried in its graveyard?

I'd dared to hope – once. I have been blind to this poisoned landscape, to danger that's followed me to this garden.

'Can you save her?'

I am lifted onto a stretcher. The world is still on its side. The sun turns a blind eye to my suffering and pain, so I close my eyes and try to breathe more slowly. Half extinguished thoughts come and go. The shine of Adam's shoes. The wind chime tinkles.

Inside the ambulance, I wish I were a cabbage butterfly following the light to the wood. I wish I had travelled there to gather a feast for Adam. Then I and my unborn child would still be safe and well.

41

I've grown used to waking up by myself and the sound of the heating coming on. It has given me time to think about a future without fear. Almost a month has passed since Adam left. I need to act before I get too big and uncomfortable to think beyond my baby. She has given me a deadline because it will be too late if I leave it until after her birth. If I leave it until I am swollen and bloated with the feel of her, I might not be strong enough to withstand his poison. My feet will be bound and I won't be able to run.

If Mum and Dad were alive, I'd tell them that I am not a bad person. I'd tell them that the action I am about to take pales into insignificance beside the prospect of their granddaughter being harmed. My reflection is unchanged because I am a good person doing a bad thing. I know the distinction. The same way I know fear.

Adam answers my call on the second ring. His voice is breezy, as if he is expecting to hear from me at that precise moment. 'Rachel.'

I have rehearsed my lines. 'I want to strike a deal with you, but not over the phone.'

'What?'

'What happened is – for now – between the three of us.'

'As it happens, I'm not far away. I'll be over in a couple of hours. No Shirley. Just me and you.'

'Fine.' As soon I hang up, I slap on my wellies, grab gloves and a plastic bag, and head to the woods.

My legs carry me to its familiar depths where the trees are so thick and dense that the sunlight barely finds its way to the earth. I pass like a shadow beneath the trees, merging with them, moving further and further away from Maple Cottage.

I forage in amongst the chaos of trees and rotten wood, the flora and the deadly. My wax jacket has ample pockets.

I prepare our lunch and lay cutlery for two on the gingham cloth on the table overlooking the garden of rooms, where so many meals have been eaten before. I add berries like black grapes to the salad, mushrooms to the pasta, and I mix my salad dressing especially for the occasion. Then I wait. It is a colourful meal, seemingly healthy too – just Adam's thing. I plate up a small amount and make it look like I've eaten my lunch already. Breathless, I sit in the rocking chair and wait for my pulse to slow.

I remember a trip to the supermarket where the berries and mushrooms spoke to me from their shelves. I remember imagining Adam's mouth open, a prelude to this moment.

He arrives and seems stunned to see me, perhaps because I look healthy and my shape hasn't altered. I am still pregnant.

The memory-muscle of our marital roles helps smooth the way. 'Do you want some lunch before we talk business?' I ask him. 'I've just had mine, but there's plenty of leftover pasta and salad.'

'I'm ravenous.'

I watch him place his car key in its usual place in the hall. At the table, he helps himself to everything. The hands that held my throat pick up a knife and fork and gently cut into his last meal. The businessman is a sucker for a deal.

'Where have you been staying?' I ask as I pour us glasses of water.

'Oh, the usual – hotels.' He gestures to my index finger. It is wrapped in a plaster from a cut sustained while chopping ingredients for his salad too quickly. 'You've cut yourself.'

'Nothing serious. Would you like some more salad dressing?'

'Yes, it's rather good.'

He is eating my secret. It is in his mouth, melting on his tongue, sliding down his throat. It is dissolving, my dark-velvet secret, and it is blooming inside him.

I try to undo my apron but the knot is too tight. Adam sees me struggling, moves behind me to untie the strings so they fall loose at my sides. I hold my breath so that I won't flinch. He sits down again while I lift the apron over my head and fold it in two before joining him at the table. My chair is opposite the window and the garden of rooms looks back at me encouragingly.

'This deal, then?'

I watch him swallow each berry. Six so far. Four to go. Is his abdomen clenching or spasming yet? Is something happening under his Calvin Klein shirt? Does he feel like he's being pulled to pieces?

'Yes.'

And as the ninth berry goes inside his mouth, a fly buzzes inside the window. The air feels humid and close, and I am counting backwards from a hundred.

His strong fingers push the serving spoon into the potato salad to add a dollop to his plate. 'This potato salad is spicy. I'm open to discussion.'

He coughs a hoarse, dry cough. Sweat beads form on his forehead like blisters. Through the window, there is a block of pure yellow from the roses planted tightly to honour his love of gold. Money. He worships money like Midas did.

'The Bullion Room,' I say, 'it's your room. The variety is called Anniversary Wishes. They'll flower all summer long. See the double petals. All I want is this house. You–'

He coughs again, as if something is wedged in his throat. Is it burning? Does it feel as if the air is being constricted by throttling hands?

'Drink,' he gasps.

I have gone to great pains to make tea from the seeds of brugmansia, so the very least Adam can do is to sip some before the angels' trumpets sound his exit from this world. I have bleached all the surfaces to remove all traces of my preparation.

'Do you take sugar?' I have forgotten if he does or not, and I really couldn't care less.

I watch him undo the top two buttons on his shirt and pull it out of his trousers, then he lifts the fabric and wafts it. I see a vein throbbing in the side of his forehead. His lips are swelling. He looks smaller, as if he has drunk a shrinking potion. I like his dismantling, his unveiling. I like this fashion show in reverse.

His face is starting to swell and has a tinge of blue-tinged brie, which reminds me that I haven't had my lunch. 'Here, take the last one,' I say, and I pop the last berry into his mouth then close it for him. Shut.

'It's hot in here,' he gasps.

Suddenly he pushes the chair away from the table so quickly it's as if a camera flash has gone off. I hear the scraping of the wooden legs on the stone floor and him trying to lift the back door latch.

'You prostituted your heart, Adam. You gave it away, sold it when you arranged my affair. I'm surprised you've lived this long without it.'

His hand rests on the latch waiting, perhaps, for my footsteps, my hand, a kind word, a kind look.

I see him as a skull, delicately papered with skin, smooth and colourless. His eyes loll in his head, and the serene hush between us is blissfully funereal.

I feel intimate with his imminent death.

The latch lifts as decisively as the cutting of an umbilical cord. The back door is thrown open onto another world of light and birdsong and insects flying. But I stay in the rocking chair, as a future pinpricks my finger.

I watch Adam lurch into the garden, his head jerking this way and that like an escaped hen. I love all the creases in his untucked white shirt. An invisible rope is pulling him out of my house to the garden of rooms, to his room. That is as it should be.

Can he hear the jubilant birdsong from Shirley's place? Can he smell the lavender in Mum's room? I don't think he can appreciate the aroma or the fertility of the soil; he is submerged in a world of pain and confusion. He is walking like he does when he is drunk; he has lost his self-assured posture, his cockerel stride.

White foam forms at the edges of his mouth and dribbles onto his chin. I watch him heave and clutch at his stomach as he leaves this world. I take a sip of water as he takes his final few footsteps. He turns and gazes at me through the window. I mouth, 'I hate you.'

I feel I am a beautiful still life, an expectant woman framed by her favourite window, a mother-to-be full of power. He takes a last terrible lingering look at me – a look of horror – realisation still vertical in the vulva of the sky. Then there is a flurry before he collapses headfirst into the gold rose bushes. A perfect tableau of yellow petals and pointed thorns.

It is so still and quiet. I stroke the skin on my cheeks, on my neck, my arms, my hand. I read my unblemished skin like braille; it will never be bruised or burned or violated by him again.

I imagine Shirley's garden, her lawn crowned by fallen apples. Outside, a wood pigeon summons the breeze to cool the parched orange mouths of the dahlias. My spade is resting in Dad's room. The cottage waits patiently for me to act.

I call the ambulance, feigning a frantic, desperate woman, pregnant, vulnerable and distraught. 'Ambulance! My husband is trying to kill himself! Hurry!'

I lay the document detailing his fraud on the table beside the card he sent me years ago. 'Sorry, Rachel. Forgive me, Adam.' Luckily I'd kept it, not thinking I would need it to kill the bastard but because I used to think I'd imagined his cruelty and violence towards me.

I can see why my dad, a quiet, taciturn man, chose poisoning. No gunfire. No rope. No bystanders to interfere.

Adam is dead and not a leaf has flinched; not a single cloud has moved out of view. The sun is playing hide and seek between the leaves. Nothing more.

A pheasant dashes from the undergrowth, its head jutting and pacing, then its long-feathered tail snatches flight. It calls as if it has just found its voice after living in hiding. There is a dash of bottle green and golden chestnut; its beauty has survived the shooting season. Perhaps like me, it is cannier than it first thought.

EPILOGUE

There are twice as many people milling around the gardens at Maple Cottage this summer and I am delighted to see so many of my friends enjoying the stunning garden of rooms. It has become quite well known in local circles as a unique creation and a legacy to my parents. It gets better every year.

The fifth room is planted out in soft pinks; like the other rooms, it has a name, 'Hope', after the birth of my daughter, Dilly, and an end to living in fear of Adam.

'I was here the last time you kindly opened your garden. I can't quite believe the dramatic change.' Harry, an elderly gentleman in a cream linen jacket, steps backwards. I shake his soft, warm hand. His wife was once friends with Mum and I remember seeing him in the graveyard and here last year. 'This room in particular – I see you've named this one "The Bullion Room" – it's particularly colourful. The soil quality must be excellent.'

Dilly chatters and babbles in my arms, sensing my happiness. A tiny life I have longed for. When I gaze at her little face nestled in my arms, I am struck by the bow shape of her mouth and her dainty chin. It is as if I am holding up a mirror to myself.

She makes me feel blessed. And powerful. Vindicated.

I had Adam cremated at the earliest opportunity and put his ashes to good use. Very few attended – they knew about the fraud, the wife-beating, and I think no one wanted to be associated with him. It made the final arrangements much simpler, once the palynologist confirmed the poison was indigenous to this area. Based on the microscopic compounds on his clothes and skin, they said that Adam had ingested it himself. After what he'd done to his employer and me, suicide was a logical end for a man like him.

'The roses are beautiful, aren't they? Like a block of gold and the scent from them is heavenly.'

'Sunshine,' he says. 'Complete sunshine. You can't put a price on that!' He smiles at Dilly. 'And you're a pretty child! I can see you're going to have green fingers like your mummy here.' He loses an arthritic finger in her small palm. 'I'm sad to see the maple tree has gone.'

'Me too. We've planted a sapling in its place, though. Twenty years from now, it will be back, stronger than ever.'

'I shan't be here then, but you and Dilly will be, which is what matters.'

His silver hair glints in the sun as he kisses Dilly and me goodbye. 'It's always a pleasure to come here. See you next year!'

Dilly giggles as I nod to the wood, thankful for its protection and its feast.

THE END

ACKNOWLEDGEMENTS

I want to thank Karen Holmes for her astute editorial probing and suggestions, and Kate Linehan and Niall Lambkin for the wonderful support and confidence they showed in me and Rachel's Garden.

Thank you to my husband, Nigel, for helping me to pursue my dream.

Thank you to the team at Bloodhound Books.

Most of all, thank you to the people who read my books. I hope you continue to enjoy my stories.

ABOUT THE AUTHOR

Louise Worthington was born in Cheshire in the UK and is the author of *Distorted Days*, *Stained Glass Lives*, *Rachel's Garden* and, forthcoming, *The Entrepreneur* (April 2021).

She taught English before becoming a full-time writer. With her husband, daughter, furry and feathered friends, Louise lives in Shropshire.

Her debut novel, *Distorted Days*, was described by Kirkus Review as 'a formidable work'. Louise is currently working on a psychological thriller.

https://louiseworthington.co.uk/

Printed in Great Britain
by Amazon

41494803R00148